CIVIL LINES

CIVIL LINES

Radhika Swarup

SIMON &
SCHUSTER

London · New York · Sydney · Toronto · New Delhi

First published in India by Simon & Schuster India, 2021

1 3 5 7 9 10 8 6 4 2

Simon & Schuster India
818, Indraprakash Building,
21, Barakhamba Road,
New Delhi 110001.

www.simonandschuster.co.in

Hardback ISBN: 978-81-947520-8-0
eBook ISBN: 978-81-947520-4-2

Typeset in India by SŪRYA, New Delhi
Printed and bound in India by Replika Press Pvt. Ltd.

FSC
www.fsc.org
MIX
Paper from responsible sources
FSC® C016779

Simon & Schuster India is committed to sourcing paper that is made from wood grown in sustainable forests and support the Forest Stewardship Council, the leading international forest certification organisation. Our books displaying the FSC logo are printed on FSC certified paper.

For Amarendra,
who believed when I wouldn't.

I

Tasha-di had called so early that even now, hours later, I wasn't sure I had spoken to her.

My phone had flashed fluorescent—a night-time precaution mandated by Benjamin's light sleeping—and as I reached for it, I thought I saw an Indian number on the display. I swallowed hard. It wasn't Maya. No, it wasn't her number, and besides, she and I weren't in the habit of phoning each other. There would be a joke shared by email or WhatsApp, or contact on a birthday, but beyond that, no real communication.

I blinked groggily, staring at the display. I couldn't think of anyone who would call me at this hour. The phone stopped ringing. It instantly burst into colour again, and I rushed to answer it. The voice at the other end spoke my name softly, and with some hesitation, but there was no mistaking its identity.

'Tasha-di?'

'It must be early at your end,' she said. 'I'm sorry. I should have waited.'

She spoke more haltingly than I remembered, her voice breaking mid-speech, and I asked her if she was all right.

'No,' Tasha-di said. 'No,' she repeated, and then, 'I'm worried about Maya.'

I couldn't remember the last time I had spoken to Tasha-di. *Di*, I thought. Older sister, but the truth was, she was Ma's sister, and that too by marriage. She really was Papa's controversial cousin; a firebrand liberal, a feminist before feminism went mainstream, and a woman who had run away from an unhappy marriage and insouciantly weathered all the scandal that ensued. She was marginally older than Ma, but Ma had always called her Tasha-di, and when Maya and I came along, so had we. She was an older sister to a generation or more, and now she roused me from my sleep to talk to me about my own older sister. 'Siya,' she was saying.

'Tasha-di, it's so nice to hear your voice.'

'Good, good,' she said perfunctorily. Her voice was back to its usual gruffness. 'Now listen, Siya.'

'Tasha-di.'

'You sure you're up?' and I knew she was thinking of our childhood when I would resist the mornings, pulling the covers over my head even as the day's heat rose. They would come in, one after the other, Papa, Ma, and Tasha-di on her visits, parting the curtains, switching off the air-conditioning, and then the low hanging fan in an attempt to rouse me. I would refuse to rise, even as the sunlight streamed in and the room grew clammy, until finally, Ma would sit herself down next to me, and with infinite tenderness, peg my nose with her fingers. How I would then squeal, spluttering for breath, sitting bolt upright, telling Ma she could have killed me. Tasha-di, watching from the doorway, would smile, 'But she got you up, my darling.'

'Siya?'

'I'm up,' I said to her. 'Tell me about Maya.'

'When did you last speak to her?'

I fell silent, but the truth was clear. I couldn't remember when I had last spoken to my sister.

I had only remembered Maya's birthday on the day itself. I had been at a café choosing my lunch, and the person in front of me had ordered a coronation chicken roll, a combination so derived from India, and so equally divorced from any real concept of it that I smiled. How Maya would hate it.

And then I started.

It was the second of March. I took out my phone to confirm the date, and saw that it was past two in the afternoon. It would be nearing dinnertime in India. The woman in front of me was vacillating over her drink, and I typed a quick message to Maya:

Happy Birthday to the best sister in the world!

I pressed send, cursing myself for having forgotten, and for having thought of nothing more than a cursory message. Had anyone else remembered to mark the day? Had there been cake bought, or the luridly bright balloons she had always loved? I would order something to send to her—half a dozen pineapple pastries, or some flowers. Something to show I cared. The queue cleared, and I stepped forward to place my order.

The day turned out to be a long one. The press had heard reports of store closures, and my phone was ringing until late in the evening. It was past ten by the time I returned home hungry and crabby, and the thought of Maya had slipped my mind.

'Siya,' came the call, Tasha-di's voice impatient. 'When did you last speak to your sister?'

'I don't know,' I replied. There was a sigh across the phone, and I knew I was being judged. The silence stretched thin, and I wondered if Tasha-di had hung up. But there it was, another sigh, and I said, 'We haven't spoken in a while.'

'I'm worried about her, Siya.'

'Is she ok?'

'That's just it,' said Tasha-di, the softness returning to her voice, and I began to worry. How long had it been since we had last spoken? Had it been this year? When Ma was alive, the main days were marked—birthdays, Diwali, the turn of the year—but now, as I thought of when I had last spoken to my older sister, I realised I couldn't pin down a date. I had last seen her in India, when Ma's affairs were being dealt with, and she had been fine. Tight-lipped, unwilling to show frailty, but fine. I had asked her to come to London with me, for a holiday, for a break from the house and its ghosts, but she had refused. She had the family around her—Tasha-di, the cousins who remained in India, and the house. And, I thought, Maya was Maya. Inscrutable, obstinate, slow to embrace change, but essentially resilient. She would be fine. 'I'll call her,' I said. 'I'm sure you're worrying about nothing.'

'Siya,' Tasha-di was saying, 'Maya has retreated into herself since your mother's passing. She was always quiet, but I thought that was your Ma's influence. But the girl hasn't written an article in months, and anytime I offer to visit, she tells me she's busy.'

I tried to think of something positive to say. Maya would be fine. And yet, I was back in the past, trying to think of the last time we had spoken. How long had it been since Ma's death? A little over a year. We must have spoken recently, must have messaged each other a joke that Ma would have disapproved of. Ma, I thought, and then, 'When did *you* last see her?'

'That's just it,' said Tasha-di. 'I can't remember.'

The room was still shrouded in the night. I looked at the window as we spoke, and saw that a light rain had begun to fall. The window was open an inch, and I shivered as the wind blew in. Such weather, and just as spring was beginning to flex its muscles! Just yesterday, I had found daffodils sprouting out in the pavement outside the flat, like so many wayward weeds, and had found myself filled with hope. The air had been crisp, and though they had swayed in the breeze, they had remained sturdy. I had found myself laughing, smiling at passers-by, but by the evening, chill had settled in the air.

I watched the rain splatter against the windows of my room, bringing a fine mist, and I rose to shut the window.

'Yes, Tasha-di,' I said as she told me I needed to get in touch. 'I'll do more,' I promised. 'I really will.'

I looked out again. It was a deluge now, the downpour, like the Indian monsoon, until my ears were suffused with the noise. It would be the work of a moment to look up a flight. I could be in India within a day. Benjamin could wait; my job search could too. Then I blinked as a raindrop splattered against my hand and shook my head. I was rushing to conclusions. Tasha-di's alarm was ludicrous and Maya was fine. I wasn't needed. My sister *was* fine.

And my life was here. Maya would have to get used to being without Ma, but that would have to be her solitary journey. I could provide a distraction, a stay of loneliness, but no concrete assistance. The thought of my upping sticks just because neither of us had thought to contact Maya was as needlessly self-indulgent as my aunt's night-time call.

There it was again, that loaded sigh. 'I'll call her,' I said to my aunt. I could do no more. Tasha-di grunted her displeasure, and I said reassuringly, 'I will, Tasha-di. I will check in on Maya.'

We must have exchanged parting pleasantries. I must have found my way off the call, and then, improbable as it was, I must have found my way back to sleep, as I found myself waking up long after my usual time. My back hurt, and I saw that I had slept in an awkward position. Had I been in India, Ma would have massaged my neck. The thought of Ma brought with it the memory of her passing, and I gulped. It was still new to me, in spite of our silences. For years now, we had barely spoken. Any interaction we did have was usually bookended with fights. There were stilted calls on birthdays or Diwalis, then a desert of quiet. And yet, after a year of her passing, the thought that I would never wake to rage against her filled me with a sadness I couldn't quite understand. I could laugh. No, I could cry. All this emotion for a mother I had neither looked after nor missed.

II

We had fought the last time we spoke. It had been three months before her passing, or maybe six; I forget. The weather had been cold, and the day overcast, and though it wasn't one of the usual days for reaching out, I had called the landline at home.

It was slowly starting to grow clear to me that the business I worked in didn't have a future. All around me, I saw the casualties of the malaise hitting the UK high streets. Stores closed, jobs were lost, and in the head office too, I saw endless colleagues look around for new opportunities. Every week, a friend handed in their resignation, and their position wasn't filled again. The rest of us worked as we pleased. We weren't working to deadlines any longer, and there appeared to be no one around to give us direction.

It was an unsettling time, and though I wasn't in the habit of unburdening myself to Ma, I wanted to hear someone ask after me. Still, my expectations were low; it was a weekend, and the two were sure to be busy. And yet, Ma had picked up on the first ring, surprising me, and as I stumbled for a reason for the call, she asked me, 'How are you, Siya?'

There it was, the question, some interest expressed, but it caught me off-guard. 'I, uh, well,' I began, but she was already carrying on. There was work that needed to be done to the wiring of the house, and she worried about giving builders access to the home.

I broke in, more forcefully than I intended. 'Ma…'

'I don't even know how long it will take…'

'Ma.'

'And the mess…'

'Ma,' I said again. My voice must have risen, as Ma paused. 'Ma,' I said again, and then, as I wondered what to say, I stopped. Too much had happened, and too much time had elapsed since we had confided in each other. And as far as Ma knew, I was happy with my life in England. It had been years since she asked about my plans to marry, and whenever she asked me how I was, my responses were monosyllabic. And now that I needed to ask for advice, I didn't know how to broach the topic. 'Siya,' Ma was saying, her voice impatient, and I quickly blurted out, 'that house is too big for the both of you, Ma.'

A shocked silence followed. I knew I had made a mistake the moment I had spoken the words. This was not the time to bring up the issue, and Ma was sure to think I was after my inheritance. I had only spoken as a diversion from my worries, but the truth was she rattled around the house, avoiding the stairs, ignoring cracks in the wall, and missing leaks and crumbling plaster. The truth was it was a house built for another time. The servant's wing at the back of the house itself was over five times the size of my London flat, and had once housed families of retainers. Those same quarters now housed Shanti, our old nanny and Ma's most faithful companion.

'Na, na,' Ma was saying. I could hear the irritation in her voice. 'Leave it.'

'But Ma,' I said. 'You know I'm right. It was too big for us even when Maya and I were young.'

'Leave it, na,' Ma said, adding the words that always ended all our arguments. 'You and your sister can do as you please after I'm dead and gone.'

Maya hadn't been party to the argument, but her presence hung over the conversation. She had sat right next to Ma, I knew, on the musty sofa outside our bedrooms, or on the straight backed dining chairs on the ground floor, her truest support and champion, the voice on her shoulder, her angel, her one true, unwavering, unquestioning confidante and child.

My fingers hovered over the phone through the day, and though I dialled the Delhi home's number several times, I always disconnected the phone before it could ring.

It wasn't a big deal, just a catch-up. I wasn't moving to India, after all. It was just a chat. But we hadn't spoken in months, and I was wary of breaking the succour of the walls that we had so carefully built around us.

My phone rang in the early evening. I fretted it was Tasha-di ringing to scold me, but I needn't have worried. It was Benjamin, calling as he often did as he finished his work for the day. 'My fridge is empty,' he announced. 'Do you fancy meeting up for dinner?'

I paused. He was still living an adolescent's life, letting someone else feed him, refusing to take responsibility for the future, not thinking of my needs, and I knew we couldn't carry on as we were. Something had to give, but then he laughed, nagging me to go out for dinner with him, and I found myself giving in and giving way to him.

Benjamin had studied the menu by the time I arrived, and had suggestions for what I would enjoy. It was a new place we were trying out, a restaurant in his neighbourhood, and as the waiter—Italian, effeminate in his show—ushered me to our table, he said, 'Your boyfriend has just arrived.'

Benjamin looked up at the term. He didn't respond, but I could see the word bothered him. I smiled. He hated classification of any sort: boyfriend, relationship, commitment, family, marriage. Expectations made him feel claustrophobic. He had told me when we had first met that he performed poorly in exams for the same reason, and cited his mediocre degree from his mediocre university as proof of his resistance to labels. 'Who is to tell me that I do or do not understand Shakespeare or *Beowulf*? Who is to tell me that I can or can't love or care for somebody?'

I had wondered then if his explanation had been a coded warning, that it was I who would have to ward off expectations. I sighed and looked across the table. Benjamin was telling me he had a piece due in the following week, and that he would have to spend the weekend on it.

'I won't be around much for a few days,' he said apologetically. He didn't ask about my progress with my job search. In part, he assumed I would share any news that arose, and in part, I suspected, he didn't want to put a dampener on the evening. I had been unemployed for several months now, and though I had been casting my CV out for at least a year, I remained unemployed.

The vigour with which I scanned job sites had dimmed of late, but it was a dispiriting process. I had to personalise each covering letter, researching the company and the role and setting out my unique suitability for the job, and often, I wouldn't even be called in for an interview. More often than not, I wouldn't even get a response to my application, which had a knock-on impact on my willingness to keep applying for jobs that I was never going to be considered for.

My time away from employment hampered me too. My CV now had a dreaded gap in it, and away from the structure of an office routine, I no longer showered first thing in the morning, no longer needed to get dressed as soon as I was up, and no longer saw the need to log on to job sites before the working day began. I grew lethargic, and the few jobs that did come on to the market were filled before I could so much as register my interest. My early failures paralysed me, and now, my paralysis ensured my failure.

I watched Benjamin as he complained about work. 'It's just as well,' I said. And as he looked up, bemused, I added, 'You being busy this weekend. I need to get a move on with my job applications.'

'Don't worry,' he said. He set his bread stick down on the table and took hold of my hand. 'Something will turn up.'

I shrugged.

'It will.'

'Maybe.' I could see him frown. There it was, the dampener cast over our evening. 'I've been thinking,' I carried on. His hand had been snaking back to his bread, but now he looked at me. 'I can't really afford my flat.'

He looked away. He didn't speak for an instant, for longer, then as I refused to elaborate, he nodded. 'No,' he said.

He'd chosen the flat with me after my last tenancy ran out. It was a two bed flat, larger and more central than my last place, and though nothing had been articulated, he had enthused about the space, telling me we would be able to entertain better there, and that we would be able to have guests over to stay, and I had assumed he had wanted to move in. But then, he hadn't said anything, and I hadn't asked. Now he nodded as I told him I couldn't justify the flat's expense, but no solution appeared to strike him either. 'No,' he said again, nodding sagely, and I marvelled at how civilised our exchange was. This is what our interaction consisted of, nods and shrugs and polite agreement. I tiptoed around the edges of my discontent, and if he ever felt any cause for complaint, he never let on. There was no space for disagreement in our interaction.

'The lease,' I told him, 'runs out next quarter. I'm not going to renew it.'

'No,' he said, breaking off a chunk of his breadstick. 'No, I don't think it makes any sense to.'

Laughter drifted up towards us from the other diners, the sound of someone else's happiness, and I nodded. All this hate Benjamin professed for classification, when he had never paused to ask how I felt about the phrases he was so disdainful of. Boyfriend. Relationship. Commitment. Family. Marriage.

'In any case,' I said. He looked up, surprised. All the big blows had been landed already, I saw him think. The lack of a job, my giving up the flat. What else was left? 'Tasha-di called earlier today.'

'That's your aunt, isn't it?'

All those years of togetherness, of intimacy without belonging, and he still needed me to signpost the relationships I did have. 'She's worried about Maya,' and as he frowned, I added, 'that's my sister.'

'I know who your sister is, Siya.'

'Tasha-di wants me to go back to India.'

This wasn't strictly true, but I wanted to jolt Benjamin. He had been complacent about my unsuccessful applications, and about my giving up my flat, and I wanted him to realise that we couldn't go on the way we had. Something had to give. Benjamin spoke now, his voice light, 'It might do you good to go there for a bit. Get a break.'

'No,' I said, my voice raised. There had been a lull in the restaurant, and my voice emerged high-pitched and strained. The table next to us turned to see if all was well. 'No,' I said again, 'If I go back, I'll be going back.'

He ran his hands through his hair, and as I smiled, happy to finally see him ruffled, he asked, 'What does that mean?'

'My life isn't exactly going anywhere, is it?' I paused, waiting to see if he spoke, but he remained silent. 'I have no job, I can't afford my flat, and things between us…' I trailed off to see him wince. He didn't speak, didn't rebut my words, and I repeated, 'I think it's better if I just go.'

'Well,' he said in a careful voice. He blew air into his cheeks, then pursed his mouth. It appeared a suggestion was on his lips, but he didn't speak. His cheeks puffed up again with his breath before he expelled it with a large sigh. I was reminded of our earlier, smoking days, when we would stand outside restaurants in the cold, blowing perfect smoke clouds into the night air.

He still hadn't spoken, and I arched my brow. 'Well,' he said unwillingly. 'If you're absolutely sure, Siya.'

I think I laughed a little. 'I am,' I said, bent on misery, on drawing blood if he wasn't prepared to give any ground. 'It's not as if we're going anywhere, is it?'

He smiled a slow, small smile, his mouth turned down, his

lips cast in a half-pout. How I had loved that pout! What insight I had claimed to have into his childish self, into his tantrums and foot stomping, into his ceaseless entreaties for attention, but now, as he made that same small face, I saw it as an admission of defeat.

'There's an evening flight to Delhi,' I said. 'I'll pack up my things and book myself on a flight leaving tomorrow.'

'Well,' he said, and as I hoped without hope for something from him, I scarcely knew what, a concession, an admission of love, he added, 'I'll help you pack.'

'No,' I said, shrill again, sounding unreasonable. People were turning to look at us again, and I knew I sounded like the aggressor. 'There's no need.'

'I really would like to,' he said, his voice earnest, and here it was, the easy act of charity, the line cast into the water, 'You won't be able to take everything with you. You can leave whatever you want—boxes, suitcases—with me. I'll keep them safe until you return.'

III

The plane began its descent over Delhi, lowering itself over the town of Gurugram. Many of the capital's technology hubs were located here, and as I peered past the child sitting next to me, I saw freshly manicured lawns bordering luxury apartment complexes. The green was vivid, even from where I sat, dotted with bright pinks and reds, and I could almost forget that this was a country that prayed for its rain. This was modern India then, the new land of opportunity. Lush at first sight, and sparkling. This was the Asian century, they were saying, and the new giants of the world were all close to this land. Fortunes were waiting to be made, a new future imagined, and a fresh, thrusting identity readily furnished for an old, tested land.

I heard someone call out my name as I reached the arrivals hall, and for a brief moment I wondered if Maya had come to receive me.

She hadn't been enthusiastic when I had called to tell her I was coming to Delhi. 'I don't know if now's the best time,' she had said to me. 'It's very hot here.'

I told her that I remembered Delhi's summers, but she continued to try to dissuade me. 'You're not used to it,' she told me, her tone measured and reasonable, and my voice acquired the younger sibling's whine. 'It's my home too,' I said, and she submitted with the firstborn's fatalism.

'As you wish,' she said nonchalantly, as if she didn't much care whether I visited or not.

I turned towards the exit, but there it was, my name being called out again, and a diaphanous chiffon dupatta being waved out towards me. I shook my head. Of course it wasn't Maya. 'Siya,' she was calling, and before I could walk towards her, Tasha-di was moving forward, bustling aside other people waiting for loved ones, straining over the balustrade, and reaching out to take hold of my baggage.

There was a man waiting patiently beside her who now darted forward. 'Namaste,' he said to me with a shy smile.

'Do you recognise him, Siya?' Tasha-di asked, and as I paused, she said, "This is Pradeep.' I still looked uncertain, and she added, 'Arre, child, this is Shanti's son.'

'Of course.' He had been a constant presence as we had grown up, staying close to his mother in the kitchen. They were a quiet pair, Shanti and her boy. There was a husband in a village somewhere to the East of Delhi, but I knew nothing further about him, and had never thought to ask. Pradeep himself was unobtrusive, avoiding notice by us, either through reserve or some sense that he was intruding on our space. I often saw him as I returned from school, peering into the garage and performing odd jobs for the driver. He would polish the cars and dust out the car mats we littered with crumbs from our after-school snacks. He would change the oil as the driver directed, and watch rapt, a toolbox in his hands, as the driver disappeared under the older cars to perform repairs. He always carried the smell of car oil with him, even when he was in the house, and now, as he reached out to hold my luggage, I was sure I identified the same aroma. He smiled again at me, a slow, shy smile, and walked on towards the parking bay. He called the lift for us, clearing a path through the others walking towards their transport, but didn't attempt any further conversation.

'He's working as a driver, isn't he?'

'He is,' Tasha-di confirmed. 'But he insisted on taking a half-day off to help me receive you.'

Pradeep was a few yards in front of us, and I asked Tasha-di, 'And Maya?'

Tasha-di shrugged. This could encompass a multitude of complaints—her failure to pick me up, or her retreat from her work and her friends. I had looked her up online after my conversation, and Tasha-di was right. Maya hadn't written in months. Her work had been sporadic even when Ma was alive, of course. She had been called on anytime Ma had a medical complaint, and inasmuch as I could have helped out too, neither had thought to call on me. Ma had contracted Tuberculosis, and Pneumonia, and had suffered accidents without anyone having informed me. They had formed an impenetrable band, Maya and Ma, and Maya's writing had suffered as a consequence.

Her other relationships had too. Ma had discouraged Maya from romantic liaisons, and though she was beautiful, Maya—with her wide eyes, full mouth and long, straight hair—she had followed her mother's counsel. And so, while I, four years Maya's junior, and plain looking, found it possible to attract interest from boys, Maya held herself aloof. There had been a boy at university, a tall, laughing law student with slicked-back hair, and I was never sure if interest had been expressed or reciprocated, but he had stopped visiting abruptly, and I suspected Ma was behind the rupture. Tasha-di sighed now, and put her hand behind my back. 'You've come home, beta,' she said. 'You don't know how much that means.'

Tasha-di dropped me off at the door, but refused to come in. 'I'll visit soon,' she said, and as I opened my mouth in protest, she added, 'I'll come tomorrow. But you'll want to catch up with your sister now.'

I entered on my own, then, and stood still for a moment in the hallway, reorienting myself. The lighting was dim here, the shapes in front of me a haze, and I blinked to focus my eyes. The clutter seemed to have grown in the year since I'd last been here. Unopened mail lined the hallway, and was piled up both under and on top of the leather armchairs that had once been repositories for our sports bags. Maya and I would dump our tennis kit—rackets, headbands, water bottles—on top of them as we came back home with bursting bladders. Our belongings would land where they did, on the armchairs or beside them, and we would race to the bathroom, praying for our bodies to not betray us. We would return to find Ma on the warpath. 'Everything must have its place,' she would drill into us, even as we complained that we had been desperate to relieve ourselves. 'Cleanliness is next to Godliness.'

'Yes, Ma,' we would repeat, chastened, rushing to tidy away our things, but as I looked around at the accumulated debris of my mother and sister's lives, I wondered who had first forgotten to heed Ma's old homily. There was a noise overhead, a muffled footstep, Maya's perhaps, and I moved forward. There were the public areas of the house in front of me; the living rooms and library and the kitchen, but I walked towards the staircase.

How large those stairs had seemed in our childhood! I looked up and gulped. The steps were still large, and the flight of stairs in front of me felt like it was double the height of any I had encountered in London. The ceilings were high on every floor, and highest here, at the ground level, where the sun seemed to dart in through every window. We had clung onto the bannisters as we climbed, terrified of hitting the floor after a fall and breaking our heads.

I began to climb the staircase, my hand creeping out of habit to hug the bannister. This space was cluttered too, serving as a repository for books and magazines. There was paper everywhere, parcels still in their boxes, and months, no years of dust gathered on top. Everything seemed dull brown, the carpet and the bannisters and the piled books, and as I lifted my hand off the staircase, I saw it was coated in a thick, furry film.

The first floor was where all the family's bedrooms were, but on an impulse, I climbed until I reached the second floor. This had been an unused space for as long as I could remember, and whenever Maya and I had the chance, we would make our way up here. We had built worlds for our dolls in the cavernous rooms in here, and by and large, we had been able to play undisturbed. I had a great curiosity to revisit these spaces, and to see if they were as big as they had been in my memory.

There was a door I didn't remember at the end of the landing. I applied pressure on the handle, but it didn't budge. I bent down; it appeared to be locked. I tried once more, putting my weight behind me, but it was no use. I was looking around for a light switch when I thought I heard a voice call out my name. This was Maya, surely, but the voice didn't repeat its call, and I paused outside the door for another moment. The entire corridor smelt musty, as if devoid of life, and when I tried to turn the door's handle, it remained unyielding.

I walked back towards my room. Shanti, Ma's old maid, looked up at my approach, and smiled broadly. 'Baby!' she said as I towered over her. 'You've come home.'

Here was one thing that hadn't changed. I folded Shanti into a hug. She smelt of the smells of the kitchen; of ginger and onion and of sharp tomato, and a little of sweat too, and I breathed the scent in deeply. 'Tell me,' I said to the woman. 'How are you?'

There was more grey in Shanti's hair than I remembered. She had a sweet tooth, and I would make sure to buy her chocolates on my visits back. It would never be anything special; just whichever box of chocolate was on offer at my local Tesco, but Shanti was always grateful for the present. Now I said guiltily to her, 'I didn't bring you your chocolate.'

The woman shook her head toothily at me. 'Bas, beta,' she said. 'It's enough that you've returned home.'

She didn't say anything about Maya. There was no sign of her, in spite of Tasha-di's complaint that she never left the house, and I hoped she wasn't trying to avoid me. 'Shanti,' I said, but the following words, 'Where is my sister?' felt like such an admission of failure that I didn't utter them.

Shanti was studying me. I smiled at her, and she said to me, 'It's so good to see you.'

'Yes,' I replied, then fell silent. The room was as I remembered it; large, spare, and high ceilinged. My old desk was pushed into one corner, and above it, set into the wall, was a shelf holding my favourite books. I got up from the bed and walked to the shelf, reading the spines of the volumes. It was as if I was taking a trip into the past, and though I began my inspection objectively enough, I was soon conscious that an earlier me had inhabited these alien worlds. How many hours I had spent reading these works in those early, happy years, and how many times I had reimagined my own fortunes. I would be set homework, and Ma would expect me to work until dinnertime, but the minute I was done, I would reach up for one of the titles on the shelf. How far I travelled with those books—to small town America, to Caribbean plantations and archaeological digs and quiet English villages. Nothing had been disturbed. Not the books, not the curtains, not the bed, and not the magazine rack by the door.

I was conscious of Shanti's gaze fixed on me. I smiled at the maid and turned towards the shuttered windows. There was a slight noise, a rustling from outside perhaps, and I looked out. There was no one there. Another noise followed, and I glanced up at the ceiling. The fan was whirling weightily around. It had come loose from its fitting, or maybe it had always hung low. As a child, I had been petrified of it falling on me, and had insisted on having my bed placed by the end furthest away from it. 'You must be tired, Siya,' Shanti was saying, but my eyes were fixed on the ceiling. There the fan whirled, slowly and insistently, forever threatening destruction. The sound was calming, hypnotic almost, and I found my eyelids growing heavy.

'Baby...'

I saw a flash. A long-tongued lizard stalked swiftly up the wall, and having reached the ceiling, was still. Its bulbous eyes seemed trained on me, as if observing me, but I was unused, after all this time, to the heat, and to my surroundings. I would have to acclimatise. And then, just by a corner, near where the waiting lizard lurked, I saw a patch of damp trailing down the wall.

The events of the day were beginning to catch up with me. The long indirect flight, the queue at immigration, the heat and the crowds. Maya had still not turned up, and I assumed she was out of the house. Shanti was shuffling about, tidying my scarf from the bed, telling me I needed to rest, and I nodded. Shanti would be off to her quarters soon. 'OK,' I told Shanti, as she frowned. 'I'll be fine.'

'But baby.'

'Enough, Shanti,' I told her. 'I grew up here too, remember?'

'Maya hasn't even called?'

There was a disapproval in her tone she didn't bother to disguise, and I tried to silence the urge to defend my sister. 'It's still a working day,' I told the woman. She still shook her head, but as I repeated that I was able to occupy myself in my own home, she found another worry. 'You'll have to turn on the geyser if you want hot water for your bath,' she told me, and I pretended to be affronted.

'I've had thousands of baths in this house, Shanti.'

'Ok, ok,' she said unwillingly. She offered once more to make me tea, or to fetch me lemonade, but as I continued to refuse, she finally conceded defeat. 'Stubborn girl,' she scolded me. 'I'll see you in the evening.'

~

Maya would return. In an hour, in two, once she was ready, and then we—sister, best friend, confidante—would be forced to talk to each other.

~

I had thought of taking a short nap, but I worried that Maya would return and not want to disturb me. I hadn't slept for over a day, but each time my eyes closed, I roused myself. It grew darker. The shadows from the trees outside the window pooled together, and still Maya wasn't back. I caught myself on the verge of sleep once again and rose from the bed. I walked to the kitchen in search of food, and once I was downstairs, I began to inspect the room.

This too was just how I remembered, from the steel utensils that had been given to Ma on her marriage to the blue glazed dinner set Papa had bought. I picked up a plate and thought of the day of their arrival. Papa had just returned early from a work trip and had seen fit to purchase a new dinner set. The fact that the blue, a proud, unapologetic azure, didn't match our furniture or our tablecloths, hadn't occurred to him. In he had walked, weighed down by a cardboard box, calling out to all of us to gather in the living room for the grand unveiling. He had expected adulation, and when Ma didn't speak, when she didn't rush over to him with congratulations on his choice, he knew he had miscalculated. Slowly, the rest of the house adjusted to its presence. New tablecloths were bought. In a year or so, the dining chairs were reupholstered a deep red, and the blue plates began to feel like they had always been part of our home.

The one I held in my hands had a chip, and as I looked through the range, I saw signs of damage in several others. I set the plate carefully back alongside its siblings and left.

I haunted the house unhurriedly, wandering through rooms I had loved and forgotten. It was my own past I was exploring, and I got a strange sense of time standing still. There was the storeroom that was the depository for all the toys we had outgrown, and as I peeked in, I saw our old bikes stored carefully by the wall. Outside, near the kitchen, I spotted an old calendar. The writing had faded, and I had to strain to make out that it dated from 1995. The calendar hadn't been taken off or replaced for over twenty years.

I heard a noise, a soft crack, a footstep on a dry leaf, perhaps, and I started. I immediately wandered back to the hallway to meet Maya, but I had been mistaken. No light came on in the porch, no key scraped against the lock, and no Maya appeared in front of me. I thought of our neighbours. There had been a family, the Kapoors, to our left with daughters roughly our age. We would meet after school, taking walks in the evening as the weather turned cool. I hadn't met either of the girls for a decade or more, and now as I struggled to recall their names, I walked outside. Their house seemed different—larger, with several cars parked outside it—and though I wanted to walk towards them, to ring their bell and learn of how their lives had turned out, if there had been successes and marriages and children, I didn't. Try as I might, I couldn't recall the names of the girls. They had both had long hair they wore in braids down their backs, and both had a dimple on their left cheeks. Both were conventionally pretty, slim and neat and cheerful, but I couldn't for the life of me remember what they were called.

'They're both married,' I heard a voice say, and turned. There she stood, still and solemn and unyielding, my unsmiling older sister.

I smiled, smiled broadly to see her in spite of her lack of emotion, and she nodded. 'I thought you would be in bed by now.'

I had been on the point of stepping forward to hug her but held back. 'I wanted to wait for you.'

'Good,' she answered, nodding briskly. 'Good.' She walked

to me, putting a hand gingerly on my shoulder. She looked at me as if to gauge my response. 'It's good to see you, Siya.'

We stuck to neutral topics—the weather, the change in global politics, and it was clear Maya wasn't comfortable in my presence. She had been skittish when she had first arrived, standing on tiptoe, keeping a tight hold on her bag, and I half-expected her to fly at any minute. Her hold on me had felt uncomfortable, and though she had led me in, towards the living room that led to each bedroom, she didn't make an effort to converse.

The conversation trailed off, and I saw Maya look towards her room. 'Maya,' I said, and as she looked at me, I blurted out, 'It's so good to see you!'

She surprised me by smiling, and I thought how lovely she was. Her hair was still long and thick and left loose. When she was at college, she had grown it till it skimmed her waist. For a while, she had come back in the evenings—always at an acceptable time, always before dinner ended—with a flower in her hair. The flower changed with the day. Sometimes it was a yellow rose, and sometimes some pungent jasmine, and she took care to remove it before she entered the house, but I stationed myself by my bedroom window, and always caught sight of her looking furtively around before she dashed the flower from behind her ear. These adornments coincided with the time she was friends with a male law student, but the excitement ended almost as soon as it started; the evenings out, the flower in her hair, and the mention of a boy.

I thought of asking about him, but instead, she asked, 'I hope it's not too hot for you?'

'It was snowing last week in London.'

'I heard,' she said, and then, 'I sometimes check on the weather in London.'

'Right,' I said.

She was thrown by the admission, for she swiftly added, 'I have so many friends in London, you see.'

'Of course.'

She was patting her hair, looking around the room as if upset by her admission, and I knew our time together was coming to an end. Her hands rested next to mine, and I turned to her. There were bags underneath her eyes, and I saw lines beginning to appear on her face. Maya had turned forty last year. She smiled, patting my hand, and I thought for the first time of my sister as a middle-aged woman. She looked tired, and there appeared to be a downward bent to her mouth I had never previously noticed. Her jaw hung slacker than I remembered, and I noticed a few strands of white hair near her ear, just by where the evening flowers would have rested. I was so instantly reminded of her in her college days that I asked, 'Are you still in touch with that lawyer friend of yours?'

'Who?' she asked. She had been on the point of sitting down, but now she straightened herself out. 'Are you in any trouble?'

'No!'

She was looking disbelievingly at me. 'Is that why you had to come here in such a rush?'

'No,' I said. 'I hope you don't mind, but I would see you come in some evenings with flowers in your hair.'

There was no reply.

'Please don't be angry,' I rushed to add. 'I was too young to think about privacy, and I thought you looked so beautiful.'

She waved a hand in the air. 'It was nothing.'

'*Didi*,' I said, using the word for older sister I had abandoned years ago. 'What was his name?'

She knew immediately who I referred to. 'Kunal,' she said. 'We were at college together.'

'Was he your boyfriend?'

She paused. 'No,' she said. She played with her hands, lacing her fingers through one another, and I knew she was thinking of the past. Her emotions flitted across her face—there was a smile, followed by a frown, then a slow pat of her cheek—and I knew she was considering her response. How beautiful she still was, despite the slackness of her face, and despite the lines the years had etched on her features. These would ordinarily have been mitigated with creams, with advice from someone close going through the same changes, but there didn't appear to have been anyone around for her to turn to. She was expressive, majestic and solitary, and she reminded me of a heroine of a Greek tragedy. I shook my head to free myself of my morose bent of mind.

Maya looked up at me. 'No,' she replied resolutely, 'He was never my boyfriend.'

There was a host of possibilities in her response that gave me hope. 'But,' I said, armed with my memories of evenings out, of calls and visits, but she was rising. 'You'll be tired,' she said to me.

'But,' I protested, unwilling for the evening to end. We hadn't shared confidences for as long as I could remember, and I had felt then that I could unburden myself to her. I could lay out the whole sorry saga with Benjamin; I could tell her how I had struggled to find employment. The French doors to the veranda were open, and I inhaled the smell of Delhi's summer evening. The bougainvillea, such a lurid pink in the day, wafted gently towards us. 'Tell me how you've been,' I said to my sister. 'I want to catch up on all I've missed while I've been away.'

She laughed a little at that, her mouth parting to reveal her small, even teeth. 'While you've been away,' she echoed, and then, just like that, the wind shifted. Gone were the smiles, gone were the brittle peace and the stilted reminisces. 'On that note,' she said, 'I meant to ask. When do you plan to go back to London?'

She looked at me with an unwelcome intensity, her eyes focused on mine. 'Well?' she was saying, nagging and insistent. I shrugged, and she asked again, 'Well?'

I rose then and smiled at her. It was hot, despite the hour, and humid. It would rain in the morning, but for the moment, I was bathed in perspiration. 'You were right,' I told my sister who continued staring at me, 'I think I am a little tired.'

I turned to my mobile phone the minute I went to my room. I typed out a message to Benjamin before deleting it. Contacting him was a bad idea. He had pestered me with calls after our break-up, showing more commitment in our separation than he ever had during our time together. He had carted bin bags full of old clothes to the charity shop, he had packed my clothes into my suitcases, and when I had run out of suitcase space, had offered to keep an eye on my things.

I could hear Maya readying the home for the night. I heard the water running in her bathroom; heard her switching off the lights in the living room. I had thought I had broken through her reserve, but as I closed my eyes I saw her hard stare. She hated me. I shook my head, telling myself her antagonism wasn't my fault. I had tried my best; there was nothing more I could do. I thought of Tasha-di's call and her worry. There was nothing more I could do.

I checked my messages. There were the usual group chats, but nothing from Benjamin. I typed out a quick message to him—*Have landed*—and sent it.

I told myself I didn't expect a response, but a moment later my phone lit up with his words: 'Fantastic. Have a great time!'

It was all very cordial, and all so pedestrian. And yet he had replied instantly. I turned my phone on its face and watched as the room of my childhood grew indelibly dark.

IV

Maya remained in my thoughts as the dark slowly took over. It was not the Maya I had last seen that I dreamt of, but the companion of my childhood. The sister, the best friend, the partner of all my infantile crimes. The pre-pubescent Maya with the smooth dark skin. The Maya with hair as dense as a winter's night; the Maya with the irrepressible smile and the dimples that deepened for a frown as much as for a smile.

Early in my fourteenth year, I had believed myself in love. There had been a boy at school. He was of average height and build, and there was nothing about him to attract attention, but he had always seemed to be around. I had noticed him smiling at me, and then one day, he had handed over a letter he told me was written in his blood. I had laughed when he had made the claim, partly out of nerves, but then he had turned his wrist over. I had seen the scar on his arm and had told myself I was in love. If I'm honest, I hadn't believed myself capable of inspiring such devotion. I hadn't been taught to think of myself as particularly lovely, and my greatest vanity was my pride in my even features. My nose was neither overly large nor small, nor were my lips or eyes. There was nothing exceptional about me, and still here he was, this boy, prepared to dip a pen in his own blood for me.

We had arranged to meet late one Tuesday evening. It had been his idea, and I had worried about how I'd get out of the house at that hour, but I'd been too flattered to refuse. In the end I had invented an excuse—a study evening at a friend's house—but in my excitement, I had revealed my plans to Maya.

I had expected my older sister to encourage me, but Maya had been against the idea from the start. She had put her hands on her waist and had paced rapidly around the stone patio to the front of our house. It was a quiet October evening, the ground she stepped on was strewn with dark bougainvillea, but I still worried that her movements would attract notice. There were a dozen people coming and going from the house—guards, cleaners, drivers, suppliers. There was danger beyond our gates too. We were a tight-knit community in those days; everyone knew each other, and crucially, we knew each other's patterns. The Kapoor girls next door had their harmonium lessons on Tuesday evenings. Their tutor was due to leave at any moment. We addressed all our elders as uncle or aunty, and in exchange for our unconditional respect, the uncles and aunties didn't consider it intrusive to weigh in on personal issues. There was no keeping a secret. There was no privacy.

'Ha!' Maya had said, reading my thoughts. Her skin had been dewy with the warmth of Delhi's evenings, dark and glowing, her teenage breakouts neatly masked—or so we thought—with Ma's kohl. Her eyes had sparkled with conviction. 'You worry that someone might spot me, and yet you're happy to take such a great risk to meet this boy.'

I had stayed mute, but I could feel my jaw set.

'All this for a boy you've just met. You didn't even know his name last week.'

'I did.'

'And,' Maya interrupted. 'You won't even remember his name in another twenty years. Is he worth risking so much trouble for?'

I had held firm. I had ranted, accusing Maya of being jealous. Maya had laughed at the accusations. 'You're an idiot,' she had said. 'But I'm not going to let you go alone.'

We set off on foot to the edge of the neighbourhood. On our way we passed by countless aunties on their evening walks. 'Beta,' we were asked repeatedly. 'What are you doing out so late?'

'We've been revising all this while,' Maya said. 'We wanted to take a walk before it was too late.'

'Hurry,' we were told. 'It'll be dark soon.'

We rushed gratefully on, both now uncomfortable to be out. It had begun to grow dark, and here, in the outer reaches of our neighbourhood, the streets were empty. Two of the lights weren't working, and we raced through the pools of dark. We ran to the main road, coming to a stop by the taxi stand where I was to meet the bloodied author of my love letters. It was late in the evening now, and the hour Delhi's workers returned home. Daily labourers, shop boys, guards, and gardeners, and drivers and cooks made their slow way back homewards. They exited overcrowded buses by the taxi stand, relaxing for the first time in hours. They milled around, taking in the air, talking amongst themselves and picking up last minute provisions. Some wandered near us. Curiosity about two unaccompanied girls drew some, while others were attracted by the smells of snacks cooking at a food stall just behind us.

'Really?' hissed Maya. 'You two geniuses had to choose a spot near all these people?'

The air was close, and still hot. The fumes from the food

seller grew strong, and each time a new bus passed, we inched closer together. Soon there was a huge crush around us; men closing in, leering and pushing.

'God!' I cried, as one jostled against me. Maya quickly pulled me towards her and put a protective hand in mine. I looked around for signs of the boy I was to meet, but we had set off early, and the traffic was chaotic. He wasn't due for a while yet. It was growing hotter and closer, the noises and the shoving more oppressive with each passing moment. We were both thoroughly tired of our adventure, when we suddenly saw a familiar face. It was Malik, the neighbourhood watchman on his way home after finishing his shift.

'You girls,' he shouted. 'What are you doing alone here at this time of the night?'

There was no time to answer. The crowd melted at the sound of his voice, and now he leaned forward, took us each by the arm and marched us through the neighbourhood. We had gone from being the objects of attention—too much attention—to parcels to be dumped unceremoniously at Papa's door.

'I'm telling you, Sir,' Malik said to a surprised Papa. I looked at him, dark, sinewy, capable, and normally so deferential. The neighbourhood's residents pooled together to give him his annual bonus. It habitually exceeded his monthly pay, and now that he was looking to save up for his daughter's wedding, he was counting on the families' generosity. It was the old-fashioned system of *bakshish* that kept us all—master and servant—dependent on each other. Supplicant and benefactor. We'd all noticed the change in Malik's manner. A smarter salute when our car passed him by. A wider smile than usual for us children. A sweet—a chocolate éclair, or the tangy *hajmola* digestives we all hankered after—as we got off the school bus at the end of the day. 'I'm telling you,' he was repeating, his face foreboding, 'There's a boy involved in this.'

I muttered something about revising for an exam, but Papa raised his hand to silence me. 'What revision were you doing by the taxi stand?'

Malik was in full flow. He lifted his arm, revealing the sweat patches under his shirt. 'I've never seen the likes of it, Sir. The two of them, standing in full view of all those men, like two common dancing girls. No shame, Sir. I can't say what would have happened if I hadn't come.'

The noise was loud, the lights were on, and Ma, vigilant watchwoman of the family's affairs, stepped out. 'Hai Ram!' she cried. Others were starting to pay attention to our woes; the guards at the gate, part-time staff in other houses heading home, and residents on their evening walks. She turned to the watchman, 'If it hadn't been for you, Malik.'

'Bas, Ma'am,' said Malik unctuously. If he had been ruffled by Pa's unresponsiveness, he revived in the face of Ma's ostentation. 'I was only doing my duty. But,' he said, returning to his dark theme, 'if I hadn't been there…'

'What were they doing there?'

The adults turned their scrutiny on us.

'It's a boy, I tell you,' repeated Malik.

'Hai Ram,' echoed Ma. She swooned. The night grew closer, I saw more lights go on down the street. The grown-ups stared at us suspiciously, and after long moments of uncomfortable silence, Maya stepped forward. 'It was me,' she said. 'I was going to meet a boy.'

Ma was surprised. For Maya, too biddable for her own good,

to be swayed by a boy was unexpected. The watchman was looking at her expectantly, as were the guards at the gate. Our neighbours lingered on their way home, and Ma swung into action.

'Of all the idiotic things,' she began. 'Do you know what could have happened to you?'

Maya kept her head meekly cast down.

'Do you?'

Maya refused to speak up for herself, and as Ma swiftly ran out of steam, she reverted to the outlet favoured by the subcontinent's arbiters of justice, landing a stinging slap on Maya's cheek.

Maya had never been in trouble before. She didn't cry or complain, and appeared suitably chastised at dinner. It was only later, when we were alone, that Maya said to me, 'All this trouble, and for a boy whose name you will soon forget.'

'No,' I told her, trying to excuse his no-show. 'He must have been held up,' but the truth was Maya was right. I never tried to meet the boy again. He did approach me at school, but I ignored him. I struggled to place him now, all that remained was the memory of a broad nose in a wide face. Sweaty palms too, and that proudly scarred wrist, but that was all that remained of my maiden adventure.

In the months that followed, Maya grew more studious. She was in her last year of school, and was revising for her exams, so the schism was understandable, but we both sensed our night-time outing had been a step too far for her.

In a few months, she would start at college, and I would gravitate towards the nameless girls next door. It was with them that I would learn to practice applying make-up, and with them that I would time my evening walks for when other boys from the area were venturing outside. Maya didn't recede, exactly, from my consciousness, but I began to associate her company with a more innocent time in my life.

~

She never stepped out of line again. She studied well, breaking off her burgeoning relationship when Ma counselled it. When she was awarded a scholarship to study at university in America, she turned to Ma again, who told her that she would find all the by-lines she needed in India itself.

The scholarship was turned down, then, and when I won my own scholarship, Ma expected me to follow my sister's example and reject it. Her anxiety was palpable from the moment the acceptance letter arrived. She drove to school to pick me up, which should have tipped me off. Normally, the old po-faced driver, Bahadur, waited at the school gates for me, but there Ma was, waving to attract my attention, and tapping at her watch to hurry me up.

'Why are you here?' I asked gracelessly, but she just rushed me to the car.

Once seated, she pulled out the envelope. 'It came with the morning post. I've been picking it up every two minutes, and once or twice, I was tempted to open it myself.' She noted the arch look I shot at her and held her hands up. 'But I didn't, ok? It's been killing me since the morning, but I knew I had to respect your privacy.'

She thrust the envelope in my hands, as I squealed, out of nerves and anticipation, she said, 'It's thick. Maya's acceptance letter was thick too.'

Once the letter was opened, once it was scanned and snatched out of my hands by an impatient Ma, and once it was retrieved and re-examined, Ma asked, 'When will you reply?'

'Immediately.'

'That's my girl,' she smiled. 'You know how proud I am of you, don't you?'

I blushed. 'Thanks, Ma.'

'My brilliant girls. But there are enough great colleges in India too.'

She was leaning across the clutch and hugging me, and it dawned on me for the first time that she meant for me to refuse the offer.

'Ma,' I said. 'I want to go.'

'No, darling,' she replied. She held me at arm's length, taking an indulgent survey of my features. 'No, no,' she repeated.' She turned to start the car. 'We'll write the letter together.'

I fully expected Ma to get her way. I told her I was not going to reject the offer, and she suggested I sleep on the decision. One day turned into two, and then a week passed, and still Ma's rhetoric remained unchanged. There was no need to leave home.

I was sure Papa would side with her, but when he didn't, I grew more resolute. 'Listen to me,' Maya advised me after a particularly fraught evening's arguing. 'Ma knows what's best for you.'

'And what,' I asked my shocked sister, 'if she doesn't?'

I did go, in the end, and even though Ma claimed she supported my decision, she cooled in her treatment of me. Increasingly, she would leave me to decide matters for myself.

'You know best,' she began to say anytime I asked her for her opinion, and it felt to me that if she was to have no rights over my future, she would take no interest in it either.

For as long as I could remember, Ma's world had revolved around the three of us, and central to that world was our presence in her house. She seemed not to have any interest outside of us. She was there at every school play and debate, was a committed cheerleader at annual sports days, and if she had a social life outside of us or Tasha-di, we didn't know of it.

She found it difficult to deal with the changes that my move brought, and though she was always cordial when I called, she herself never rang. There was always an excuse ready—the time difference was too great, or she worried about disturbing me at my studies—but we both knew her behaviour had changed. She was no longer the hovering, over-protective mother I sometimes found stifling. After a while, I grew resentful, and called her less. Papa and I still spoke, but a week would pass, and then two, between calls with my mother. As for Maya, she never stepped out of line again.

V

I waited to speak to Maya in the morning. She had been stand-offish as we ended our evening, but there had been moments in our conversation when I had sensed a chink in her reserve.

I thought of how worried Tasha-di had been about her, and I thought of all the questions I had been on the point of asking her about her writing and how she spent her days. I didn't know who her friends were, or if she had any. I didn't know if she missed Ma, if she still idolised her, or if she could conceive of a life away from her shadow. She didn't know the challenges I had faced in London, and in some ways, hadn't seemed curious about a world outside her own. I didn't know if this lack of interest was personal. I didn't know enough about her to know if she meant to offend.

I waited till noon, then knocked on her door. There was no response. I debated going in but was wary of entering unbidden, and instead, I returned to the lounge and tried to occupy myself. My phone was no use to me; there was barely any reception available, and I spent a little time refamiliarizing myself with the country's newspapers.

Shanti came by asking if I was hungry, and I told her I would wait for Maya.

'Maya baby,' she said uncertainly. 'I thought she would have been with you.'

Shanti hadn't seen her all day, hadn't heard the car start or the front door open. I walked to the veranda, opening the windows, and as Delhi's sun hit me, I looked out. There was no sign of my sister.

A framed photograph caught my eye, and I wandered in its direction. Our pictures hadn't been updated in over a decade and I knew all the items displayed by heart. I had looked at the same faces and smiles all my life, and yet, here was a dusty print on the mantelpiece opposite where Ma liked to sit that I didn't recognise. I walked towards it. The photograph was indistinct behind the layers of dust that had gathered, neither the faces nor location discernible, and I began to wipe at the glass of the frame with my hand.

My palm was soon thick with dirt, but the faces grew clearer. It was a graduation scene, the students in caps and gowns, and as I peered, I recognised the senate building at my university. 'It's from your undergraduate degree,' I heard Maya say, and as I turned towards her, I saw she had come from the staircase. I smiled. She hadn't been avoiding me, then, or at least not ignoring the calls from inside her bedroom.

'Ma,' Maya was continuing, 'was so proud of you.' She smiled, half embarrassed. 'Kept telling everyone you had achieved a first class degree.'

Maya was shaking her head as if Ma's preening about me was habitual, but the truth was she hadn't attended my graduation. Maya hadn't either, and it had only been Papa who had flown across to see me receive my degree. Ma hadn't called after the ceremony, and I had told myself I hadn't expected her to.

But here it was, right in front of where Ma sat, my graduation photo from the university Ma hadn't wanted me to study at.

'She was very proud of you, you know.'

I snorted.

'She was,' Maya was insisting. 'We both were.' Her face scrunched up a little. 'I still am.'

And there, unbidden, were the tears I hadn't cried for a year or longer. The tears that should have been shed at Ma's passing, at the loss of my job, at the continuing troubles with Benjamin, at my failure to check in on my bereft sister. She was reaching forward, for all her prickliness of the night before, and with infinite, excruciating care, she was putting a hand around my shoulder. 'What brought that all on, silly?'

'It's all such a mess.'

Maya was shaking her head.

'It is,' I repeated, the younger sibling again, insisting my voice was heard. 'My job has gone…'

'There will be other jobs.'

'No,' I said, tinny, high-pitched. 'I've been applying for jobs for a year or longer. No one is hiring.'

'Well,' she said, detaching herself from me. She sat down on Ma's old seat. 'It's a tough world out there.'

'It's never been this hard before…'

'It *is* always harder for us.'

I blinked dumbly.

'Come on,' she was saying, nodding in emphasis, impatient at my lack of comprehension. 'You know that it is always harder for women.'

I stared. She was only a few years older than me, and yet her attitudes—her opinions, her passiveness, her fatalism, her willingness to admit defeat—were pure Ma. Where had this note of sexism crept in? Was it an explicit prejudice, or the fears Ma had poured into her? Or had she ventured out into the world after Ma's passing and found her path blocked?

'You've always been so idealistic,' Maya was saying, 'But you have to face facts. Life is always just that bit harder for a woman.'

I tried the door that led off the landing again, to no avail. It was a broad, thick old structure, and though I pushed hard, and then ran at it as I had seen in the movies, I didn't make an impact.

There was, I remembered, another staircase on the other side of the house, from behind the kitchen. I had never climbed it in all the years I had lived in the house. There was something Shanti had said to me as a young girl, something about ghosts lining the service staircase, that had filled me with fear, and I had never attempted to tackle the stairs. The second floor was where she carried out her housekeeping duties. This was where the bedsheets and clothes were taken to be ironed after they were washed, and I had seen her all the time, scurrying away with basket-loads of air-dried washing, and had never once followed her.

Even now, as I tried to penetrate the areas of the house that were closed to me, I didn't think of climbing up the stairs behind the kitchen. Still, Shanti must have seen me hover in the area, as she asked me if I needed anything.

'No,' I said to her, and then, 'I tried to get into the second floor, but found it locked.'

Shanti sighed. A strand of hair escaped from her bun, and she tucked it swiftly back into place. 'Baby,' she said. 'That floor has been shut for months.'

'Why?' I asked. I could feel my mouth turning down with a juvenile petulance, and she nodded patiently.

'What can your poor sister do?' she asked. 'The house was crumbling before your mother died, and if I'm to be honest, it needed work even before you left for England.'

By the time I visited after Ma's death, the walls were a study in shading. The gardener came and maintained the garden, just as Shanti took care of the house and its inhabitants, but the bigger issues that transcended maintenance were overlooked. Plaster peeled off the outside walls, and there was no mobile reception in any room barring the living room on the ground floor and a certain spot in my bedroom on the floor above. A bookcase had caved in the library and had not been repaired. And that was just a brief list of what I had seen. I had largely refrained from marching into Shanti's kitchen, and as for the floor above the one I slept in, I couldn't think of the horrors the locked door masked.

Shanti shook her head, lowering herself gingerly onto a chair. She rubbed her knee slowly, as if rubbing ointment on a bruise, and I said to her, 'You need to slow down.'

She waved her hands at me.

'You do,' I insisted. There it was again, the petulant tone in my voice. Somehow, I always ended up sounding like a child in this house. These were the ghosts Shanti always warned me about, but they weren't the shadows of strangers. They were the spectres of my own infancy. 'You do too much around here,' I said. 'Running up and down all those stairs.'

'The ghosts carry me around,' she laughed, but I refused to join in her hilarity. This was not the same household I had grown up in. There had been two chefs when I was at school, and two boys to help Shanti with her labours. There were the cleaners who came in every day, and Shanti largely had a managerial role in the house; keeping all the staff in order. She saw me shaking my head, and put her hand in mine, 'The house is getting old, baby,' she said. 'Just like your Shanti.'

'You're not old,' I replied stoutly. Then I remembered I had said the same about the others I had loved; Papa and Ma. I thought of her house in the village. Every year Ma would give Shanti a bonus on our birthdays, and it was with these supplemental gifts of money that Shanti had built her home. One year's gifts would pay for the shell of the house, the next for the doors and windows. She furnished her house the following year, and slowly, added to her possessions; kitchen utensils, a coir *charpai*, and then, after much encouragement, an outdoor toilet. 'Maybe,' I said to her, 'you could retire to your house in the village?'

'Maybe,' she said, smiling. Her hand remained in mine, and she gave it a squeeze.

'But seriously,' I was saying. I got up from where I sat, removing my hand from Shanti's. 'Why don't you?'

'I can't leave my girls.'

'What's stopping you?' I asked. 'Are you worried about Pradeep? He can live with us for as long as he wants to. This is his home as much as it is ours.' I looked at her nodding patiently, as if she were indulging me, and a new thought occurred to me, 'You do want to go back to your home and your husband, don't you?'

Shanti rose from her chair and came towards me. Once more her arms straddled mine, as if I were the one in need of comfort. 'No,' she said to me with immense kindness. 'No baby, I don't want to go home to my husband.'

I had begun to take a walk of a morning. There was no exercising in Delhi otherwise; we drove everywhere, and that too was often a production. The car had to be retrieved from the garage, and by the time we had the ancient motor running, Shanti would have run out of the house, offering Pradeep's services or requesting we pick up provisions from the market. Most days we would only be able to leave an hour after an outing was first spoken of. On my walks, my time was my own. There was no need to remember to take the keys, no need to return within the hour or with staples. I was largely guided by the heat, which began to grow unbearable earlier in the day as my stay continued. I adjusted by starting my walks earlier in the morning, leaving at six and before breakfast.

I asked Maya several times to accompany me, but she was always busy. She told me she was writing, or that she had to meet a friend, but I never saw her leave the house, and I never saw her byline appear on any publication. Our interaction was civil enough, but stilted, and there was no reprising the intimacy I had so briefly sensed at the start of my visit. I walked, then, on my own, and started to bump into other regulars; workers on errands, and residents from neighbouring houses. I didn't recognise most of them; the houses I had grown up next to had invariably been turned into palatial flats. There were many more families around than I ever remembered, and I was often joined by a grandmother on her way around the locality. The woman, a Mrs Bhatnagar, lived with her daughter and her young family in a house a few doors down from ours and went out for her exercise as soon as her grandchildren had been sent off to school for the day. Her day out started towards the end of my walk, but she would fall in line with me, giving me unprompted snippets of her life, and in return, asking for details of my life and prospects.

For all Mrs Bhatnagar's prying, I began to enjoy her company. There was a familiarity to her prejudices; telling me to cross the road to avoid a black cat, scolding her little errand boy when she saw him dawdling outside. She was always skittish around stray dogs, clutching my arm as if that offered a talisman against an attack, and this homely claim was welcome. This woman, with her constant diets and frequent calls to her religious guru was a mother unlike my own had ever been. She was credulous and silly and superstitious and endlessly fallible, but there was a warmth to her that I found hard to resist.

She was handy with gossip too, and after Maya's froideur, I found her loquaciousness refreshing. We passed by a stationary car, and Mrs Bhatnagar told me about the Bollywood starlet who was inside. 'She went to Modern School, you know. She's very much a local girl.' And then, around the corner, her voice dropped, her words grew worshipful, and she pointed at a large, freshly painted house. 'And that's Raja Singh's palace, of course.'

'Raja Singh?'

'You know, the angel guy…'

'Angel?'

'Angel, you know.' She wiped sweat off her upper lip as she searched for the right word. 'Angel investor. He's made a ton of money as India has changed. He's invested in online delivery companies, in TV stations, in those mother-in-law-daughter-in-law TV serials. He's like a modern day Midas. Knows everyone who's anyone. And his wife—what a woman.'

Mrs Bhatnagar paused in front of the house, and I looked through the gaps in the gate.

'She is gorgeous, of course. Always dripping with diamonds…'

I was still peering at the house, and Mrs Bhatnagar pulled at my sleeve. 'Who?' I asked.

'Why, Mrs Singh, of course.' Mrs Bhatnagar pursed her mouth at my inattention. 'What lavish parties she hosts! What clothes she wears! She's just back from Santorini, you know!'

'Santorini must be hot at this time of year.'

Mrs Bhatnagar looked pensively at me. I thought she was on the point of walking to the Singh house to introduce me to Mrs Singh, but she turned away. 'I'll have to ask my maid,' she was saying. 'She knows the Singhs' maid, you know. She keeps me up-to-date with all the goings on in the household.'

I worried that I had embarrassed Mrs Bhatnagar, and rushed to change the topic. I guessed her daughter was around my age, and asked her if she ever joined her on her walk. Mrs Bhatnagar let out a loud hoot. 'Rashmi,' she told me, 'thinks that walks are too common.'

'Too pedestrian,' I offered, but thc irony appeared to escape her.

'She only likes to go to the gym,' she told me. 'She drops her children off to school, and then is in the gym until lunchtime.' Mrs Bhatnagar swerved past a champak tree, and though I paused to smell the fragrance, she tugged me on. 'She will spend all morning there, going to her classes, sitting in the sauna. Sauna!' she cried, 'As if Delhi itself isn't a sauna! And then,' she said, 'She'll visit the salon and have some food at a restaurant. She never returns home to eat,' she sniffed. This more than anything seemed to affront the woman, 'Says Indian food is too greasy. Bah!' she cried, holding me back from a speeding car, and I wasn't sure if she was more affronted by the motorist or her child. 'The kids follow her lead too, and they will only have pizza or pasta for dinner.' She sniggered. 'As if there isn't any grease in all that fancy, fancy food!'

Every word she spoke was laced with judgement. The

'modern generation' came in for much of her ire, though I refrained from pointing out I too belonged to it. I wasn't immune from her questioning for long, though, as she soon asked me, 'And you, child, are you married?'

'No,' I replied. Her gaze continued intent on me, and I added, 'No, aunty.' The pharmacist passed us, bowing to Mrs Bhatnagar, and she pulled at my arm to talk to him. 'I will be visiting you soon, Kapoor,' she pronounced, and as he bowed, telling her he would await her visit, I hoped the topic of my spinsterhood would be forgotten. But then, as we walked on, she said to me, 'Not married yet?'

'No,' I replied. I looked overhead. The heat was intensifying; perhaps I could get away at the next turn.

'Tell me,' she said. She yanked my hand, 'How old are you?'

I didn't dare pretend to be offended by the question. I had turned thirty-seven the previous month, but as she stared unblinkingly at me, I gulped. 'I'm thirty-six, aunty,' I answered humbly.

'Hmm,' she said thoughtfully. 'You're old.' She looked at me dispassionately, and I lifted a hand to my face in defence. 'Rashmi was married at twenty-five. But then,' she added, 'I've heard you had an unorthodox mother.' This was pronounced with greater disdain than usual, and I was on the point of speaking up. 'And,' she continued, cheering up. 'Things are changing. Maybe there will be some divorcé or widower who will be willing to take you on.'

She stopped in her path and stood looking at me with benevolence.

'Besides,' she told me, 'that's some serious real estate you sisters are sitting on.' I looked away, embarrassed by her words, but she carried blithely on. 'Of course, your sister is too old for marriage, but with you, the real estate you bring with you will add to your attractiveness.' We had paused, taking up the entire pavement, and I saw other pedestrians dip down to the street to swerve around us. Mrs Bhatnagar took hold of my arm, shaking it in emphasis. 'Yes,' she said thoughtfully. 'That would make you quite the pretty package.'

She was looking at me expectantly, and I knew I was expected to be grateful for her idea, but I saw a turn I could take, and pointed in its direction instead. I could have stood up for Ma, or could have told her I was in no hurry to marry, or that Maya wasn't too old, but I just told her I had to get back, and rushed off towards home.

Back at the house, I kept thinking about what Mrs Bhatnagar had said. We were one of the only houses on the street that remained whole. Most of the rest had been divided—through family settlements, or through sales to property developers—and the few that remained whole had been recently restored and sold to large business families. Here too, several families co-existed; brothers running different arms of a large conglomerate occupying separate wings of the same house. It was only our house, it seemed, that was occupied by so few. Once, when I had been out in the evening with Tasha-di, I had returned to the area to see all the other homes ablaze with light. Most of the floors in each dwelling were lit, and in many, fairy lights twinkled in the garden. Our house, in comparison, felt funereal. I could see the light on in Shanti's kitchen, and then, lights on in the veranda where Maya sat. If Pradeep was in his quarters, signs of his habitation were hidden from view by the gloom of the main house. Tasha-di must have read my thoughts, as she said, 'This house hasn't been alive for years.'

'It's too big,' I said.

'Yes,' she said. 'But who is to tell Maya?'

They had been sure, mother and daughter, that I was after money. All the reserve that had permeated our relationship had solidified after I suggested that the house was too big for them. I looked up to see Tasha-di studying me. 'Yes,' I echoed, 'who is to tell Maya?'

VI

Shanti fell down the stairs late one afternoon. She was rushing from the ground floor with some ironing when she slipped. I had been in the library reading a book, and trying to stay out of Maya's way, when I heard her cry. I rushed first to the kitchen, but finding no Shanti, I moved towards the staircase that had terrified me for so long. There I hesitated, reluctant to tackle it, when I heard a cry, 'Is someone there?'

I started. Then the call echoed again, and I yelled into the gloom, 'Shanti?'

There was a panic in her voice that I had never heard before. 'Hurry, baby.'

I ran up the stairs two at a time. It was dark, and a narrower space than the staircase we used, and as I neared the first floor, I found Shanti crumpled against the wall. Her torso rested at an angle to her legs, and I was hesitant to touch her for fear of causing her harm. Piles of clean sheets lay a few steps above her.

'I was in a rush,' said Shanti. She looked in pain but smiled reassuringly when she saw me. 'I should have looked where I was going.'

I asked her if she could walk. She nodded, rising on her feet, but then she yelped, a little like a trapped animal. Her arms circled mine, and I told her to rest on me. I took her carefully back to her room, asking her all the time if she was in distress, but she insisted she wasn't. 'You've come back home, baby,' she kept on saying, but I saw how ragged her breath was. Pradeep was out at work, and I settled her on her bed. Maya was told of the accident, and she ran across to Shanti's quarters with water and paracetamol. 'You've fallen again?' she asked Shanti, who nodded shamefacedly.

'Again?' I asked, but Maya appeared not to have heard me.

The doctor was called, and he recommended a trip to the hospital. We both went with Shanti, and as we waited for her to emerge from having her back X-rayed, Maya said to me, 'You're not going back to London, are you?'

I hadn't had a single reply to my job queries. Benjamin had sent that one breezy text, but there hadn't been any further communication. The lease on my flat was up for renewal in a few months, and I would have to decide what to do then, but in the meantime, there was nothing dragging me back to the life I had called my own. I didn't respond to Maya, and she said softly, 'You were right about the house.'

I didn't dare speak. I wasn't sure if she was trying to make me feel better, but I scarcely dared believe she meant her words. For so long, both Ma and Maya had suspected that my suggestion was driven by greed, and now that Maya herself had brought the topic up, I was wary of saying anything. 'I was thinking,' she said. 'It is too big for us.'

'I don't know…'

'It is.' She looked at me, nodding animatedly, as if to invite agreement, and I saw what a watershed moment her admission was. She had resisted any interference for years, but now that she had admitted that things had to change, she couldn't stop talking. 'Most of the rooms are boarded up, and we get lost in the rest. That poor Shanti falling…'

Maya trailed off. I was cautious about offering my opinion, but I needn't have worried. Maya was speaking again.

'I didn't want to listen to you. Ma didn't either. She thought it would be an admission of weakness, somehow, to accept the thought that we couldn't afford the house's upkeep. And after Ma...'

Here Maya stopped. She took a deep breath, and then another, and I put my hand on her arm. This touch felt as awkward as our first meeting a few weeks back, and Maya rose. She walked up towards the X-ray department and peered in through the glass panel on the door.

'Maya,' I said, but she didn't respond. I didn't bring up the house again, and after Shanti emerged from the X-ray, our focus was on her. She hadn't broken any bones, and the doctor prescribed painkillers and a week of rest. But relations between us seemed to have improved, as Maya joined me on my walk the next day. We avoided Mrs Bhatnagar when she came out and waved at us, and as we walked, we mulled through various options for the house.

Neither of us wanted to sell. The house, behemoth though it was, was part of our lives, and we were loath to part with it. The best option, then, was to partition it and either rent or sell bits off. We would have to call in a builder. Typically, Maya told me, they would work for free in exchange for taking a chunk of a house—a floor or a wing. 'My old school friend's parents,' she said, 'were only left with a floor of their house once they called a builder in.'

I frowned. I told her I had some savings, and though I didn't tell her a large part of this was the redundancy money I had received, she shook her head. 'It will take millions,' she told me, 'everything needs doing.'

The idea of parting with the house was anathema to me, and I saw for the first time the struggle Ma and Maya must have endured. 'I have some money too,' I repeated, in the hope that my savings would at least kickstart the work, but she refused to let me offer my money.

'I've been resisting this for years,' she said to me. 'But it makes sense to call in a builder. They'll value the property, so getting them in will be worthwhile even if we change our minds.'

VII

Shanti was back in the kitchen two days after she fell. Maya and I had gone out for our walk, and returned to find her preparing breakfast.

We told her she was meant to rest, and that we could prepare food, but she waved our concerns off. We told her that her back needed to heal and she laughed. She continued to chop her onions and tomatoes with a manic zeal, and it was clear from watching her that she had built up a good head of steam. 'My back,' she said, 'has survived much worse than a fall.'

'Come on, Shanti,' Maya said. She spoke with great tenderness, and I suspected such outbursts were a commonplace occurrence.

'All my life,' Shanti said. There were tears in her eyes, through her contact with the onions, through her agitation, and Maya tried once again to put a hand on Shanti's shoulders. Shanti was having none of it. 'All my life I have served people.' She was looking at her board of chopped vegetables with distaste. 'I have cooked their food, bathed their infants, cleaned their shit.'

This was so unexpected that there was an intake of breath from both Maya and me. Shanti huffed, putting a hand up to the small of her back as she returned to her work, and as I rushed to bring her a chair, she told me to stop. 'All his beatings,' she continued, glaring at me, 'I withstood all of them. And now you want to send me back to him?'

'Shanti…'

I was confused, but Maya remained by the woman's side, running a hand on her back. 'Nothing is going to change, Shanti.'

'All these things you're planning…'

'What are you talking about, Shanti?' I asked.

'Are you not planning on bringing a builder in?'

Maya and I looked at each other. They would have heard us talking, mother and son, and worried our plans meant change for them too. 'Well,' I said, on the defensive, 'you yourself said the house was too big.'

'It *is* too big,' she agreed, 'But I don't want to be made homeless.'

We both laughed at her hysteria, and she fixed us with an angry stare. 'Come on, Shanti,' I said.

But she wasn't done. 'I don't want to have to go and live with that wretched husband of mine.'

'No one is going to make you homeless, Shanti,' Maya was saying, but I had a question.

'Why are you calling your husband wretched?'

Shanti laughed. 'He's struck the lottery with me, that's why.' She finally let go of the knife she was using to chop vegetables and sat down on the chair I held out for her. She grimaced with pain. 'I send all my money home to him, and he spends it on alcohol. He has hangers-on around him all day long, getting drunk and making trouble for other villagers, even when Pradeep and I visit. Now tell me, is this a good example to set for the boy?' I looked sombre, but Shanti was carrying on. 'If I say anything, he beats me.' Shanti thumped at her right thigh, wincing with pain at the contact. 'He brought out a rod the last time we argued.'

'Oh Shanti…'

'Guess who won that argument?' She let out a mirthless laugh. Turning to Maya, she said, 'Remember I wasn't able to sit down for months?'

Maya nodded.

'Even now,' and Shanti's hand rose to her waist. 'Even now it hurts when I'm rising or sitting. It is painful when I lay down at night.'

There was a shudder that passed through her frame, and I asked, 'When was this?'

'Last winter.' This could have been before or after Ma's death, before or after my visit, but Shanti didn't provide further details. 'I'll live my life here,' he told me. 'And you have your fun in Delhi.'

'Shanti…'

'Fun!' she sniffed. She brought some phlegm up through her throat, and I half-expected her to spit it out, but it remained in her mouth, neither expelled nor absorbed. Her face puckered up, as if she had ingested something unappetising, but at length, she held her nose and swallowed. Maya and I looked at each other, and Maya rolled her eyes at me. It appeared Shanti had behaved erratically before. 'Fun!' she said again, bringing our attention back to her. 'And now you want to bundle me off to that savage!'

I came to where Maya knelt, putting a hand on Shanti's shoulder. She started at the contact. 'No one is bundling you off,' I said, and though she sniffed again, she didn't move away.

A builder visited, a broad, waxy-moustached man who had carried out work for her school friend. He inspected the property thoroughly, shaking his head at the layers of books and magazines on top of every surface, tutting at the collapsed bookcase, wrinkling his nose at the musty smell in the abandoned rooms. He grimaced at the cracks spreading thin fingers across each ceiling, and we worried the problems with the house were insurmountable.

'It's a lot of work, I know,' I said.

He laughed. 'A lot of work?' he said, still convulsed with laughter. He shook his head, his face flushed from his exertion, and pointed at the exposed wiring, and at the damp rising up the walls. He tapped at the ceiling, coughing as dust rained down on our shoulders. 'The entire structure needs to be taken apart.'

'Oh.'

'I could,' he said, smiling benevolently, as if the honour was ours, 'make it easier for you and just take the thing off your hands. I've done this before, you see.' He pointed towards the west. 'There is another house in Civil Lines I have taken into my hands. Tore the whole thing down. Number 2, you know,' and Maya nodded.

'The new one,' she told me, wincing. The builder smiled proudly. 'The one that's all chrome and glass.'

'Yes,' he said. 'That's the one. We put in two floors of parking, and a rooftop bar and swimming pool. It houses six families now, all top-notch executive sorts.' He nodded. 'That was a very worthwhile project.'

'Thank you,' I said. 'You have given us a lot to think about,' but the builder wasn't done.

'We need to talk numbers,' he informed us. A price was

named, a figure so low that Maya balked, and the builder was swiftly told we would revert to him with our thoughts.

'They're all sharks,' she said to me. 'They see two women alone and know they can take advantage.'

'He would destroy the house.'

'Glass staircases, just imagine. As if this was a Cinderella fantasy, and not a heritage property.'

'Well,' I said. 'He's not getting the job. What are we going to do?'

Maya shrugged. 'You left,' she said, and though I worried she was signposting a return to her early froideur, I began to bristle. What had I been expected to do, tie myself to Ma forever? Remain as Maya had, the protected child, pampered and safe and invaluable? She could have tested her wings too, and if she had, perhaps I would have felt less alienated.

Nothing had ever been said, not explicitly, but things changed the minute I was out of the house. They told me I was overreacting anytime I pointed this out, but it felt to me like I was swiftly written out of the family. Suddenly, the unit at home seemed not to include me. New Year's cards sent by friends were addressed to Maya, Ma and Papa, and not me, and it made sense. I no longer lived at home, but it appeared as if I never had. Ma never asked when I would visit. They all, and in particular my mother and sister, developed their own vernacular. There were trips I wasn't party to, meals and movies and jokes that I hadn't partaken of. They had to be reminded—time and time again—with a regularity that soon grew fractious, that they could visit too. If they had shifted on purpose to flush out the space my absence created, they never said so, and to me it felt like the unit I looked at with such longing from afar was the only one that had ever been. There I was in England, bitterly homesick and friendless for the first few years, and life seemed to be carrying on just fine without me in Delhi. 'And Ma,' Maya was saying, and I looked up at her. 'Ma,' she continued, 'took your move very badly.'

'Sure,' I said, the most aggressive response I felt capable of, but Maya appeared not to have noticed my tone.

'She didn't leave her room for days,' she said. 'Didn't bathe, didn't come out and order the staff around, didn't come out for breakfast or for tea or for dinner.' Maya flashed an involuntary smile. 'For days, she left off her invasive questions—*Where are you going, and who are you going to see? Will there be boys there?* I was quite relieved, to be honest, but Papa was worried. He said Ma's grief was ridiculous—you had won a scholarship to one of the best universities in the world, after all.'

'Ma just stopped talking to me, Maya.'

'Ma lost a bit of her sparkle after you left.' She looked across at the library, where Papa had been in the habit of returning with his briefs. 'And Papa didn't say anything to her either.' She looked at me with her hands held out. 'I mean, he wouldn't, would he?' and I nodded in my turn. 'And then,' she said, 'when Papa passed away, it was like the ground had shifted from under Ma's feet.' She looked at her hands. Her fingers were long and slim, and unadorned with either jewellery or polish. 'She didn't talk for days.'

'Ma…'

'It was the shock, I think.' Maya looked at me, then at her hands, and with an impatience that felt unnatural in her, she dashed her hands.

'It was a shock to you too, of course.'

'And to you,' she said.

'And to me.'

'And,' she said, pointing towards the clutter, 'I don't think she ever tidied up again. There were no more guests. Well,' she said, 'Tasha-di occasionally, but she was limited to the public rooms of the house. She never saw the worst of it.'

The words were out before I could stop myself. 'And you never thought of sorting things out after Ma...'

She looked at me sadly. 'I didn't know how, Siya.'

Papa was laid back by nature. He met Ma in college, and when Ma suggested he might want to invite her out for a meal, he was grateful to comply. She was beautiful, Ma, and ambitious, topping the college's annual exams, writing for India's leading magazines even before she graduated, and Papa was surprised to be noticed.

After marriage, he would defer to Ma's judgement on most matters. Ma chose schools for us. She chose which activities we would take part in; she chose which friends were suitable, for Papa as much as for us. She decided the food we ate, the books we read, the schedule we kept. She was organised and articulate, and even if Papa had had the inclination to provide a counterpoint, he would have found it hard to get a word in.

The only time I really remember there being an altercation was to do with my education. Ma argued there were colleges in India too, but Papa was convinced that taking up the scholarship would broaden my horizons. They fought bitterly, Ma using her usual imperatives, but Papa remained resistant for the first time in my memory.

They usually began after dinner, and after we had all retired to our rooms for the evening, but I tended to dawdle in the living room outside our bedrooms. I knew my future was to be decided over the course of these arguments, and I was fearful of Ma winning. She was the vociferous one in our family, and on the night when the matter was decided, she was especially voluble. 'I want to protect my girls,' she said.

'My sisters,' he countered as Ma sneered, 'all prospered by embracing the world.'

'My world exists in these four walls.'

'It never used to,' he countered. 'You were the bravest soul I had ever met.'

'Yes,' said Ma, and I leaned forward. This was all news to me.

'All your plans,' he was saying, and each word felt like a body blow. Ma didn't respond, though I heard a deep intake of breath from behind the door. 'You were my hero, Rupa,' he said, as if he was the bereaved one. 'You were going to go and conquer the world.'

There was no reply for a minute or longer, and as I told myself to remember to breathe, I heard the sound of Papa's feet on the ground.

'Well,' Ma was saying, when Papa broke in.

'They can't spend their lives hiding from shadows.'

I didn't hear much of what followed. There were tears from Ma, which surprised me. She was usually phlegmatic, but here she was, weeping audibly. I half expected Papa to mollify her, but he said in a resolute voice, 'We have to think of what's best for Siya.'

Silence followed. It was quiet outside, and as I waited, refusing to breathe, I heard the sound of crickets chirping outside. A bead of sweat formed on my neck, and I realised I hadn't switched the fan on in my anxiety. I walked towards the switch, then heard the floorboard creak underfoot, and froze. 'It's Siya we're talking about here,' he said. 'Siya, and not you.'

'Fine,' Ma screamed. She seemed restored to her vigour and this reassured and terrified me. 'Fine!' She was furious, I could tell, but I scarcely dared believe she would relinquish control. Her voice fell in timbre and acquired a terrible poise. 'That's it, Ratan,' she said. 'Do as you please.'

'Come on, now.'

'She's your daughter,' Ma said, as if it didn't much matter.

'She's yours too.'

'No, she's not,' Ma said. Her voice was loud, and even if I hadn't been just outside their room, I would have heard them. I looked towards Maya's room, but her door didn't budge. 'She looks like you. That nose,' she said, and my hand rose self-consciously to my nose. It was broader than Maya's or Ma's, and I had long been conscious of it, but Ma had always told me it was beautiful, and that her own snub nose had often been a source of embarrassment to her. 'That nose,' she was screaming, in a tantrum to challenge any of our childhood ones, and then, 'You know what's best for her. I'm washing my hands of the whole thing.'

The week after our clear-out began, we ventured to the second floor. Maya tried different keys in the lock before running into Ma's room. She emerged, carrying a rusty bunch of keys. One of these finally fit. 'To be honest,' she told me, 'I didn't know if we even had one that would work. I haven't been up here for years.'

We entered a dim passage. Our entry disturbed the dust that had collected on the surfaces, and both Maya and I coughed. I reached out to Maya, but she was stumbling towards the light fixtures and pressing down on a switch. The lights must not have been switched on for years, as there was a pause, and then an arthritic wheeze as the hallway came into flickering view. We proceeded with the aid of the wavering light, stopping in front of the first room we came to. This was locked too, and Maya tried a few keys before the door yielded.

'Do you remember?' I asked, but here too Maya was switching on a light, and the room came into focus. It was exactly as I remembered it; the large wooden bed against one wall, and then the doll's house we had set up. We must have been playing at doctors the last time we were up here, as several of the dolls lay on their backs with bandaged arms or legs. One had a plaster on her nose, and I asked, 'When were we last here?'

'I don't know,' said Maya. 'Not for years.'

We must have fallen out of the habit of playing upstairs, though I couldn't remember the actual moment we outgrew our dolls. And yet, here they all were, preserved and unchanging, as they had been all those years ago, in the throes of a fever or healing from a fractured wrist. 'Maybe,' I asked, 'no one ever came up here after we stopped playing?'

Maya didn't reply. She walked towards a cardboard box half-buried under the bed and pulled it out. Clouds of dust rose in the air, and I abandoned the dolls to rush towards her. 'I've never seen this before,' she said to me. 'Is it yours?' and as I shook my head, she began to brush the dust off the box's surface.

She scraped at the surface with a focus I didn't normally associate with her, and I wondered if the box contained her possessions. The thought of love letters from her lawyer friend rose in my mind, but as I saw her, attacking the dust, her forehead furrowed with her effort, I knew not to voice my thoughts.

And then the box caved. It had been held in place by a heavy band of tape, but this must have been opened and reopened over the years, as Maya's brushing caused it to collapse. I was struck again by the thought that it contained papers that were personal to her.

'Oh,' she was saying now, surprised, and I knew it wasn't one of her own treasures she had uncovered. Her mouth widened, and I leaned forward to see what she had found.

'These are Ma's,' she was telling me, and sure enough, I saw Ma's round, looping script on several large unsealed envelopes.

'Yes,' I said to her, 'But what are they?'

'Estate papers?'

'Or,' I said, 'a will perhaps?' There hadn't been one among the papers we found in her room, but I saw how Maya looked at me, the old suspicions rising to the fore, and I hurried to add, 'Well, hand me a pile, then.'

Ma had given me a small box when I was a little girl. It was brightly coloured, its purple and green sploshes gem-like in my young eyes. She had probably received it as part of a gift, and had stripped it of its inserts, but it was the most magical thing I had ever seen. I was a little bit of a magpie in those days, and soon, anything I deemed to be of value, an abandoned receipt, a theatre ticket, a trinket, would find its way into the box.

Ma seemed to have had a similar impulse. As I peered into the box, I saw swatches of colour beneath the paper. There were long strings of beads, corals and amethysts, silk scarves and other, neatly folded items of clothing. These we hurried to tip out, and as a white shirt fell out, Maya exclaimed, 'This was her favourite shirt!'

It had tiny blue polka dots on it, and Maya told me that Ma had worn it nearly constantly for years. 'She absolutely loved it,' she said. 'There was a huge panic once when it was lost. Shanti must have mislaid it in her little ironing room, and for days, Ma asked for the shirt only to be told that Shanti couldn't find it. There were tears,' and as I raised an eyebrow, she insisted, 'No, really. She was convinced Shanti had stolen it for herself.'

'But that's just bonkers!'

'I know,' said my sister. 'But Ma wasn't making any sense. Eventually the shirt was found, and Ma was restored to herself. But it was a tense few days until it was found.'

I took the shirt from Maya and brought it up to smell. It smelt musty, and of mothballs, and if the shirt had been party to happy moments of my mother's life, it betrayed no sign of it. I picked up one of Ma's strings of beads. A hazy image flickered in front of my eyes, of Ma in bright lipstick, high heels and silken scarves. I smiled at the thought. Ma, my unchanging, dependable Ma, in such glamourous wear! Now I twirled a scarf around my fingers, imagining a trace of a fragrance to go with the mustiness of the fabric, when Maya turned to the envelopes.

The first one was full of notepads and pencils. We rifled through them, trying to glean clues to Ma's existence independent of us, but nothing was obvious. 'They're just notes,' I said to Maya. 'Leads on stories, quotes she had been given, that sort of stuff. Nothing interesting.'

Maya nodded. She turned towards the next envelope, which contained a sheaf of papers held together by a rubber band. We scanned them, Maya reading each page first before handing it to me. Most related to articles Ma had written, and mentioned citations or prizes she was being nominated for.

Further down the pack, there began to emerge correspondence relating to a new magazine.

'I thought I'd dreamt this!' Maya cried, stabbing a finger at a page circled with a crimson marker. She looked up from the paper and sang the little tune we had made up all those years ago. '*A political, satirical magazine for political, satirical girls!*'

I laughed, moving closer to her. I skimmed through the words, focussing on the letters written in red in our mother's hand. *The Satirist*! The words were circled in the same emphatic red, and then underlined thrice.

'This must have been it,' said Maya. 'This must have been the magazine that Ma and Tasha-di planned.'

Our scanning of the papers grew more frantic, and it felt a little like we were on a scavenger hunt. We were bloodhounds, the two daughters of a woman we had known only as Ma, and were on the search for signs of a life that existed beyond ours. There had been no sign of it in my memory, but here, as we read, delicious words spilled out offering us glimpses of promise, and more, of hope. There were more letters between the two women discussing staffing and costs, and I said to Maya, 'I never knew that Tasha-di…' when Maya interrupted me. She pushed a new letter at me, saying, 'This is a new writer.'

The letter was written in a hurried, fluid script, the sentences generally short and urgent. We quickly surmised that the author of these letters was a mentor, and potentially a source of funding for the venture, though the writer's name remained unclear. There was no reference to their name or profession in the letter, which was signed simply with a large scrawl.

I looked at the last letter that had passed between Ma and Tasha-di, and the closest it got to referring to a third party was a line that said, 'I think we're ready to talk funding.'

'R,' Maya said now, pointing at the scrawled signature at the bottom of the letter. It was an untidy sign-off, the writing half-smudged, and could have represented a number of letters, and I shook my head at her. 'Look,' she said, tracing out the letter with her finger. The paper was pushed towards me, and in the end, I nodded half-heartedly.

'It *is* R.'

'It could be.'

'It is,' she insisted.

'Does that narrow the field, though?' I asked. 'Do we know an R?'

'I don't know,' she said. She had followed Ma into the field of journalism, and though a new generation was writing today's stories, some of the old guard had progressed to positions of eminence. She considered the page in my lap. 'It could be a last name,' she said.

'It could,' I said. I looked carefully at the handwriting, taking in the large, florid script. 'It feels like a man's handwriting.'

She shrugged. We were none the wiser. There was no person with a name beginning with R we could think of, no hidden or declared benefactor we knew about. 'But it is an R,' she said insistently, and I shrugged. The writing was too uncertain.

We began to look at the other papers in the pile. They continued to be written by the same hand, and were authored in the same didactic manner. It told my mother what to do, demanded progress reports and staff changes, and it appeared that Ma complied, as following letters contained praise interspersed with further demands.

The last letter in the pack, however, saw a change in tone. The writing itself was neater, more measured, as if some thought had gone into the author's words. Where normally half a dozen sentences were spread out over an entire page, this letter was succinct. There was no opening greeting. Maya read it first, and then passed it wordlessly on to me. I bent over the words:

I saw last night as a meeting between old friends. That you considered my conduct overfamiliar fills me with endless regret.

There was no scrawl at the end of this letter, and though the tone of this missive—both the words and the writing—were so at odds with what had passed before, I was in no doubt that the author was the same nameless person who had earlier corresponded with Ma. I looked towards Maya, who was rereading the last letter over my shoulder.

'It is the same person, isn't it?'

She nodded. She brought out the previous note, tracing out the scrawled signature at the bottom, and put it next to the letter in my hand. 'It's the same.'

We pored over the letters. It was the same person writing both, and I read the final words out loud. 'That you considered my conduct overfamiliar fills me with endless regret.'

'Overfamiliar.'

I didn't ask her what she thought the words meant, but there she was again, tracing out the signature on the letter in her hand. 'Overfamiliar…' I trailed off, but she didn't look up. I found I couldn't articulate my suspicions. I hardly knew what to make of the words I saw in front of me. Ma had always been just that, our mother. She was there to scold us about untidiness, and to make sure our homework was done. She organised classes and holidays for us, she managed our clothes and our schedules and our futures. She grew grumpy towards the end of the day, and was easily incensed by an irreverent word, but for the bulk of our childhood, she had been a solid presence in our lives. She had always been the foundation we built our lives around.

Papa's sisters, our brilliant aunts, had been the ones we aspired to emulate, but Ma had been our bedrock. We had never had to think of a time without her, not while I was still under her wing, and the thought that she had ever faced conflict, or a challenge filled me with dread. It was sadness at any pain she had felt that I experienced, but also an unsettling sense that the truths I had taken for granted as a child hadn't been wholly valid.

Maya was silent, and I tried again. 'Do you think,' I began, and then, 'Have you any memory,' but she was shaking her head.

'You know Ma,' she told me. She weighed her next words, then said, 'She was Ma,' and I nodded. 'But then again,' she said, before trailing off. Maya was silent a while longer, and I knew she was trying to make sense of the letter she had just read. This sentiment I took for gospel, though I myself had no real memory of it. The only Ma I remembered was the one I had known, and that Ma had been stolid and unimaginative and unwilling to change. 'But then,' Maya was saying, rubbing at the scrawl at the foot of the letter, and I knew she was remembering a different Ma.

After the funeral pyre had been lit, after we had dressed and adorned her for the last time, and after we had watched the flames take her into their embrace, we had made our way to our local temple. The cremation itself had been a small ceremony, with Shanti, Tasha-di and Kitty Bua, Papa's favourite sister, in attendance, but the gathering at the temple had been open to a larger number. Half-forgotten relatives turned up, ostentatious in their profession of grief. A woman whose name I couldn't recall hugged me close every time she saw me. 'You remember, beta,' she said to me, 'how cute you were as a baby?' and I could only nod in reply. The nameless lady was overcome with sadness at the passing of Ma, and more so at Maya having been left alone.

'It'll be fine,' I said, passing her a tissue from my pocket. She sniffed, and I said, 'Really, it will. Maya is a survivor.' The lady stared at me expectantly, and I wondered if she expected me to appear more distraught. 'Really,' I said finally, prising myself from her embrace, and then, as she continued to stare, 'It really will, Aunty.'

We were soon thronged by others; neighbours, old associates of Papa's, classmates and childhood friends, and a small group of journalists who had once known Ma. Neither Maya nor I recognised many of these last faces, but Tasha-di occasionally provided an introduction. It was all a haze for us though, and in spite of the chill of the season, I soon found my face flushed. I threw off the shawl Shanti had insisted I carry, and though I wouldn't find it again at the end of the afternoon, I wouldn't notice the loss until long after the day had passed.

People filed past us, expressing regret, offering us a hug or an anecdote about Ma. Towards the end, some journalists walked up to us. Tasha-di was swift in leaning forward and offering us details of how they knew Ma, but all I could absorb was the knowledge that they had known Ma before her world had been limited to ours. One of these journalists, suave, poised, their voice deep with authority, said to me, 'Your mother's passing fills me with endless regret.'

I handed Maya the letter and closed my eyes. Who had it been who had spoken those words? As the memory struck me, I had felt sure that it was a man, but as I focused, on the heat of the temple and rush of the mourners, I found I couldn't be certain. Maya had been convinced the letter writer was a man, and perhaps my memory was coloured by her conviction. What if it had been a woman, confident, successful and glib, who had mouthed those words?

My head swam, and I looked up to see that the fan hadn't been turned on in the room. The air hummed with humidity, the ceiling was laced with damp, and as I inhaled, I saw a lizard streak past the lights overhead. I looked at Maya, who was carefully folding the letter in exactly the same manner we had found it.

I thought again of the words I had heard in the temple: 'Your mother's passing fills me with endless regret.' Had it been a man? I closed my eyes again, trying to remember the voice that had articulated the sentence. I retained an impression of ease, of words that carried an effortless heft; were they definitely spoken by a man? There had been a richness to the voice, a huskiness, but that didn't necessarily make the speaker male. And if the speaker was male, who had it been? Had it been an old man, a tall one, or one with a moustache? The words buzzed in my head.

The heat rose, and I leant back towards the wall. Surely I would have remembered. The words, extraordinary as they had been, had stuck in my mind. Perhaps, if I focussed, I would be able to remember a detail; a scar, a mole, a distinctive scent. I tried again to identify the owner of the words Maya cradled in her lap, but it was no use. I only remembered the rush of the evening, and an interminable line waiting to pay its condolences. Faces blended into one another, as did genders and clothes and colours and ages. There had been a polished smile, a grimace, that distinctive sorrow expressed, but all else remained stubbornly amorphous.

VIII

We visited Tasha-di at the end of the week. Ordinarily, it was she who came to us, but she didn't ask us the reason for our visit, busying herself instead with bringing refreshments out for us, and I took the chance to refamiliarize myself with her living quarters. These remained the same as they always had been, bohemian and a little chaotic, with books and photos of friends lining up on each shelf. A woven sari was flung over her coffee table, potted ferns dotted the space and crystal acquired through trips to Europe sparkled on her dining table. Bright scarves hung off sofas. As a child her flat had seemed magical to me, every item precious and deliberate in its presence, and the passing of time had done nothing to diminish my wonder. 'It's still the same,' I whispered to Maya. 'It's like nowhere I've ever been before.'

As I looked around, I was struck by the photos on her mantelpiece. There was a photo of her in a sunlit terrace in the Mediterranean, one of her hiking in the mountains, then one of her with Ma in a sequinned sari, but what I noticed for the first time was that most were photos taken in the past. I remembered when the photo with Ma was taken. It was for a family wedding, and both women had gone to the salon to have their hair and nails done. Maya and I were both still at school, and this photo from well over a decade ago seemed to be the latest one taken.

There had been nothing since, and I realised for the first time that Ma's passing had been a loss for Tasha-di too.

We tiptoed around the topic of the letter. I raised an eyebrow at Maya as I sipped at my tea, and though she nodded, she made no move to introduce the subject. Talk turned to Ma, which provided us with the perfect opening, but nether Maya nor I spoke about the letter. We hadn't discussed it between ourselves, and we both had kept our thoughts on the subject to ourselves. I surmised that an unwelcome advance of some sort had been made, but wasn't sure if Maya had reached the same conclusion. There was an unwillingness on both our parts to broach such personal matters, and we now hesitated to raise them with Tasha-di.

It was Tasha-di in the end who broke the logjam. She saw me looking at her sari-decorated coffee table and smiled. 'It's so nice to see you here, Siya,' she said. 'When you were little, you would love to hide under this table.'

'It was like Aladdin's cave for me,' I told her. 'Your entire flat was.'

'But,' she said. 'That's not why you're here.' She spoke kindly, but there was no disguising the wistfulness in her voice.

'Tasha-di,' said Maya, as if to reproach her, but no further words suggested themselves to her, and she reached instead for the letter she carried in her bag. This she now presented to the older woman, biting her lips as she waited for a reaction.

Tasha-di didn't speak for an age. Her eyes moved slowly down the page, and though I grew impatient at the time she took to read through a couple of lines, she didn't hurry. She looked up at us, then at the page again. This she perused once more, taking her agonising time. At length, she folded the paper neatly, placing it on the sofa next to her. She nodded, once then again in quick succession, and then she rose. She looked at us for a moment before leaving the room.

Maya looked at me. We didn't exchange a word, and we both felt as if we were waiting for Tasha-di's verdict before committing to an opinion on the subject.

Tasha-di returned, holding up a pair of glasses, which she slowly put on. She didn't look at us or speak. Returning to the letter, she read it through one more time, her fingers tracing the lines as she read them. She finally looked up, and I realised I had been holding my breath.

'Well?'

'Well,' replied Tasha-di. She smiled at us and dragged her chair to between us. She took our hands in hers, and said, 'Do you children remember your mother as a journalist?'

'No,' I replied, as my sister stayed silent.

'It was a long time ago,' Tasha-di said slowly. She seemed to be composing her thoughts. Her speech had a measured air, and I wondered if her trip to the hallway had been more to consider her words than to find her glasses. 'But,' she was saying, smiling broadly, squeezing our hands, and I found myself smiling in spite of myself. 'She was one hell of a journalist, your mother.'

'What about…'

Her smile widened. 'Did you know, girls, that she planned to launch a magazine?'

Maya half nodded. She looked at me, and then said, 'I thought it was a dream, like the dolls we played with, but I have an impression of a magazine, and Ma in her white blouse…'

'It wasn't a dream, darling,' Tasha-di was saying. She rose again, letting go of our hands, and walked into the innards of her home. There was a louder noise now, a dragging out of a heavy object, then the turning of a lock, and both Maya and I were up on our feet and in her room in an instant. Tasha-di smiled to see us, gesturing us in. She waved an old magazine at us, and asked, 'And this. Do you remember this?'

I looked at Maya, who shook her head. The magazine was placed in her hands, and as I huddled in for a better view, I saw that it wasn't a glossy production. The colours were a little less vivid than I normally saw, the paper thicker, and the whole thing felt like a magazine had been photocopied and stapled together. 'Look,' Maya was saying, pointing at the title, and I saw the words '*The Satirist*' emblazoned on the cover.

'This was your Ma's baby,' Tasha-di was saying, but we barely registered her words. We were turning through the pages, noting the contents, flipping through the articles and the comment section before turning back to where Ma had penned her first—and it appeared, last—ever editorial. I leaned forward in my eagerness to get a better view, jostling against Maya, but she appeared not to notice. 'Look,' she was saying again, indicating towards the words Ma had written, and I read:

The future has never looked brighter. The Cold War has ended, the Berlin Wall has fallen, and it seems like the dream of peace will finally become reality.

At home too, I see shoots of promise. Our economy is opening up to the outside world, our computer scientists are joining the engineers and doctors who have long been associated with excellence across the globe. The fires of communal tension that raged so violently earlier this decade appear firmly to have been vanquished. More women are entering the workforce than ever before, and everywhere I look, I see new possibilities. I see dialogue, I see tolerance, and I see openness. I see hope for myself and my colleagues, and for the two daughters I am bringing up to be fearless inheritors of this earth.

As we throw off the shackles of an insular, socialist past, The Satirist *will reflect a modern, confident India. By focussing on agents of change, whether in the fields of law, medicine, cinema or gender equality, we will seek to inspire a new generation. By championing the invisible—the poor, the uneducated, the unrepresented—we will hold a mirror up to ourselves. And by poking fun at ourselves, we will make sure we don't take ourselves too seriously.*

I found it for all of us who have dreamt of a brighter tomorrow. And I found it to show my daughters that the new dawn I tell them about is firmly within their grasp.

We stayed with Tasha-di late into the evening. The magazine sparked endless questions. How many issues of *The Satirist* had been published? Who worked alongside Ma? How had it been received, and why had it been shut down? And, the question we seemed not to have received any answer to: who had written the letter that had lain among Ma's most treasured belongings?

Tasha-di insisted on cooking for us before talking further. I was impatient, and worried she was being evasive, but she took me to the little square kitchen that remained as it always had. She made me open a cupboard and take out the Maggi noodles she had always prepared for us as children. 'These you remember, right?' I nodded, and she set to preparing carrots and peas to drop into the boiling mix. 'We need to add some nutrition,' and I thought of how much Ma had hated Tasha-di cooking us the snack. 'They're full of rubbish,' she'd complain, but Tasha-di would throw in some vegetables to pad out the food. 'There,' she was saying, 'Even your mother can't complain now.'

'Tasha-di,' I said. Maya had been silent after reading the magazine, not contributing to the conversation or pressing Tasha-di to answer my questions, and I asked her again, 'Why aren't you telling me about the letter?'

'You were both so young.'

She had been impossible to pin down all day. 'Tasha-di!'

She held her hands up. 'Really,' she said, placing her hands on my shoulders. 'You're focussing on unimportant things.'

'But…'

'What you haven't realised is how magical what I showed you was.'

'I know.'

'Your mother single-handedly founded a magazine.' Tasha-di saw me beginning to speak, and shrugged. 'I helped, of course, but my main contribution was organisational. I was a glorified secretary, if you will.' She waved away my protests. 'Really, Siya, you won't remember what your mother was like then.' I shook my head, and she said, 'She was a star. She was driven and determined, and she was the one who put together the staff and raised the funding for the entire magazine.'

I was on the backfoot, but I tried again, 'But…'

It was no use. Tasha-di was ploughing on. I heard the scraping of a chair from the living room, and Maya emerged to join us. 'What's taking you so long?' she asked, before she spotted the three steaming bowls of Maggi. 'Ooh,' she cooed, thrilled at being allowed a frowned-upon treat, and I wondered if she had ever indulged in a forbidden passion in her life.

'Come, come,' Tasha-di said. 'I was just telling Siya about how spectacular your mother was.' Maya nodded. 'She was the one, girls, who put together all the layouts. She was the one who chose all the cartoons and who managed all the deadlines.' I nodded, trying to reconcile my memories of Ma with the picture Tasha-di painted. 'She called me her partner, but really, it was she who was running the whole show.'

I tried. Several times after we had finished the food and washed the dishes, I would try to reintroduce the topic of the letter, but Tasha-di seemed unwilling or unable to provide more information. Maya's curiosity seemed to have fixed on the magazine itself, and it was on this subject that Tasha-di proved most communicative.

'We had offices,' she told us. She smiled as she spoke, stretching out in her chair, and it was clear the memory was a happy one. They would have chosen the space together, her and Ma, and have decorated it. Trips would have been made to the shops around our school hours to choose all the paraphernalia of running an office; desks, chairs, lamps, paper, printer, and Tasha-di's ubiquitous ferns. 'We weren't far from your school,' and as I frowned, trying to picture an office complex nearby, Tasha-di said, 'There was an army officers' site nearby. They had blocks of flats, and one of the officers rented his space out. Each room was an office housing a different company, and the kitchen was a communal space. We had the use of the balcony and living room for meetings. It was a nice space,' she said, 'but I don't think you would remember it. It was a five minute walk from your school's front gates.'

She was looking at us, and though Maya nodded to indicate

she knew the location, I shrugged. 'There were five of us working for *The Satirist*,' she said. Tasha-di was smiling again, revisiting pleasant memories, 'It was me, your mother, and three women journalists your Ma had met along the course of her career.'

'An all woman office, then,' said Maya thoughtfully.

'See,' I called, triumphant, but this didn't square with my memory of my mother. The Ma I had known had filled Maya with all her fears. The Ma I had known had taught Maya that women always faced obstacles. This fearless, pioneering woman seemed a chimera.

'Yes,' Tasha-di was saying, smiling as a memory returned to her. 'There *was* a man, Jitu, who came in to do the illustrations, but he was only there on a part-time basis. Most of the time, it was just our merry band of wonderful women.'

'Sounds fantastic,' I said.

'It does sound fantastic,' echoed Maya. More than me, it was she who was struck by the life Ma had once lived. I knew Tasha-di wasn't lying, but I still only half believed her account. For Maya, though, the pages she had seen earlier in the week had awoken in her the earliest memories she had of Ma. It was the Ma in crisp white blouses she remembered, and the Ma with strings of beads and bright red lipstick she thought of. 'Yes,' she repeated softly, 'it does sound fantastic.'

'It was, girls. How proud you would have been to see your Ma then. And how proud she would have been…'

Maya interrupted. 'Why was it shut down, Tasha-di?'

A sad smile followed. Tasha-di straightened out her kameez and sat up. 'It never really took off, beta.'

'Of course,' agreed Maya. 'It's such a hard path for…'

With a forlorn shake of her head, Tasha-di said, 'The funding your mother was promised never materialised, and everything had to be given up. The offices, our brave band of journalists, everything.' She was nodding, as if to convince us that the end she described hadn't been as catastrophic as it sounded, but I saw her lips tremble as she spoke. There was a brittle shrug, and another quiver in her lips as she said, 'It happens all the time in business apparently.' An over-loud laugh, and her hands thrown up in the air. 'Deals fall through all the time.'

She was looking at me, waiting for my reaction, and I frowned. Incredible as it had been for Ma to have launched a magazine with two young kids in the house, it felt more remarkable still that she had let it die. I would never have done the same. I would have laid off staff; I would have let go of the offices, I would have pared down my offering, but I wouldn't have let my dream die. Deals did fall through all the time, but for Ma to have allowed her business to fold showed a lack of resilience. This was the Ma I knew; living in shadows, so scared of disappointment that she never took risks. And then I thought of myself in my over-large flat in London, unable to change out of my pyjamas, unable to muster the enthusiasm to apply for jobs I knew I was unlikely to get.

'Yes,' I said, my voice rising. 'Of course, it happens all the time.'

IX

Despite the exclusiveness of its location, Civil Lines market often felt like a microcosm of India's chaotic and aggressively inclusive democracy.

The first stop for most was the street food restaurant, where customers were fed food with unswerving efficiency, strangers rammed onto tables together, and in a most un-Delhilike exercise, drivers and menial staff being sat next to tongue-tied young lovers being sat next to society matrons. The shop played the volume game, but the food was exquisite, the tangy chaat as moreish as the Punjabi spiced chickpeas, and though the society matrons huffed when the bearer asked them to budge up to make room for new customers, they promptly did.

Normal order was restored past the restaurant, as the eateries grew more elite and more uninspiring. The shops the market was famous for—high end jewellers and art galleries and tea rooms and antique stores—were then laid out in all their glory, and it was here the matrons usually repaired to after getting their fix of street food. The hoi polloi generally weren't visible now, but as I was to learn, they had a little section—an annexe to the market, so to speak—all their own.

Now that Shanti understood that our plans didn't obstruct her way of life, she grew cheerful. Every day brought a new idea;

sometimes a proposal to change the whole edifice into a grand hotel, and on others, plans to rent out wings of the property. She grew in energy, taking trips to the market she had previously been wary of, and one morning, as I started on my daily walk, I saw her set off too.

She nodded at me, motioning for me to precede her, when I asked, 'Where are you off to?'

'The market,' she said, 'I'm picking up some supplies.'

'Good,' I said, 'I'll walk with you,' and she fell in step with me.

We made our way towards the market, ambling peaceably when Shanti yanked my arm. There was an elderly man—silver-haired, trim, dressed in a dark grey Lacoste tracksuit—power walking on the opposite side of the road, and Shanti stood on tiptoe to whisper to me, 'Do you know who that is?'

The man had passed by us, and I turned to inspect him. He didn't seem familiar to me, but Shanti was saying, 'He's a very big man, Baby. Big, important man.'

I nodded, disinterested, and then Shanti added, 'He has a big house beyond the market,' and I snapped my fingers. 'That's the local celebrity, isn't it?' and as I scoured my memory for the name Mrs Bhatnagar had mentioned, I turned again to look at the retreating back. He wasn't tall, and looked like he was in his sixties or seventies, but he walked briskly, and had an erect bearing that gave him an air of purpose. 'Raja!' I said, clapping my hands, 'That's Raja Singh, isn't it?'

Shanti nodded. 'He used to know your mother.'

'Ma?' I asked. How had their paths crossed? Mrs Bhatnagar had said something about Raja Singh owning a TV station, but Ma was a print journalist. 'Are you sure?'

But then Shanti shrugged. 'I don't know, baby,' she said. 'I seem to remember your Ma talking to him when they passed each other on morning walks, but I may be wrong,' and I turned away from my scrutiny of the retreating back. He was just a social acquaintance. It wasn't him, then, who had written that letter to my mother. We walked towards the market, and when I slowed down in front of the convenience store, Shanti cleared her throat. 'Not here, baby,' she said, and pointed towards an antique store at the corner of the market. There was a tiny lane past the shop, so small that I had never noticed it before, but Shanti gestured towards it, and I slipped in through it. There was a smaller set of stores through the lane, a sort of a slapdash bolt-on to the main market, and as I walked in, I saw baskets bursting with aubergine and okra and guavas and mangoes. There was a riot of colour around me, and of smell, more vibrant than the packaged produce we normally picked up, and as I walked in, I saw a little child, three years old, maybe, resting on its haunches. Its gender was unclear, as it was dressed in a greying vest and shorts, but it eyed me with an unblinking, frank curiosity. I smiled at it, and Shanti, who had been silent during our walk to this smaller market, called out, 'Gautam, what are you doing out here alone? Where is your mother?'

The child blinked, and then returned to his survey of me. 'Come,' Shanti said, leading me by the elbow. She took up a basket and began to load it with vegetables.

'Okra!' I cried out, and as the child moved to get a better view of me, I felt my churlishness. Shanti smiled, and I added in a softer voice, 'Must you?'

'Baby,' she said kindly, 'these are our vegetables.' I must have looked bemused, as she added, 'This is food for Pradeep and me.'

'Yes,' I nodded, embarrassed, 'Of course,' and watched as Shanti proceeded to add food to her basket. She picked long stems of green beans and potato and mustard seeds and curry leaves, wrinkling her nose at a papaya, and I thought to myself how little I knew of the tastes of the woman who had been responsible for so much of our childhood. She paused in front of a carton of eggs, and I wasn't sure if she ate eggs or was worried about their cost. I thought of purchasing a carton for her, then worried about causing offence, and in the end, I made an excuse and fled. The little boy shuffled to the entrance of the shop to watch me leave.

I smiled at the child, but he didn't acknowledge my greeting. His eyes were glued to my face, his eyes unsmiling, and curiously wary, as I turned quickly away.

I had just left the store when I heard someone greet me. Hands were folded, and a small, wiry man bowed his head as he said, 'Namaste Didi.'

I was so taken aback that I didn't recognise him for an instant, but then he looked up, and I smiled back at him.

'Namaste,' I said, 'Your mother is just inside buying food.'

He nodded at the news, and folded his hands again. 'I'll take your leave, then,' he said, and hurried away.

I returned home to a text from Benjamin. There hadn't been any communication for weeks, and as I checked my phone, more out of habit than any real expectation, I saw that he had written. The message itself was short: 'You back?' and I switched my phone off. I wasn't going to reply.

Maya and I hadn't returned to the second floor since our last excursion, though the words were never far from my mind.

Often, when I was drifting—my eyes heavy in the midday sun, or as Mrs Bhatnagar accosted us on our walks—the script flashed through my eyes. I could close my eyes and imagine the words were there, right in front of me, tangible almost, urgent and overbearing like a fruit on the turn.

I saw last night as a meeting between old friends. That you considered my conduct overfamiliar fills me with endless regret.

'Well?' Someone would speak in a raised voice, looking as if they had been expecting a response, and the charm would break. I would shake my head and laugh. 'It's too hot,' I would complain. 'I'm still getting used to Delhi's heat.'

There would be nods, or a joke about how foreign I had become, but occasionally I caught Maya looking at me, and I knew she was thinking of the letter too. Once she said to me, 'I wonder what the words mean,' and I pretended not to hear her. Maya's world had been so cloistered that I wasn't sure she read the same meaning into the words as I did, and I worried, after all her losses, about disturbing her equilibrium.

She persevered. The next time we were alone and on the veranda, she recited a phrase from the letter: '*that you considered my conduct overfamiliar*,' and I knew she was as haunted by the note as I was. Did she think Ma's benefactor was male? Did she think he had suggested onerous terms for the deal? Or did she think his familiarity had been more personal in nature? And that was where I grew more unsure in my mind. Had there been a spurned advance? But it was Ma. *Ma.* Dour and unadventurous and unfriendly. She barely changed her clothes, never wore perfume or makeup. She was hardly likely to be the object of anyone's attention.

'What do you think the words mean?' Maya asked, turning to me as if I was the older one, as if I could read into the meaning of those opaque, impenetrable words.

I tried to ask Tasha-di about the letter when Maya wasn't there, but she didn't provide any colour on the letter. She claimed a loss of memory, focussing instead on the magazine. She gave us the proof copy to take home, and told us she was happy to answer any questions we had on *The Satirist*, but it was clear she was unable or unwilling to divulge information on the letter or its writer.

We followed her lead then, and when we were alone after dinner, Maya often pulled out the proof copy to peruse it. Her wonder zeroed in on Ma's passion, and on her entrepreneurialism. 'Just imagine,' she said to me, 'Ma set up a magazine all on her own.'

'Yes.'

'Her own magazine!' She looked at me, nodding as if to spur my enthusiasm, and said, 'She wasn't content to just sit there and work for an organisation. She wasn't going to do an editor's bidding.' Here my sister fell silent, and I briefly debated asking her about her own patchy writing. Had she not enjoyed the stories she had been assigned? Had there been creative differences? Had her sexism proceeded from her experiences and not from Ma? Maya had been a promising writer all her life. As a child, she was always running off to write in her notebook, or to send her dolls off on assignments, and when she had gone to college, she had edited her student newspaper. She had won several journalism prizes, and had been offered jobs by India's leading dailies, but somehow, over the years, her output had fallen.

When I asked, Ma usually muttered something about print journalism dying out, and I knew enough about their lives to know that the demands Ma placed on Maya's time were incompatible with a career. Maya always agreed with

Ma's analysis—yes, things were terrible in print journalism. Newspapers were shutting down daily, as were magazines, and instead, the only news that was flourishing was run out of online ezines. She nodded, Ma mourned a changing world, and I made soothing noises, but now, as I watched her gush about Ma's initiative, I wondered if she thought of the career that could have been hers.

Delhi's heat was relentless. I wore looser clothes, sticking largely to the whites that were preferred by most of Delhi in the summer, and tied my hair up in a bun. And still there was no relief. It intensified overnight, raking the grass, drying the petals on the bougainvillea in our veranda to a crisp, and burning my scalp anytime I was outside until I began to long for the relief the monsoon brought. The sun rose before I did, and by the time Shanti was in my room, drawing open the curtains, complaining about the dust that had already accumulated in the room, I knew rest was impossible.

We began to take our walks earlier. At this hour, we were untroubled by Mrs Bhatnagar, though we came across joggers completing a quick circuit of the area. 'Corporate people,' Maya said in explanation. 'They're getting in their exercise before work.' She nodded at a few, though no one stopped to make conversation.

'Lots of new faces around.'

Maya nodded. 'There are so many corporate rentals in the area now,' she said. 'The place has grown transient.'

A grey-haired man speed-walked past us, and I nudged Maya. 'That's Raja Singh, isn't it?'

She nodded. 'He's not a common sight as he travels so often.

But whenever he's in Delhi, he'll take his morning walk. Very often he'll invite a colleague or business associate to join him, and they will have a business meeting as they walk.'

'A true power walk, then.' I watched as he zoomed on into the distance. An idea was beginning to form in my head. It was nothing concrete, not just then, but I asked Maya, 'Are there any offices in the area?'

She laughed and asked who could afford the local real estate prices, and I replied, 'We could.' It took a while to explain to her that we were both unwilling to let go of the house. Maya frowned at me as I spoke, arguing that she had agreed to let in builders, and I had to point out to her that she hadn't met any she had liked.

Maya paused. Raja Singh had vanished from view. The day's heat was rising, and I spied a bead of perspiration above her lip. Her hair, tied into a tight bun, was starting to escape from its restraints, and under the sunlight, I saw white strands of hair. She flashed me a thin, strained smile, and said, 'We can't just let anyone in, Siya.'

'Of course not,' I replied. 'But Delhi must have *one* trustworthy builder.'

She remained unsmiling. 'You don't know how unscrupulous these people are.'

'Come on…'

'No,' she said. Her eyes flashed. 'You don't know what India is like.' I bristled at her words, but she carried on. 'They'll make endless promises to get the contract, and then deadlines will slip. You'll have to monitor them constantly to make sure they aren't using substandard products…'

She was ready to carry on, but I held up my hand. Ma had been paranoid and resistant to change, but I hadn't realised how closely my sister resembled her. There she was, hands on hips, blowing air out through puffed up cheeks, and I said, 'You're probably right, Maya. And maybe there's another solution.'

It took a while to communicate to her that we could hire out the ground floor as offices. Maya complained no one had ever done that before, and when I told her about the room Ma had rented out near our school, she had more objections. That was a middle-class area, and ours was more exclusive. There was sure to be resistance from the neighbours. I pointed out that our neighbours were transient now, professional families out during office hours. Chances were they wouldn't even know of any change we made. Maya then worried about the permissions required to change the use of a domestic building.

'We'll have to think about builders again if we're to partition off the ground floor,' she told me triumphantly, and I sighed. 'We'll be back to square one.'

'But maybe not,' I said. It was too hot to walk now, and though we remained standing as we had been when we started the conversation, we were beginning to attract attention. A few boys passed us by on an errand to the market—to pick up milk or bread or eggs—and noticed us rooted to the same spot on their return. They dawdled, hoping to catch a whiff of drama, some sighting of a scandal or a tiff. Little urchins gathered around them, as did stray dogs, and I saw that we had gathered an avid audience.

I guided Maya back to our home, and once inside, I took her around the ground floor. 'This,' I said, pointing at the library. We both winced at the sight of the caved-in bookcase, but the space itself was large. Papa had come here of an evening, sitting among the leather clad books until he was called in for dinner. There was a small drinks cart—untouched for years—in one corner. The crystal decanters, dusty now and unpolished, still contained inches of an amber liquid I took to be scotch.

We often came in here, Maya and I, after our homework was done. Ma was stricter, worried if our homework was finished too quickly, always mindful that our reading materials shouldn't simply consist of comics and glossy magazines, but Papa, more laid back, and more content in our company, was the parent we gravitated towards. He would let us munch on his snacks, even as Ma warned they would ruin our appetite, and as we wandered into the room that still carried so many memories of Papa years after his passing, it felt a little like we were returning to our childhoods.

'This?'

'Yes,' I said, though I paused before I replied. This room had been our sanctuary, but as I looked around, I saw it was big enough to accommodate our old dining table. An idea was forming in my head, and as Maya was shaking her head in her instinctive denial, I said, 'I keep thinking of Ma's magazine.' This held her attention, and though she didn't reply, I took heart from the fact that she hadn't rebutted me.

'*The Satirist*,' I said, painting the words with my fingers. I felt a little like a salesperson, an estate agent, a seller of fantasises, and as Maya paused, expectant, I began to circle the room. The thrill of possibility was beginning to course through me, and I saw now, not simply a use for the house, but a path for Maya, and one for me. 'Just imagine,' I told her. I ran to the window, and pulled open the curtains. Light spilled in through the dirty panes, and I leaned forward to open the latch on the windows. These had been untouched in years, probably last cleaned when Papa's decanters had been, and a plume of dust swirled towards me as the ancient fittings were disturbed. I coughed, rubbing my hands on my trousers, and turned cheerily towards Maya. 'Just imagine,' I said, as she smiled and pointed out a dust smudge on my forehead. 'We could restart the magazine.'

She smiled still but didn't interrupt.

'We could hire in journalists.'

'Really? Who?'

'Come on,' I said, turning my eyes on her. 'You must have friends from your college days you can rope in.'

She shrugged.

'Tasha-di will have contacts. Or,' I said, warming to my theme, 'We can get in some fresh graduates. You can be the editor.'

I expected her to pick up on the million holes in my logic, our lack of funding or experience, but she didn't seem to notice them. '*The Satirist*', she said in a ponderous voice, and I nodded.

'I can do the marketing.'

Maya didn't ask if I planned to remain in Delhi, and I rushed to say, 'We can bring in the large dining table we never eat at. That will sit ten, twelve easily.'

'Yes.'

'I can help with copy editing, with the layout for the early magazines. We can ask Tasha-di to join us too. And really, we only need one or two others then.'

'There will need to be distribution channels.' Maya was starting to frown. '*The Satirist* folded before it had even begun.'

'We *will* launch.'

'When Ma failed with all her contacts and all our experience? We don't stand a chance.' Other doubts, most of them valid, were beginning to assert themselves, but I ploughed on. 'Sure,' I said. 'And we'll have to think of budgets, but surely this is an easier way to use the house, isn't it?'.

She inclined her head. I knew what she was thinking: this was no solution to the problem of the house, but it was something. The magazine would bring some unused rooms into play. Some problems would be fixed. The cracks in the ceiling would keep spreading, more of our ancient furniture would buckle under the weight of Ma's books, but this was a small step towards recovery. It *was* something. And, I thought, it was something for the both of us to do while we thought of how to rescue our decaying home.

'Think about it, Maya,' I said, as she walked towards the bookcase. Many of the books had spilled out, and were lying on the floor. They hadn't been gathered up, or stacked in any sort of order. She lifted one, fingering its spine, before laying it flat on a side table. She bent down, picking another volume before placing it on top of the first book. She repeated the process until she had piled four books on top of one another, and then began another stack next to the first.

She worked quietly, and I was unsure if she was unaware of my presence, but I was unwilling to disturb her. Maya created six low piles of books on the circular table, and paused to see the effect. She looked up at me and smiled. There was a light in her eyes, though I couldn't work out which way her thoughts tended.

'This,' she whispered. Her voice was wispy, as if she didn't dare to articulate the thought, and I moved closer to hear her say, 'This is where we'll keep the layout of each issue before it goes to print.'

'Maya…'

'Wait,' she said, holding her hand up. She pushed the table to the end of the room, opening the doors to the garden room. The plants had long since withered and been moved out, but both of us thought instantly of Ma and Tasha-di sitting on the old wicker armchairs of an evening with their whisky and pakoras, and the late-night rasp in their voices, the backdrop to our childhoods.

'This,' Maya said, then trailed off. I nodded. Her voice had grown heavy, choked equally by memory and potential. Ma was still here, another ghost, and another ruin. She had died in this room. She had been reading a magazine in the morning, a cup of tea by her side, and the rest of the house had only been alerted to her passing by the sound of the cup clattering against the table. They had run in, Maya and Shanti, to find Ma, hands outstretched, head flung back as if at the commencement of laughter or a speech, and a tea stain spreading fast on the floor below.

I saw Maya looking at the ground, and at the stain that had resisted all attempts at removal. I reached forward to put my arms around her. We hadn't been overly tactile since my return, and she stiffened against me, but didn't fight against the contact. That, I told myself, was something. That was a start. We remained together, still and uncertain, as the morning's shadows stretched their fingers across the room.

X

Maya vacillated for days, developing doubts when she was alone, and I had to spend my days walking her through the rooms on the ground floor, painting the picture of the future that could be ours. The house would not have to be partitioned. We would not have to bring in builders, nor tenants. It would just be the both of us and our team—Tasha-di, a second mother, and others we vetted—bringing to life Ma's old visualisation. By evening, she would be as enthused about *The Satirist* as I was, but overnight, the gremlins of doubt would set in. She would wake up conscious of the competition we faced, of her own lack of experience, and of my having abandoned her and Ma in the past. 'I'm not leaving,' I would repeat to her every morning, but still, she found it easier to bank on disappointment.

At length, I began to action decisions in the evening after Maya had been worked up into enthusiasm and confidence. We would sit out on the veranda after dinner with our wine, and as the smell of jasmine rose from the garden, we would make our plans. The old library was slowly converted into the magazine's office. The broken bookcase was relieved of its burden. I suggested to Shanti that we hire a carpenter to fix the woodwork, but she told us Pradeep was more than capable of the work. He came in then, early one morning while Maya and I were on our walk, and by the next morning, he had restored the bookcase to its original structure. The books were neatly arranged on the shelves, the volumes all sorted by size, and as I praised his work, his face flushed deep.

'It's nothing, Didi,' he said. He was solemn, his head bowed, but it was clear he was pleased at the praise.

'No really,' said Shanti. 'The boy laboured hard. He wouldn't stop until his work was done.' She beamed, patting her son on the back, and though he refused to look up, she added, 'I offered so many times to bring him a cup of tea, but he wouldn't take a break.'

'He's a hard worker.'

Pradeep looked up at this. 'There is so much more to do, Didi,' he said. He spoke earnestly, and he looked not at me or at Maya, but at a fixed point between us. 'The floor below the carpet.' He rushed to a corner of the room, got onto his knees and pulled up the end of the carpet.

'Pradeep!' called out Shanti, a recrimination ready on her lips, but Maya and I were following him to where he knelt, and looking at the flooring he was pointing at.

'Look, Didi,' he said. 'Pure marble.'

I looked at Maya, who shrugged. For as long as we could remember, the floors across the house had been carpeted. The patch Pradeep was motioning towards was grey, and I couldn't be certain of the material. Maya looked similarly flummoxed, but Pradeep nodded forcefully. He scrubbed at the exposed floor, lifting some dirt onto his palms, and smiled proudly. 'Really Didi,' he said. 'I can set the flooring to rights in no time.'

I looked again at Maya, who didn't speak. Pradeep was looking at us now, his eyes flitting from one face to the next, and I said, 'What about your job?'

'Yes,' he replied, his face downcast. 'You're right, Didi.'

'See how much your Didis care about you, Pradeep?' said Shanti. She shuffled slowly forward, looking uncertainly at the grimy floor. 'They are right,' she added, 'you need to get back to work.'

He nodded. He looked at us, and as we both spoke again, telling him how grateful we were to him for fixing the bookshelf, he rose.

'Go, beta,' Shanti called out. 'You have to go to work,' and he made his way outside the house.

'This boy,' said Shanti. She looked distastefully at the exposed floor. 'All this mess he's made.'

'Come on, Shanti,' Maya said. 'He was a big help to us.'

'He's a good enough boy,' she said. She brought out a broom and began sweeping the dust her son had unearthed, and as she worked, her complaints continued. 'He's become distracted of late. His father is insisting he marries, and has chosen a girl for him, a good girl from the village.'

'But that's great, Shanti!'

'Yes, well,' the woman sighed. 'The girl is good, the family is good, but it's become harder than ever to get a word out of the boy.'

Maya asked, 'Is he not happy with the match?'

'No, no,' said Shanti. 'The girl is very good.' The dirt had been swept up, and the carpet replaced, but Shanti kept working, running her broom over new parts of the floor. 'She is pretty too,' she said unhappily. 'And it's high time the boy was married.'

'But...'

Shanti was speaking over me. 'He keeps lurking around.'

We'd both noticed the same, but I moved to reassure Shanti. 'Have you spoken to him?'

Shanti tutted.

'Maybe he isn't ready to be married.'

She shifted on her haunches.

'Maybe,' Maya added, 'you could talk to him.'

Shanti huffed again, but didn't disagree with us. She picked up her broom and dustpan, and though she looked around the floor with dissatisfaction, her eyes lingered on the restored bookshelf. 'OK,' she said to herself as much as to us, and made her way from the room.

Our next stop was to see Tasha-di. She was the family oracle, and we wanted her involvement with the magazine, but I told Maya I had to send off a message before we left.

I ran up to my room, searched out the spot that offered good reception, and picked up my phone. I looked at Benjamin's message, still perfunctory, and still expecting my return. I had told myself I wasn't going to reply, but I typed out a quick text: 'Staying in Delhi. I'm launching a new magazine.'

We were sure Tasha-di would be quick to fall in with our plans. She had worried for months about Maya, and since my arrival in Delhi, had begun to ask me what my plans were. I pretended to complain that she wanted me gone, but her concern was clear. I made no mention of my ex-boyfriend, no mention of my work, and no mention of the life I had led in London. I had arrived in Delhi, ostensibly for a few weeks to check in on my older sister, and had made no mention of returning.

But when Maya told her that we were thinking of launching a magazine, that we wanted, in fact, to resurrect Ma's old title, she was curiously resistant. We made a strong pitch. This was a bit of Ma preserved, of course, and a purpose for us. There was a purpose for Tasha-di too, of course, and when we asked her to come in and take over the finances and the running of the magazine, she took an age to respond.

We sat on her small sofa, the three of us, as we had since our childhood, with her in the middle. I was running my fingers through the fringes of the throw behind me, and Tasha-di addressed me directly. 'I'm surprised you want to do this, Siya.'

'It's a great idea,' I gushed, and then, as she didn't shift in her survey of me, 'it's you who says India is the new growth story. Everyone seems to be downing shutters in England.'

She nodded thoughtfully. We had come over to her place straight after our morning walk. We brought with us lunch Shanti packed in ancient steel tiffin boxes, joking that it would be our first ever working lunch.

'Really,' I said as she didn't speak. 'We've planned it all out. Staffing, budgets, everything.'

She smiled sadly. 'I'd better get up,' she said, pointing to the rug, and the empty tiffin boxes, 'and start to tidy up.' She patted me gently on the back, and I worried she considered the matter to be at an end.

'But there's more,' I exclaimed. I told her I had money to contribute towards the magazine. My redundancy pay, while not a fortune, was a comfortable sum, and it would surely pay for the running costs of the magazine for a year or more. Tasha-di listened kindly to all I had to say, and then asked me if I had set aside a budget for advertising.

'We'll build that out,' I said to her. 'But I would imagine our ad revenues will only build up as our readership does.'

'I'm not talking about ad revenues,' Tasha-di told me. 'I'm

talking about the advertising you'll have to do to get the public's attention.'

'Sure,' I said, though the enthusiasm with which I responded to her question betrayed my ignorance.

'Costs stack up,' said Tasha-di with infinite tenderness.

'Sure,' I repeated. I looked at Maya, who had been following our conversation without interrupting. She looked at me, gave me a small, thin smile, and shrugged. Another dream lost; I saw her think. We would return to our home where we would fight, as we had for weeks before Tasha-di had shown us *The Satirist*'s proofs, about how to put the house to use.

Tasha-di was nodding, kindly, so kindly, and I knew she believed the magazine was doomed. 'It's a tough business, my darling,' she was saying, 'before you know it, you'll have sunk all your money,' and I knew she was thinking of her own failed business. *It's a tough business*, the same morbid defeatism that Maya always exhibited, and I half-expected my feminist aunt to come out with some sexist trope. *It was harder for women. It was the male-led enterprises that flourished.*

I stood up. I picked up the remains of our meal, the leftover rice and gravy and yogurt, piling one tiffin box over the next, and walked towards the kitchen. There, I worked slowly, trying to calm myself, rinsing out the utensils before parcelling them back up, but as I worked, I thought. I knew I wasn't ready to give up. There would be funding we could source, of course, and in the interim, we could get to work creating the framework of the magazine.

I heard hushed voices from the living room. This was Maya and Tasha-di, then, trying to work out how to deal with my disappointment. I heard the word gentle, and in a louder voice, Tasha-di saying, 'She's been through so much,' but I shook my head. They were being too defeatist, the two in the living room. There were things we could do. We could source staff and print an issue. We could even launch online. The best magazines in India, especially in the politically charged environment we were living through, were the online ones. They were the ones at the vanguard of investigative journalism as most of their print brethren toed the party line.

'Yes,' I thought, jubilant, mutinous, unwilling to admit defeat. We could do it. Tasha-di was wrong to be so dour. We could create an online presence and we could print our magazine. And then, as we gained traction, we could seek outside funding. We could present a tangible product as opposed to simply a half-baked idea.

There were holes, I knew, in my argument, and hurdles I wasn't anticipating. Sourcing funding would be harder than I expected. We had no pedigree. Maya's journalistic career had been lacklustre, and my last role had been in marketing for a company that had failed. Tasha-di, for all her wisdom, had always operated behind the scenes. She had no background to speak of, and as a team, I could see we wouldn't inspire unstinting confidence.

Footsteps approached the kitchen. Tasha-di came in with a smile on her face. As she made eye contact with me, her smile stretched wide. I knew she was terrified of what I would say, but I went up to her. 'Don't worry, Tasha-di,' I said, and as she swallowed in surprise, I added, 'I'm not going to be downhearted.'

'No,' she said, still surprised. 'Exactly.'

'There's plenty we can do.' She was staring, nodding but not smiling, wary of disagreeing and disappointing me further. I said, 'We have some money, Tasha-di. It allows us to hire a small team, and to print an issue. We'll do everything in-house to minimise costs—the design, the layouts, the artwork. It won't be the most polished publication, of course, but it will get us into print. And,' I added, 'we can publish online too, like all those new outfits Maya admires.'

'That won't work.'

'Of course it will.'

'You have to have significant funding before you launch online. I have seen it with others in the industry.'

'We'll manage.'

'No, we won't,' she maintained. 'The internet is full of noise. To emerge above the clamour requires serious financial muscle. 'No,' she repeated, looking at my crestfallen face. 'Focussing on the internet will mean throwing our existing money down the drain.'

'But...'

'Listen to me, beta,' Tasha-di said. She was looking at me with love, and I knew she was thinking of the past. 'You print an issue,' she said. 'What then?'

'Well look, you never know.' I smiled at her, but she still had a worried look on her face. 'We don't start off online, and we limit ourselves to a small print run. The first issues will be distributed locally. They'll be free if it gets people to read then. And hopefully...'

'Siya, child...'

'Hopefully,' I continued, my smile wide. My cheer felt forced even to me, and my jaw was starting to ache. 'Hopefully, Tasha-di, *The Satirist* will be a runaway success. Hopefully,' I said as she pursed her lips, 'it makes so much money that we never need to worry about money again.'

Maya hadn't come in, but I knew our voices were carrying.

Tasha-di looked towards the living room, sighed, then asked, 'And what if the magazine fails?'

'Then,' I said, still smiling, though I knew I sounded unrealistic. Tasha-di was looking at me with concern, and I knew she was beginning to worry in earnest. 'We will still have options,' I said. 'We can look outside for funding. We can go to a bank, or to a media house.'

Maya came into the kitchen, a quizzical look on her face, and I shrugged. 'Look,' I said. 'You can be all doom and gloom if you like. But I'm not going to give up.'

'But darling,' said Tasha-di, 'you could lose all your money!'

'I could,' I agreed. 'But it's not a life changing amount.' Maya was frowning, and I said, 'You're being too defeatist. What's the worst that could happen? We spend a year building something. We'll learn a bit more about ourselves and what we are capable of. We could fail, of course, but I would hate to not try for the fear of not succeeding.'

'Well…'

'Think of *The Satirist* as an adventure. We'll have fun, if nothing else.'

Maya had been quiet for most of our discussion at Tasha-di's. She was quiet in the car on the way home, and anytime I tried to speak, she pointed to the road ahead. She was a careful driver, and skittish in Delhi's congested roads, but we were encountering empty streets, and she still insisted on focussing on her driving. She was always easily daunted, ready to give up at the first sign of a challenge, and I worried she had lost heart.

As we turned into Civil Lines, I saw her relax. She smiled at me through the rear-view mirror, and echoed a phrase I had shot at Tasha-di: 'What's the worst that could happen?'

I smiled in response, but there was no time to talk. We had arrived back home to the sight of Shanti at the front door, waving her hands at her downcast son.

It emerged that Pradeep had been fired from his job. His employers had given him a warning the day he had come to the airport to pick me up. He had been spending too much time, apparently, away from his work and in our service. I thought of the innumerable occasions when he would offer to run an errand for us. We had always been grateful to accept, but then, we hadn't once thought to see if his helping us was putting his employment in danger.

'This stupid boy!' Shanti was crying. 'He never even said a thing to me!' Apparently, she had grown suspicious, and once we had left to meet Tasha-di, she had set herself the task of tracking him down. She had gone first to his employer's house, waiting outside the gates for over an hour, but he had neither entered nor emerged. She had asked a passing maid about his whereabouts, and it was the maid who told her that Pradeep had been fired. 'I was so ashamed when she told me he had been let go a month or more back. Just think,' she said to Maya, 'what a fool I felt like.' Maya nodded, and her affirmation reinvigorated Shanti. 'And on my way back home, who do you think I see, bold as brass, on the pavement?'

She hit at his shoulder with her palm, but as she was a good foot shorter than him, her aggression didn't much disturb her son. He remained as he was, head bowed, hands folded, and rooted to the ground. Shanti screamed in her frustration, lashing out at Pradeep again, and Maya ran forward to contain the old retainer.

'It's our fault too, Shanti,' I told her. 'We shouldn't have asked him to help us out so much.'

She shook her head. 'What is he, a child?' she asked through a spittle-filled mouth. 'Can he not take care of his obligations?'

Maya had her hand on Shanti's back. 'He was just being kind.'

'Being kind?' Shanti roared. Maya shrank back at the vehemence in the woman's voice, and seeing how Maya reacted, Shanti hit out at her son again. 'What kindness is there in letting down your employer? What kindness is there in breaking your poor mother's heart?' She kept beating at Pradeep with her worn palms, and Maya mouthed at me to help.

'Go,' I told Pradeep, who wouldn't look me in the eye. He didn't move, and I gave him a little shove. 'Go, go,' I insisted, 'Go to sleep. Things will look better in the morning,' and he finally took off, turning away from us and towards the quarters at the back of the house.

Shanti was sobbing. Tears ran down her face unchecked, and Maya lifted a tissue to her skin to stem their flow. 'Shh,' she said soothingly, patting her softly on the back, as if to calm a hysterical child. Shanti's cries grew more muted, and I reached forward, putting my arms around her. Her chest heaved against me, and as I looked down, I was struck again by the white in her hair. Once Shanti was calmer, she said, 'Now, what will become of the boy? He only has a roof over his head because you are kind.'

'No,' said Maya firmly. 'This is his home.'

'And what about his future?' the woman asked. 'How is he going to earn money? Or am I going to have to earn and provide for that great big lump until I'm dead and gone?'

'There will be other jobs.'

'Did he think about the girl he was going to marry?' she jabbed. She broke away from my embrace. Her face was full of thunder, dark and pursed, and she asked, 'Tell me, baby, who is going to marry that idiot now?'

'Come on, Shanti.'

She didn't speak then, this small, greying woman. She had been a second mother to us, scolding us when we had needed it, and comforting us too when we were ill or unhappy, but as I looked down at her, so solitary in her grief, I saw that I had never before been called upon to ease her pain.

XI

The monsoons were anticipated any day. The news channels gave over much of their hourly segments to tracking the path of the rain up the country, and in the meantime, North India held its breath. The heat seemed more unbearable; the air full with unspent moisture. We wore our crispest, most starched white cottons, but these were drenched the minute we stepped out. The grass in the garden grew bleached, the rooms indoors—airy and high-ceilinged—grew heavy with the smell of damp.

We grew sluggish too, and rose later. I bathed twice a day, and yet I felt my clothes stick to my skin the minute I was out of the bathroom. Maya, though, seemed unaffected by the humidity, and began to work as if possessed. She had the library aired out, and opened the connecting door to the garden room. The ancient wicker chairs were dusted, all the clutter from here was shifted to the living room on the first floor, and though every table upstairs heaved with decaying papers, the two rooms she had opened up on the ground floor were now spotless.

I asked Maya what had changed her mind about the magazine, and she threw her arms into the air. 'It's all falling apart—the house, our lives. And I've always been scared of change. But I heard you fight for us at Tasha-di's flat, and something you said: "What's the worst that could happen?", struck a chord with me. The worst was happening, and the worst that was happening was that I was allowing it to happen.'

Pradeep's help was enlisted in the clean up. No one spoke about the job he had lost, and he fell naturally into employment with us. His salary was paid out of the household budget, and though I offered to pay him out of my savings, Maya refused. 'Keep your money for the magazine,' she instructed, and I had a chimera, a hint of a memory of the big sister who had always guided me and led me away from trouble.

Pradeep began to come into the house, then, shortly after we returned from our morning walks, and set to unearthing the floor in the hallway. He would run errands for us, ferrying us about to supply stores and as we went to meetings with Tasha-di and potential recruits. After we were finished for the evening, he would move into the library and begin to work on the flooring there. We told him his working day ended when ours did, and though he never disagreed with us, we often heard him working as we dined on the first floor.

Ben wrote a few days later. 'Are you not coming back?'

I replied straight away. 'No. I'm launching a magazine with my sister.'

'Seriously, then,' he wrote back. 'For real?'

'For real,' I replied, and smiled. For real.

I sometimes saw Raja Singh from the first floor veranda and quelled my urge to call out to him. He was a successful investor;

a reader of the nation's tastes; an incubator of new ideas; he had known Ma. Surely we could rely on him for advice. But there was a reluctance to accost him—he was so eminent, and our plan still so unformed—and he continued to pass by our house untroubled as I continued to tell myself I would approach him the next time I saw him.

Maya was a revelation during these weeks. She had earlier told me she knew no one we could bring into the magazine, and she had been right. She had fallen out of touch with many of her college friends, and the others she had encountered were too senior to countenance working in a poorly funded start-up operating out of the founders' crumbling home. And yet, there she was, despite all her natural reservations, feeding me ideas, telling me about two old college friends who had given up working after bearing children.

'Either,' she told me, 'would be an asset. But it's Sonia, really, who would be wonderful to have on board.' We were in my bedroom. The monsoons had begun, and I woke every morning to sheets of water pouring down onto the balcony in front of my room. Everything was transformed by the rains. The grass, which had turned to straw, sprang back to vivid life overnight. Crickets chirped in the evening; earthworms moved languidly underfoot. The air smelt earthier. Birdsong seemed sweeter, there were reports of peacock sightings on a roof in the area. The neighbourhood seemed all at once lusher, fuller, and it affected us. We smiled more at each other, our pace grew more relaxed, and as I woke in the mornings, I didn't immediately rise. There was comfort in the sound of the rain beating against the walls of the house, insistent and life-affirming, and I would choose to lay in bed, my eyes shut, taking in the drama of the heavens. It might have been my imagination, but I thought that the damp patch in my ceiling had spread a little, though I chose to ignore this. Maya was full of energy for our project, the air fragrant with possibility, and I was loathe to present any problems to her.

Our morning walks were halted. Maya came into my room, instead, after her yoga, and as I lay in bed, resisting the call of the day, she would pull open the curtains, and scold me for wasting time. Shanti would bring in tea, and Maya would snuggle in next to me, and as I took my first sips against the drumbeat of India's monsoon, Maya would tell me of all she had thought of as I slept. Now she raised herself up against a pillow, and asked me, 'You remember Sonia, surely?'

'Hmm…' I muttered noncommittally.

'You must,' she insisted, and as I shrugged, she said, 'she was brilliant. I only ever lost prizes in college to her, and after graduation, she joined the best magazine in India.'

'You were brilliant too,' I said stoutly, but Maya raised her hand.

'Sonia wrote beautifully about politics and social change. I was sure she would have been a major editor by now, but after she had her children, her ambition seemed to leave her. She didn't have family in Delhi, and didn't want to leave her children in the charge of help, so she resigned from the magazine. I still see her by-line sometimes in an online magazine, but I don't think she's writing regularly.'

I looked at her for a moment. 'Both the brilliant girls from your degree gave up writing.'

'Well,' she said. She turned away from my gaze, and set her cup of tea down on a side table. 'I had my own version of care assigned to me.'

Maya had picked up the edge of my bed cover, and was running her fingers through it. She traced out the peacock pattern on the worn fabric, her fingers running through the design repeatedly, as if she was rubbing an itch, and I thought—perhaps for the first time—of all she had given up. She had been alone in that house, shrouded in the silence Ma had built up around her, and instead of relieving her burden, I had been away and unencumbered. 'I'm sorry, Maya,' I said, but she was shaking her head. Her head was bowed now, and I saw her blink rapidly, but she didn't speak. I thought of speaking again, of expressing my regret, of promising to be better, but I wasn't in the habit of providing comfort to her, and I didn't know how my words would be received. We sat in silence then, as the rain lashed down around us. If she felt uncomfortable, she didn't mention it. Our tea grew cold. I took another sip, but felt my action to be too noisy. The sip sounded loud to me, the ensuing gulp louder still, and I set my cup down on a table.

We continued quiet, and Maya made no move to change the situation. In the end, and to distract her from her thoughts, I asked her, 'So are you still in touch with her?'

This jolted her. 'Who?'

'This Sonia girl you told me about.'

It took her a moment to realise who I spoke of. She shook her head, and said, 'No,' and then, 'Yes. We're not friends, exactly, but we keep in touch as part of a group. There are the usual greetings over Diwali, and maybe a catch up at a party once a year. But no,' she said again thoughtfully, 'we're not friends.'

There was an hourglass I had once taken from a board game. I had loved to see the grains of sand slip down the funnel and deposit down the bottom of the surface, and instead of spurring me on to be mindful of time, I had found the motion relaxing. This hourglass rested on a table next to the bed, and Maya picked it up. She looked at it, turning it over as the sand ran out, and I asked her, 'Do you have her number?'

'Yes,' and then, as she turned the hourglass again and set it back down on the table, 'I called her this morning. We can go meet her later on today.'

XII

Sonia listened to our plans for *The Satirist* with great interest before telling us she wasn't able to help. Both of her children were in full-time education, and she told us she would have to be back home in time for their return from school. Sahil, her oldest, was fifteen, and reaching his crucial years at school, and she didn't want to be distracted when he was at home.

'Ok,' said Maya. I was downhearted at the rejection, but Maya made a suggestion. 'Why don't you take the local interest stories then. Any oddities that strike you. You can add the satirical tone to *The Satirist*.' Sonia was nodding thoughtfully, and I knew my sister had caught her imagination. 'And then, when your kids are older, you can move back into looking at politics.'

'Yes,' said Sonia. She had a long face, her features serious, her words and movements measured, and she took a while to continue. She had on a loose-fitting tracksuit, which she pointed to apologetically. 'This is all I wear these days. I'm a professional mother now, Maya. And Sahil does need me.'

'Look,' I said, and both women turned to me with surprise. I had been largely silent thus far, letting the two old journalists lead the conversation, and as I spoke, I worried I was breaking the rhythm of their interaction. 'This is all a little bit of a gamble. I'm uprooting myself to start *The Satirist*. So, in a way, is Maya.' Sonia looked at Maya, who shrugged. I continued, anxious to persuade Sonia. 'If we look at the world around us,' and here I ran out of inspiration. I looked at my sister, but it was no use. I couldn't think of anything else to say.

'The world,' she said, the words spilling out of her mouth, 'is changing beyond recognition. I'm not just talking about climate change and the change in the political order, though these in themselves are terrifying. I'm talking about the way news is presented, and about the way we interact with it. I'm talking about our shorter attention spans and about how everything we consume is interactive. We spend more time online, and we curate who we listen to. This has led to a polarisation of our discourse, and to an increasing shrillness in our debates and news. And this is why we need to turn to the old way of disseminating our information. This is why our columns need to be shorter, and pithier, just as we have to be balanced and unbiased at a time when so few others are.'

This was the longest speech I had ever heard from Maya. Her articles had always been persuasive, well argued, well researched and immaculately structured, and to see her talents translate to the spoken word was new to me. I surged in confidence all at once. Yes, I thought. We could do this. This ridiculous idea of starting up a print magazine as the world grew digital sounded suddenly not only possible, but urgently needed. I looked across at Sonia, who seemed similarly affected by Maya's words.

She nodded, going to where Maya sat. She perched herself on the arm of Maya's chair, and put her arms around my sister. 'I always wondered,' said Sonia. 'Why you stopped writing.'

Maya gave her a wry smile. 'Life,' she said, 'gets in the way.'

'Well,' nodded Sonia. She looked around her living room,

filled as it was with photos of her children. 'Like Siya says, you're both uprooting yourselves.'

She didn't speak further. 'You can step back anytime…' I started, but Maya shot me down with a quick look. Sonia laughed. She looked at me and then at my sister, and both burst out into loud, irrepressible peals of laughter I pretended to mind.

The purchases continued. We ordered new computers and desks, with Pradeep in charge of all the ferrying and building work. The wedding, which had been brokered and then cancelled after news of Pradeep's unemployment reached the village, was now back on.

I was with Pradeep in the library, monitoring the layout of the desks. Pradeep didn't speak much, indicating his agreement with my suggestions with a short nod. I asked for a few desks to be moved so that Maya and I were sitting opposite each other, and as he followed my instructions, I said, 'It's all slowly coming together.'

I had spoken softly, but he looked up now and nodded. 'Yes, Didi,' he said, and then, wiping his hands and reaching into a trouser pocket, he asked me, 'would you like to see a picture?'

I was caught off-guard by his question, but he pulled out a small passport photo sized image. This he now brought towards me. 'A photo of my phancee.'

I understood the word to mean his fiancée, and took the proffered picture. The image itself was out of focus, and the card lined, as if it had been folded and refolded repeatedly, and I squinted to get a better view. The girl in the picture was slim and looked serious. She didn't smile, and I wondered if the photo had in fact been taken for an official purpose. Pradeep was looking at me, expecting a reply, and I returned to scrutinising his fiancée's features. She was young, just out of her teens perhaps, and elegant. Her hair fell straight down her shoulders, her lips were full and wide. The sternness of her features couldn't hide that. There was an intelligence I thought I detected in her eyes, a sharpness, a knowledge, and I wondered how they would pair up, Pradeep, always so solemn and subservient, and this proud young creature with intelligence in her eyes.

Maya called Tania, the other friend from college she had thought of. Tania had married well and vanished from journalism. 'But,' she told me and Sonia, 'she must feel the itch of work.'

A call was placed, then, though it went unanswered, and was not returned. Maya sent Tania a message on Facebook, but there was no response to that either. 'Is it a tricky time for her, do you think?' she asked Sonia. 'An exam year for one of her kids, maybe?'

'I can't imagine so,' Sonia replied. 'Her children are much younger than mine.' She looked at us, so anxious to hear her opinion, and she blinked. 'I don't know.' She looked around at us again, straining in our seats in our eagerness, and sighed. 'I was never really very good friends with her,' she added, but what she didn't mention was that we were a rag-tag crew of associates without any pedigree. Asking an acquaintance to emerge from retirement for the sake of our little half-baked plan wasn't likely to appeal to most.

Sonia did have thoughts on two more hires. One was a friend's daughter, freshly out of college and looking for a job.

'She doesn't have any experience,' she told us, 'but she's bright, and I'm sure she will learn quickly.'

The girl, Natasha, was contacted, and called in for an interview. She had interned for a month at a daily newspaper, and as she walked into our office—the old garden room full of its bamboo armchairs—I could see her sniff. She sat through the hour-long meeting, then told us she didn't think we were the right place for her.

'But,' an astonished Sonia pointed out, 'this is an opportunity to get in on the ground floor of an amazing new magazine. You'll be working right alongside two industry veterans, and you'll get your earliest by-lines much sooner than you otherwise would.' Natasha still pursed her lips, and Sonia added, 'Think of all the experience you'll gain.'

'But this is it,' the girl pointed out, 'What would I gain from working for a magazine no one has heard of?'

Natasha had baldly stated what Tania's silence had implied, and both Maya and I were daunted. The girl was right; no one had heard of us. No one would buy our magazine. We were destined to end in failure. No offer was extended to Natasha, though it was clear it wouldn't have been accepted even if it had been made.

'How's it going?' Benjamin wrote.

'No one wants to write for a magazine started by nobodies.'

'Losers,' he wrote back.

'Yes, right,' I thought. 'Losers.'

Tasha-di, who joined us in interviewing the young graduate, began to voice fresh concerns about the money I was putting at risk, telling us not to be irresponsible, and her arguments began to sway my sister. Always credulous, always obedient, Maya found it natural to doubt herself. 'Maybe it's not such a good idea,' she told me. 'What experience do we have of running a magazine, anyway?'

It was Sonia who told us not to lose heart. She had been slow to commit to *The Satirist*, and full of disclaimers about the calls on her time, but she now refused to give way to Tasha-di's worries. 'Siya is right,' she told us. 'It's not like we have much to lose, is it?'

'We have Siya's money,' came Tasha-di's terse reply.

'It's a wonderful idea for a magazine.'

'Rubbish.'

'It is,' insisted Sonia. 'I have been asked to join magazines and newspapers for years and have never been tempted. Now I am not only on board, but excited about the future. So what if a silly child can't see the opportunity?'

Tasha-di had taken on the mantle of doom-monger once more. She didn't say anything to Sonia but her face remained downcast.

'Others will,' said Sonia. She stood up, as if on a podium, and looked at us. We were in the garden room, the scene of so many of Ma and Tasha-di's soirees, and a weary Tasha-di shook her head. Sonia sat back down, landing weightily on the spent cushion.

I nodded now, and Maya, who had listened quietly to us all this while, turned to Tasha-di. 'We've come so far,' she said. 'And we have Sonia on board. Others will join us too; you wait and see.'

Sonia's next suggestion was for a caricaturist she had once worked with. Maya and I worried about our attractiveness to an employable person, but Sonia reassured us he would be unable to resist us. 'Ajay is a contrarian. He comes from a well-off family, and turned to art, not because he had to or was encouraged to, but rather because he was told it was an unworthy pursuit. His parents would have preferred him to go into the family business, but there has always been a perverse element to him.'

I wasn't sure if I much cared for the implied analogy. 'He'll work for us, then,' I asked, 'because he shouldn't?'

'Just meet him and see.'

I hadn't replied to Benjamin's last message, but I heard from him again. 'Have you overtaken the *Times of India* yet?'

'It's a magazine we're setting up, genius, and not a newspaper.'

He sent a winking emoji, and while I attempted to decipher his purpose, he added, 'That was my clunky attempt to ask how you are.'

'Still understaffed,' I wrote.

'If you want,' he shot back, 'you can use my published articles in your magazine.'

Great, I thought. More lifestyle features in my political magazine. 'I can't afford to pay you.'

'I don't want payment,' he replied.

He was listed on the phone as typing, but no new message appeared, and I wrote, 'I'm not sure your work will suit us.'

No reply appeared for a while, and I assumed he had abandoned the message he had been typing out. Then my phone beeped. 'My holidays gone wrong series would be perfect for you.'

'Holidays gone wrong?'

'I'll send you a couple of articles,' he typed. 'You decide if they work for you.'

I didn't reply, but my phone lit up after a few seconds. 'Please,' he said, 'let me do this for you.'

Ajay came in smelling of smoke. He made no chit-chat, didn't ask how we all met or what led to the founding of the magazine, just stood looking down at us all sitting primly, hands folded over our laps in our bamboo armchairs, and smiled. I knew instinctively the kind of man he was. Sexist, elitist, entitled. He'd be ignoring deadlines by the end of the week, and would consider us lucky for having secured his services. He saw me looking at him and winked. I had never felt so inconsequential before, nor so frivolous, and I hated him on sight.

But Sonia was rising and patting him on the back. 'Ajay will never win a beauty contest,' she said, as the man laughed, 'but just wait till you see his work.'

A portfolio was produced, and sheets of drawings were passed around. I frowned as I looked at them. Ajay leaned, his back to the wall, his t-shirt rolled up on the sleeves, as if waiting for adulation. He caught me looking at him. His lips curled at the ends, and I glared. He grinned. I shook my head disapprovingly and returned to his work.

Maya and Tasha-di had been through his other work by this point, and passed this to me. 'Hmm,' I said. 'Well,' and as I opened the first page of his portfolio, I thought of polite ways to turn him down. I scanned the first image, a cartoon of a pot-bellied politician, and sighed. I turned to the next page, a caricature of a famous actor, and frowned. I looked up to see

Ajay watching me through lidded eyes and sighed again.

I turned page after page, and though I continued to sigh and make non-committal noises, the truth was clear. Ajay had a rare talent for expression.

I was determined not to praise him, though, and I knew he would grate on me and my team. There he reclined, against my wall, as if the honour of viewing his art was mine. I wasn't going to give him the satisfaction of knowing I admired his work. 'Hmm,' I said, when Sonia rose.

'Well,' she said, taking the work out of my hand. 'I remember your art being good, Ajay,' she said, 'but this is much better than I remembered.'

Maya joined the two ex-colleagues. 'Yes,' she said, nodding avidly, and I knew she was enthused by Ajay's work. 'These pictures,' she said, waving at the portfolio Sonia held in her hands, 'they're just fantastic.'

She looked around to the both of us for confirmation. Tasha-di was looking at me, but at Maya's prompt, she nodded. 'Yes,' she said, 'I agree with the others. My only worry is whether we can afford you.'

Ajay had his eyes on me, waiting for my reaction, but at Tasha-di's words, he stood straight. 'I know what I'm getting into here,' he told her. 'I fully expect the magazine to be loss making for the first year.' I bristled at his words, and he said slowly, turning his attention back to me, 'and that is the best case scenario. I've seen lots of these things start and fold.' There was a hint of a smile in his face, and I turned quickly away. 'Like I was saying, the odds are stacked against you.' I heard a noise I took to be a laugh, and turned back to see him say, 'But I'm there. I love the story, and I think this is either an inspired or deluded moment to launch a print magazine.' He was quiet for a long moment, his eyes fixed on me. 'I'm not sure as yet which it is, but I'm here for the ride.'

On his way out, Ajay bumped into Pradeep. He brushed into the driver, and instead of apologising, he laughed, patting the man playfully on his back. Pradeep didn't say anything, shrinking instead back into the shadows, but later he approached me. 'Didi,' he said.

I presumed he wanted to talk about his fiancée. 'Yes, Pradeep?'

'It's about that Ajay Sir.'

I frowned.

'You know, Didi,' the driver continued, 'I'm not sure about him working in the house.'

I didn't speak.

'You know,' he said. He was clearly uncomfortable voicing his opinion, and my silence unnerved him, but he battled on. 'You are all such nice-nice ladies working. I think this man will make trouble.'

The precise nature of Pradeep's concern was not delved into, and when I thanked him for his warning, he took it to mean our conversation was at an end. He nodded, walking back to his quarters, and as he walked, I thought I heard him mutter 'trouble'.

Ajay joined our team. Natasha had turned us down, and Tania hadn't returned Maya's calls, but the artist's enthusiasm for *The Satirist* had filled us with renewed vigour. The two new recruits agreed to work for an honorarium for the first year, limiting our costs to the actual production of the magazine.

I approached a few local shops, asking them to stock copies of the launch issue of the magazine for free. We knew it was a big ask, but we had always frequented these stores and were known to the proprietors. As we expanded our operations, first through Delhi, and then across India, we would have to face market economics, but for the moment, the shops that knew us told us they would stock our magazine without charge.

XIII

The weather turned cooler. We packed away our white cottons and brought out our winter shawls. The first issue of the magazine was taking shape. A launch date was set for the first of December, as was a launch party to mark the occasion. It was mainly Maya and Sonia who called their contacts, but acceptances were flowing in, prompted by curiosity as much as by interest, and we had to change our plans to host the event in the garden room and open out the garden beyond too.

We worked hard, then, on the event, and on the issue. Our brainstorming sessions officially took place in the morning over cups of tea in the garden room, but Maya and I began our discussions as we took our morning walks. She continued to surprise me with the extent to which she was taking ownership of the magazine. I had spent so long finding solutions—arguing against Maya and Tasha-di's uncertainty—that I hadn't thought to think about the tone of the magazine.

I knew it was to be political, I knew it would focus on Delhi in the early issues, and I knew we weren't to seek advertising until we had established our readership, but it was Maya who pointed out that our magazine didn't have anything to differentiate it from the others in circulation.

I worried she was having renewed doubts, and told her that *The Satirist* was a great magazine.

She pounced on my words. 'Exactly! But where is the satirical content?'

I paused. 'Benjamin's article fits the bill,' I said defensively, 'and Ajay's cartoons do too.'

'Yes,' she agreed. 'But that's it. Sonia's writing is fantastic, but I had forgotten her style. It's hard-hitting, it's raw and honest and empathetic, but it's not satirical.'

A woman walked past us in a blaze of pink velour. A young maid hurried behind her, carrying a bottle of water and a perfumed face towel. Maya and I both smiled. 'That,' my sister told me, 'is Raja Singh's wife.'

I turned around to look at the retreating pair.

'He,' Maya was saying, 'is the most successful investor in India. They say he's launched entire industries.'

Mrs Bhatnagar had mentioned Mrs Singh before, eulogising her glamour and hospitality. Her fragrance still lingered in the air, a sharp, citrus smell, but Maya was turning me towards her. 'He's iconic, Siya.'

I nodded, ready to reprise our walk, but Maya was still speaking. 'He's the one to copy. And he wouldn't invest in a magazine without a USP.'

I thought of Mrs Singh sashaying on her walk. 'What if,' I suggested, 'I write a short column called, "The Adventures of Arrival"?' I saw Maya studying me, and I added, 'I'll make it tongue-in-cheek. Focus on the misconceptions so many have about life in Delhi—from foreigners to our own non-resident Indians.'

'That could be something.' Maya nodded. She began walking, and as we closed in on the trail of Mrs Singh's perfume, she nodded again, 'And I can write a short column called "Today in Politics" about the most ridiculous utterances made by India's politicians.'

Back at home, we debated our feature article. India seemed more divided than it had been since Independence. Maya wanted to write an article on the controversial right-wing Prime Minister, but Tasha-di worried about alienating conservative readers.

We were stuck, arguing with Tasha-di that we wouldn't be cowed. We were going to write truth to power, but Tasha-di held firm. It was foolish, at this early stage, to set at least half the population against us. It seemed like we were never going to agree, and I had started to think of lifestyle articles we could use for the first issue, when Shanti came up with an alternative.

'Why don't you write about demonetisation?'

I remembered hearing about demonetisation in London. Over the course of one evening in November 2016, as the world focussed on Donald Trump—another populist, right-wing leader—get elected in the US, the majority of India's bank notes were rendered illegal tender. I had read an article on the internet, and as I had tried to explain the enormity of the action to Benjamin, I had told him, 'India is largely a cash-based economy. Imagine not using your credit cards in London. Imagine not having internet banking. And then, imagine 86 per cent of the currency in circulation—your £5 notes, your £10 notes, your £20 notes, heck, the equivalent of all your pound coins too—being made illegal overnight.'

I had read briefly about demonetisation in the days after it had occurred, had registered the rationale appeared to be to root out black money and terrorism from across the border, but my attention had been diverted by the events in America. Trump had been elected, and it appeared the world would never be the same again. Back in India, hundreds of millions were queueing up at bank branches to trade in their newly illegal money for new money that was being dispensed in slow, painful drips, and as Shanti now told us, a man in her village had been driven to suicide because of demonetisation.

'His daughter was to be married at the start of December,' she told us. She spoke phlegmatically, as if it was natural for these big policy rollouts to punish the working man. 'The girl's family had been saving for years. You know how it is,' and we all nodded. The rest of us lived in affluent areas in Delhi, but we'd all been brought up by our mothers penny-pinching, siphoning little sums from the monthly household budget to save. It was never for themselves, rather for an after-school activity, or for a new item of furniture, or for a wedding or for further education. Saving in India began with the birth of a child, and we could easily imagine the villager's family pilfering money from their monthly expenses to save for their daughter's wedding.

'He had all this money in cash, and he had all these expenses he had committed to—the henna-wallah, the rented jewellery, the florist for the ceremony, the shehnai musicians, the caterers, the venue, the priest. All of that had been budgeted for, and all of that was to have been paid for with money that was no longer accepted anywhere.'

There were several echoing anecdotes; labourers who went unpaid as cash ran out, people who could no longer buy their vegetables, middle-class people—the urban, those who paid their restaurant bills with credit cards but left cash tips for the waiters—who found themselves unable to pay their tips when they dined out. 'Right,' said Shanti dismissively. 'Delhi suffered. But the girl in my village was unable to get married. The shame of a cancelled wedding…' Shanti grimaced. 'The girl's life was ruined. The disgrace was such that she was never going to get another offer of marriage and the poor, humiliated father ended up hanging himself one night after his daughter had cried herself to sleep.'

We were all silent. 'So yes,' Shanti went on, 'Delhi suffered after demonetisation. But it was the working, the labourers, the poor who were paid in cash, and the poor who saved in cash who suffered the most.'

'Shanti,' I said, feeling ineffectual, 'were you close?'

'Were we close?' Shanti huffed. 'Were we close, baby? Does that even matter?'

Her testimony decided us. We were to lead with a piece on demonetisation, and Sonia, charged with writing the article, used Shanti's villager as the basis for her article. She would come in early in the morning, just as Shanti was preparing our breakfast, and set to asking her questions. 'This girl,' Shanti complained. 'She's there every time I turn around. I can't breathe, I can't cook, I can't clean for fear of her never-ending questions. Hasn't she heard of newspapers? The story was covered in *The Times*. She could look there instead of troubling me. And,' Shanti spat out, 'she eats paranthas quicker than I can make them. She's a pest, that woman.'

'Come on, Shanti,' I reasoned. 'She's trying to shine a light on how your poor neighbour suffered.'

'What poor neighbour?' Shanti scowled. 'The man was a brute. Kept on trying to build on our land.'

Shanti continued dissatisfied, then, until I urged Sonia to back off. Ajay took her off to the streets of Delhi to find some builders who had suffered with the dying supply of money, and peace was slowly restored. Together, the pair unearthed the invisible victims of a new government's macho foray into economic policymaking—the heartbroken families, the starving labourers, the unpaid workers. The feature, 'Demonetisation: An Intimate Portrait', was the lead for our first issue.

Elsewhere in the house, Shanti prepared for the launch party. She prepared and froze kebabs and samosas, and Pradeep took over the organisation. He hired waiters, he selected barmen, and he oversaw the erection of a tent in the garden.

While they worked, he and Shanti planned for the upcoming wedding too. Horoscopes were matched, earnest looking pandits consulted, and the date for the wedding was set. Pradeep was due to be married the week after *The Satirist* launched. I offered to accompany the mother-son duo to the wedding, but Shanti refused. 'You will be busy here, Baby,' she told me. It was early in the morning, and she had just brought my tea into my room. The sun was rising later, and though Maya and I had reprised our daily walks, we were beginning to leave later in the mornings. The curtains were pulled open, and as a dim, syrupy sunlight trickled in, I asked again, 'But it is your only son's wedding, Shanti. When will you celebrate like this again?'

She smiled, then carried on opening the windows.

'I should be there too.'

'Really,' she said. She came to my bed and put a hand on my head. This had been our routine since my childhood, Shanti with her hand on my head. She would use the touch to reassure, to reprove, and to caress, and I leaned into her touch. 'We'll be back with the bride in a week. There's no point in you coming all the way.'

Later that day, I complained to Maya. 'I don't see why she doesn't want us there.'

'She's in a very unhappy marriage,' replied Maya. I stuck out my lip in disapproval, but my sister carried on. 'Her husband abuses her physically. And this is the woman who has been in charge of us for all our lives. She has loved us; she has cared for us; she has wiped away our tears. Do you think she would want us to see her humiliated in her own home?'

I was quiet for a minute. 'But still, it's Pradeep's wedding.'

'We'll send him off with a nice gift. And his bride will come and live with us. We show them in a million ways that they are part of our family. Not attending one little ceremony doesn't change that.'

There was no time to argue. There was no time to feel aggrieved. There was no time, seemingly, to sleep either, as the end of November approached. Supplies took longer to arrive than we had anticipated, causing delays with the printing of the magazine. And once it was all finally done, once the product was finished and ready for delivery, one of the shopkeepers in the market had second thoughts about stocking the magazine.

'Think about it from our perspective,' the proprietor told me. He was the bulbous-nosed son of Mr Seth, the old shop owner. We had been going to the store for decades, when the old man sneaked us sweets from a jar while Ma shopped for supplies. It was Mr Seth I had spoken to about stocking the magazine, and he had scolded me for the formality of my request. 'Aren't you like one of my own?' I hadn't seen him in years; my trips to Delhi had been infrequent and strained. Whatever time I had, had been spent with Ma and Maya. The thought of visiting Mr Seth had never crossed my mind, and there he had been when I had gone to speak to him, angry at the thought he would refuse me. 'Of course we'll stock our children's magazine. We'll give it pride of place. See if we don't.'

It had been a few months since the arrangement was settled, but a week before the magazine was due to arrive at the shop. Mr Seth's son, Vivek, cornered me and led me to his desk at the back of the store. He asked his assistant to fetch me a drink. 'Coffee, tea, coke, whatever you please,' and when I refused, he launched straight into his speech. 'You see,' he said. 'Any space we are allocating to you means that other magazines are missing out.'

I thought for one delirious moment that he had been hired by an existing magazine to stop our launch. But then he spoke again, his face gleaming with regret. 'Unfortunately,' he said, 'it doesn't make sense not to allocate shelf space to magazines that sell.'

'But…'

'I know,' he interrupted. 'You'll sell. But you see, we get paid commission for every magazine we stock.' He looked at me sympathetically, as if embarrassed by what he was saying, but his eyes were hard behind his glasses. 'And, you know, if I think of how many copies of *Femina* we sell in a day, or of *Outlook*, then it's hard to justify stocking a brand new, unheard of little start-up.'

I nodded. Mr Seth had never mentioned being paid for stocking the magazine, but the economics of the transaction were clear to me. I had seen the old man's offer as a favour, but in Vivek's telling, his father's kindness was leaving the family out of pocket.

'Mr Seth,' I said, but Vivek waved his hands in the air.

'Papa,' he said, 'is not running the business anymore.'

My heart sank. I had thought of appealing to Mr Seth, but it was clear that power had changed hands. Vivek did not favour the idea of stocking *The Satirist* for free, but I looked at him as he sat behind his father's old desk, and said, 'Your support would mean so much.'

'Of course,' he replied, 'It would be fantastic to see…' he paused, as if trying to place a name, then said, 'your magazine prosper.'

'I wonder,' I said. I saw Vivek's attention waver. There was a queue building up at the till, and he looked to rise. But I wasn't willing to give up so easily, and I said, 'Perhaps I could interest you in our sponsorship package.'

He smiled at a customer, then nodded briskly at me. 'Sponsorship?'

Nothing had been planned. We faced the classic beginner's conundrum: we would continue to lose money until we secured advertising, and we would be unable to secure advertising until we had secured our readership. The spreadsheets I built and maintained in London had felt a little premature with the magazine, but as Vivek leaned forward, his forehead glistening with perspiration, I said, 'As a gesture of goodwill, we were thinking of offering our key partners free advertising in the launch issue.'

He stroked an imaginary beard. 'Key partners, you say?'

'Absolutely. All those showing faith in us by stocking us in our infancy. And all local businesses we are proud to promote.'

'Hmm,' Vivek said. I could see him picturing the advert.

Him in a photo in front of the store, and a gushing paragraph in praise of Seth Supplies. And I, I realised, would have to be the one penning the gushing paragraph. 'Hmm,' he repeated, and as someone else approached him, he waved them unceremoniously away. 'You say free sponsorship is only for the launch issue?'

'Well…'

'And *The Satirist* is a monthly magazine?'

I smiled. 'You're a tough negotiator, Vivek,' I said. 'How about I offer you free sponsorship for the first three issues?'

He thought hard. His hand rose to his forehead, then to his slicked-back hair. 'I'll tell you what,' he said benignly, 'You make it free advertising for six months and we have a deal.'

Vivek's deal disturbed all our planning. The maiden issue was already printed and ready to be delivered. Pradeep had figured out the route he would take to ensure delivery of all the copies took place in a single day. Maya was unhappy with the new arrangement I had brokered, and suggested returning to Vivek with an alternative proposal. 'Tell him these copies are ready,' she told me. 'We can give him free sponsorship in the next issue.'

Maya took seniority over me in editorial issues. In fact, she and Sonia had taken charge over most of the running of the magazine as our marketing efforts hadn't yet kicked in. I was sure she expected me to agree with her plans, but I shook my head. 'We do that,' I pointed out, 'and we risk Vivek not stocking the magazine at all.'

'Mr Seth…'

'Even if he does stock it, who is to say he doesn't let it languish in a bottom shelf? We need him on our side, Maya.'

Tasha-di spoke up. 'We can't renege on Siya's promise,' she said with finality. 'We need as much goodwill as we can get.'

'But the magazine is ready. It would take a complete change in layout to incorporate ads.'

'Maybe not,' I replied. 'If Seth Supplies gets free advertising, we really should provide it for our other stockists.' Maya threw her hands up, and I carried on, 'That makes our job easier, don't you see? We'll just print out a four page spread on advertising.'

Maya was still frowning, but Ajay snapped his fingers. 'That's doable,' he said. He picked up a large sheet of paper, folding it in half in demonstration. 'The ads go on these four pages, and the rest of your layout is not impacted.' He looked at me to be sure that his understanding was in line with my plan. I nodded, when he asked, 'Do you want to have the ad pages as a detachable insert in the middle of the magazine?'

'No,' I replied. I could see Maya and Sonia were still not on board with the plan. The concept of a detachable insert would please no one, Vivek least of all. 'No,' I said again. 'I thought we could remove the staples from the magazine, placing the adverts right inside the cover.'

'So they're the front and back pages of the magazine?' Ajay asked.

'Exactly,' I said. 'We could place them in the centre, but then I worry Vivek will think they're not prominent enough.'

'But,' said Sonia, and I spoke over her.

'I know it's disruptive,' I said, 'But it seems the least troublesome way of getting what everyone wants.'

'Actually,' Ajay said. I didn't quite trust his good offices, but he picked up a magazine from a stack, and proceeded to pry out the staples binding the paper. He worked gingerly, as if removing a splinter from a child's finger. We loomed over him, watching as he retrieved the two metal implements from their place. 'There,' he said, holding up the staples triumphantly, 'All done.'

'I don't know,' said Maya. 'I still think we should only offer advertising from the next issue onwards.'

'Siya's right,' said Ajay. Tasha-di added her assent, and he said, 'It'll be done in half a day. Let Siya finalise her sponsorship.' Maya cackled unhappily at the word, and he repeated, 'Her sponsorship, and I'll make sure the magazines are ready for their new pages.' He saw Shanti pause before the room, and said, 'I'm sure this lovely lady will help me. I've forgotten her name for the moment,' and as I barked, 'Shanti,' he held up his hands. The staples let out a small glint. 'Shanti,' he said. 'I'm sorry. I'm bad with names. But you'll help me get the magazines ready, won't you?'

Shanti nodded, Maya did too, although reluctantly, and it appeared we were all finally set.

Now that I had broached the topic of advertising, I began approaching our remaining stockists, and extended them the offer we had made Seth Supplies. There was a hotel in the vicinity, and I spoke to them too about sponsorship. 'We're just starting out,' I explained to the manager, a sleek-haired girl called Puneeta. 'But we want to support local enterprises, and are happy to offer free advertising for the first issue.'

We were sitting in the manager's office. She listened to my pitch, and asked her secretary to bring us some tea. 'We're trying to build out brand,' she told me. 'I would be very interested in discussing sponsorship. But tell me this,' she added as I smiled, 'Do you have a leisure section?'

The thought of returning to Maya with another layout change didn't appeal to me. 'Not for this issue.'

'But it's something that interests you? A column you could call something like "Delhi Beats"?'

'Maybe,' I said. We prided ourselves on our objectivity. I wasn't keen on becoming mouthpieces for a corporation. 'Though if I'm honest, I am not sure how comfortable we would be at the idea of placed articles in addition to advertising.'

'No, no,' she said in a rush. She gulped, smoothing her hair, flashing me a smile, and I realised she was mounting a pitch of her own. 'My degree is actually in communications. I want to write an article about our bar, and one about our restaurant, sure, but I'm also happy to go out and write about Delhi's food and culture scene.'

'Well,' I said slowly, 'it's something to consider.'

'I can send you samples of my writing,' she said. She brushed her hair behind her ears and waited for me to respond.

'I'm sure you're good at what you do,' I said. 'But I'm not sure I can pay you. There's no money in our budget for additional staff at the moment.'

Puneeta laughed. 'I have no plans of jacking in this job. But, if you're interested, I'm happy to go and check out different restaurants and bars in my spare time. I'll get fed for free, and I'll get to keep writing.' She looked at me, and as I paused to consider her proposal, she said, 'And after your launch issue, I would be happy to discuss advertising with you. We have some money still to allocate from next year's budget. We're very keen to get our brand in front of a wider audience.'

I inclined my head. 'We're very keen to support the local community. I'm sure we can offer you a package your hotel will find compelling. And,' I added, as Puneeta returned to nervously patting her impossibly straight hair, 'I'm sure the editors would be very happy to read the articles you have written.'

We passed Raja Singh the next time Maya and I took our morning walk. He slowed down as he approached us, nodding his neighbourly greeting, and I knew this was my chance to approach him. The plans for the launch party were ready, and though it would be too much to expect him to attend, a kind word, a plug, some advice, an introduction to a friendly influencer, any of these would be welcome. I prepared my opening words: 'Mr Singh, Sir,' but he was bending his head, parting his lips in a cursory smile, and moving on.

My time was up; my opportunity lost.

Maya must have been thinking about talking to him too, as she nudged me. 'Siya,' and I turned. 'Mr Singh,' I called as he sped away in the opposite direction. He didn't hear me, didn't or wouldn't pause, and I tried again. 'Sir,' I cried more loudly, hurrying after him, 'Mr Singh!' and he finally stopped. He turned to look at me, not smiling, more expectant than displeased, and I said, 'Mr Singh, I believe you knew our mother.'

Maya had walked towards us, and stood by my side but Raja Singh merely raised an eyebrow.

'Sir,' Maya was saying, 'our mother was Rupa Sharma.'

He opened his mouth to speak, then stopped. He broke into a smile. 'You're Rupa's girls?' he said, looking at Maya. He turned to me, then back to Maya, his smile warm.

'Sir,' I said, 'we're launching a magazine.'

'Rupa's girls,' he was repeating to himself. 'Did you know that we were great friends?'

'Sir,' said Maya, 'yes, Sir.'

Raja Singh turned towards me, 'And you're a journalist too, you say?'

'No, Sir,' I blurted out, and then, as he waited, I added, 'Maya is. And we're launching a new magazine.'

It all sounded so amateurish, my non-pitch to Raja Singh, the word 'new', my admitting to not being a journalist, but he was nodding, he was smiling, and he was saying, 'But that's great, girls.' I wondered if I should talk to him about sponsorship, then decided against the idea. This was a big man; he dealt in life-changing sums. Maybe as we began to establish ourselves I could ask him for investment, but in the meantime, there was no point asking him to shell out a few thousand rupees to support a start-up's print run.

The phone in Raja's tracksuit buzzed, and he turned to leave, but I said, 'We have a launch party in a few days. We would be honoured if you were to attend.'

It was an audacious request. He was reaching out for his phone, he was answering it, but he nodded at me. 'Send the details to my house,' he was saying, and then he was turning, and heading off back to his day.

I looked at Maya, who seemed as stunned as I felt. 'So,' I asked, 'did that really happen or did I just dream it?'

'I don't know.'

We walked back home, full of ideas we were unable to articulate. We were stunned by our encounter with Raja Singh, unable to believe his graciousness, and unwilling to trust he would attend our launch. 'But what did he say?' I kept asking my sister, and she kept answering with the same phrase: 'I don't know.'

The procurement of the sponsorship required more interaction with Ajay than I had counted on. Most of the sponsors were small enterprises and requested us to supply the wording for the ads. Several requested proprietor photos, and Ajay pointed out his skills extended to photography.

We were five days away from the launch event. I had intended to go to the shops that needed photography to take the requisite photos, but Ajay began to talk about pixilation and the optimum angles for shooting photos. 'Did you know, Siya,' he said. He came towards me, his breath reeking of smoke. I found him most afternoons in the courtyard at the back of the house, a cigarette in his hand. 'This will kill you,' I would say, and he would raise his hand in salute.

'Siya,' he was saying, and I stepped away from him. 'I studied photography at college.'

Tasha-di spat out her tea mid-sip, then set to coughing loudly.

Ajay nodded. 'I was rather good too.'

'I was thinking,' said Tasha-di. She had wiped off the tea from her mouth, but I spied a trickle on her clothes. I rose to fetch a tissue, but she gestured for me to remain seated. 'That maybe you take Ajay along for the photos.'

'I'm sure…'

She cut in. 'It'll make everyone's life easier.' She looked at Maya and Sonia. 'We're running out of time, and it helps no one if you have to return to the shops to take new photos.'

Maya looked up. 'Yes,' she said, as Tasha-di sat back in her chair. 'For heaven's sakes, just stop bickering, the both of you, and go get the photos. Your sponsorship deals have already caused enough chaos.'

We went then, Ajay and I, early the next morning. We

started at Seth Supplies, where Ajay asked Vivek to arrange himself in various poses in front of the shop. The shopkeeper was asked to squat, to bend, then to stand one-legged, all in search of the perfect angle. Vivek complied, eager to see his photo in the magazine, but as we left, I asked Ajay, 'Were all those acrobatics necessary?'

'What acrobatics?'

'Come on.'

He laughed. 'The man almost put a halt to the magazine.' I smiled, and Ajay said to me, 'I'm famished. I skipped breakfast to make it over at this ungodly hour.'

I looked back at Seth Supplies. 'Do you want to pick up a snack from there?'

'No,' he grinned. 'I don't think young Mr Seth is going to be in the mood to see me anytime soon. But I quite like that little canteen thing at the start of the market. Let's just stop there.'

I checked my watch. 'I don't know.'

'I'll be fast,' he promised. He didn't wait for my response, walking towards the restaurant, and after waiting to see if he stopped, I followed him. We were seated next to a pair of local workers, who assumed Ajay and I were on a date, and immediately began to make eyes at each other. Theatrical winks followed, and many knowing nods of the head, and if our neighbours' intention was to be subtle, they failed miserably. I grew uncomfortable, looking around for the waiter, but Ajay seemed to relish my embarrassment.

'I will always remember today,' he said, leaning forward on the banquette and reaching his hands across the table. I leant back, and he added, 'This is our very first meal together.' The workers gulped down their golgappas, and as another coughing fit ensued, he smiled contentedly. 'This,' he said, an eye on his two victims, 'is the happiest I have ever been.'

A waiter set down two menus in front of us, and I rushed to order. 'I'll have a fresh lime soda,' I said. 'We have a lot of work to do, Ajay. I'm sure you'll want to order quickly.'

Ajay made a show of studying the menu, and as I tutted, he finally raised his head. 'I'll have the chole bhature,' he said, looking at me with a pleased smile.

'Chole bhature?'

'Yes,' he replied and then, signalling to the waiter, he ordered a large dish of ice cream for dessert.

I grunted. 'I thought you were going to order a snack. And here you are, ordering a full blown lunch.' He smirked, and I spat out, 'We have a busy day ahead of us.'

He turned to our gawping audience. He raised an eyebrow, gave a martyr-like shrug. 'Yes, ma'am,' he said penitently. 'As you say, ma'am.'

The coughing fit restarted, Ajay's food arrived, and he began slowly, and pleasurably, to tackle the mountain in front of him.

I showed Maya and Sonia the articles Benjamin sent me, and they both enjoyed the writing. 'It's good,' Maya said to me. 'Are you sure there is no catch?'

'I'm sure.' She looked uncertain, potentially worried about my having second thoughts about our breakup. 'I'm sure,' I insisted. 'There's no catch.'

Ajay saw the by-line, and asked Maya who the new contributor was. 'Oh,' she said hurriedly, 'That's Siya's Benjamin. He's doing us a favour.'

'Siya's Benjamin,' Ajay repeated, his eyes glued to the page. 'He writes well.'

XIV

Everything turned us skittish; the delays with supplies, the troubles with sponsors, arguments within the team. Everything felt like an omen, and it often seemed to us that *The Satirist* was doomed to fail again. Things took too long. The news cycle changed, and monthly magazines were out of date the minute they went to print. More online news sites were being launched, and print media proprietors reported falling sales and lower profits. We were sure the launch wouldn't happen, were sure we would come across an unforeseen obstacle, were sure Raja Singh wouldn't make an appearance, and though we carried on preparing, we prepared with an eye on failure. Then all at once, and all too soon, the end of the month arrived.

The house was ready, the tent in the garden had withstood the previous night's rains. 'It's a good omen,' Tasha-di proclaimed. 'Rain always bodes well.'

Shanti cooked all day. She sliced onions, prepared chutneys, fried kebabs and samosas and pakoras, and though I worried she had too much work to do, she had a broad smile on her face. 'It's just like the old days,' she said. 'Parties all the time.'

'But it's just you to shoulder the work now,' I said. 'You must be tired.'

'Get me an army of help once the magazine begins bringing in money. Besides,' she added thoughtfully, 'Pradeep's bride will be helping out in the kitchen soon.' After the bulk of her prep work was finished, Shanti changed into a green silk sari.

'This is nice,' Maya said. She fingered the fabric, admiring the softness of the silk, 'Is it new?'

'I bought it for Pradeep's wedding.'

'Then why,' asked Maya, 'are you wearing it today? It will smell of food on the day of the wedding.'

'It is auspicious to wear new clothes for an important occasion,' said Shanti, wiping away a tear. 'And just you try and tell me that this magazine doesn't belong a little to me too.'

This was always Shanti's way. She would ceaselessly take care of us, minding our manners and our worries, and then, when we least expected it, she would launch into hysterics worthy of a film heroine. 'Yes,' Maya said shamefacedly, and I quickly nodded. 'Yes, of course this magazine belongs to you too.'

The party was full of people I didn't know. There was no Raja Singh, which was as expected, but there were journalists Maya, Sonia and Ajay had known in their working lives, and though I, as head of marketing, was at the door to greet everyone, it was usually one of the others who introduced me to our guests.

'This is hopeless,' Ajay pointed out, and as I burnt red, he added, 'I'll stand here by you and help identify people for you.'

He was wearing a suit, a proper buttoned up charcoal grey herringbone affair he paired with a pinstripe shirt and gleaming camel coloured shoes. He looked well, and what was worse, he knew it. He preened, a little like a peacock, flicking invisible specks of his sleeve, and checking his collar to make sure it remained stiff. His hands constantly rose to his hair, and as he turned to me, I said, 'No, that's fine, Maya can help me. The founders should both be at the door.'

But Maya was running around with a dozen chores. People she hadn't seen for years—ex-colleagues, potential collaborators—all wanted to talk to her, and her attention was fleeting. 'You'll be fine, Siya,' she said, 'Ajay will take care of you.'

He smiled then, and lowered his gaze to his sleeve. Another imaginary speck was discarded from his suit sleeve, and he put his arm around my shoulder, 'Come,' he said, gesturing to the empty doorway. I remained rooted to my spot. I knew my lower lip jutted out, just as it always had as a child during moments of displeasure. All in the family knew to watch out for it. Often, I'd hear them mouth to one another, 'Siya's in one of her moods again,' which only served to infuriate me further. Ajay smiled gently, and held a hand out. 'How bad can it be?'

People were arriving by the minute. Ajay, now stationed next to me, pointed out key guests, and I had to admit that I was impressed by the turnout. Several high-ranking journalists were there, editors and publishers and commentators and media grandees, including some TV news presenters I recognised. The system worked well. Ajay first introduced them to me and then led them to Maya, but what struck me most was the party's interest in Maya. 'She was always such a promising writer,' said one guest, 'I'm so excited to see what she does next.'

Puneeta arrived early in the evening. She wore a suit, the pencil trousers in her outfit tight, and had her hair up in a high ponytail. She was more attractive than I remembered, her features chiselled and accentuated with make-up, and I saw she made an impression on Ajay. 'This,' I said, smiling sweetly at him, 'Is the manager of the hotel I'm speaking to about sponsorship. She's also a gifted writer.' Puneeta had sent me some of her articles, and they were good. Good, I thought, no they had been better than that. She had been able to draw an image of a place in a few lines. 'She has a gift for description,' I gushed, and as she coloured, I added, 'I'm sure we would welcome a "Delhi Beats" column.'

Puneeta smiled gratefully. 'That's so great to hear.'

'In fact,' I added, 'Ajay here is a keen photographer. Perhaps the two of you can go out on assignment together.'

I spotted Maya talking to someone familiar. It was a man of around forty, tall and slim and balding at the crown. I was sure I knew him, but for the life of me I couldn't place him. Maya looked completely engrossed in the conversation, and I decided against sending Puneeta her way. 'Why don't the both of you go and discuss things further,' I said to Ajay, and as he opened his mouth to complain, I added, 'and when you see Sonia, be sure to introduce Puneeta to her.'

'But you need me here,' pointed out Ajay, and I shook my head.

'I'm fine now,' I said, 'and all the journalists have already arrived. I'll survive.'

They went then, the suited pair, into the garden, and I was soon joined by Sonia. She wore her hair up in a bun, and matched her trousers with a simple white shirt and a long, gold necklace. 'You look lovely,' I said.

'Thank you,' she said smiling, and I could see she was moved by the compliment. 'My uniform for years has been

Mummy clothes. The simplest salwar kameezes, or tee-shirts and whatever comfortable trousers I can schlep around in. I know this outfit must seem simple to you.'

'It doesn't. It's lovely.'

'I haven't worn anything like this in years.'

I put my arm around her. Her enthusiasm was palpable. 'It's a good turnout, isn't it?'

'Yes,' she agreed. 'I was always on board, but tonight I feel certain that we can make something of this magazine.'

All of a sudden a trim figure entered, and I knew Raja Singh had arrived. I watched as he approached, anxious to greet him, but he appeared in no hurry. His gait was leisurely and his eyes flitted through the crowd.

'What's he even doing here?' Sonia asked. She began to tell me that Raja Singh was a titan of Indian industry, that he had parlayed a hefty property inheritance into an investment empire that spanned media, entertainment and the internet, and I remembered that Maya and I had judged it best not to tell the team about our meeting with the great man. Sonia whooped with her nerves. 'He's Delhi royalty, Siya. He's the king maker.' She spoke in an awed rush, but even then, by the time she was finished, Raja was upon us. She smiled broadly, 'Sir, what an honour it is to see you here.'

'I wouldn't miss it for the world.' He hugged Sonia. 'I'm always happy to support local business. And an all-woman editorial team is an initiative worth supporting.' He turned to me with a smile. 'And I'm always happy to support my friends.'

Raja Singh had been spotted. Several people came up to him, shaking his hand, congratulating him on his latest investment. Soon he was thronged.

Sonia tapped me on the shoulder. 'Stay here,' she instructed. 'I'll go get Maya.'

Raja had a booming voice, and he spoke slowly and deliberately. 'As I told the Prime Minister,' I heard him say before someone else exclaimed and I lost the thread of their conversation. I considered backing away. Here was the cream of Delhi's intelligentsia, and I felt more than ever like an interloper. Raja saw me and held his hand up, signalling me to stay. 'Yes, well,' he told a greying news anchor. 'Let's catch up over a drink. But now,' he said, his hand on my back, 'I was just about to congratulate this young lady.'

'Sir,' I began, as several others looked expectantly in my direction. 'We're so honoured you came.'

Raja Singh smiled. 'It's nothing.' His was a wide mouth, generous and full of warmth, and he enveloped me in a hug. The air was close, the crowd thronged, and I felt short of breath. 'We're pretty much family.' I smiled and he carried on, 'Rupa and I really were great friends.'

'Sir,' I said, taken aback by his warmth. I could see Sonia nearby, watching over our conversation and keeping a lookout for Maya. Ajay approached her with Puneeta and introduced the two. He headed over to my side, and then held his hand out to Raja, 'It's so good to see you, Sir.'

Raja nodded benevolently. 'I was just getting to know this lovely young lady.'

Ajay nodded. 'Sir knows everyone in the media. TV, radio, online, you name it, he's helped set it up.'

Raja beamed. 'You're being too kind,' he said. 'But listen, Siya Sharma,' he said, turning to me, 'I meant what I said.'

'Yes Sir.'

'Your mother was a dear friend.' He handed me a business card. 'I'm sure *The Satirist* will be a great success.' I thanked him for his wishes, and he said, his voice sombre, 'But if you are ever in need, of advice, or funding, of anything at all, just remember you can call on me.'

I thanked him again. He looked at me for a long, unblinking moment, then nodded, 'And now,' he said to Ajay, 'are those kebabs I smell?'

I saw Maya again a few moments later. She was running from person to person, and held a full glass in her hand. She hadn't eaten all day, busying herself instead with the preparations, and I knew she would collapse the moment the last guest left. But I saw how consumed she was with her role, and as I looked around the room, watching Tasha-di mingle with people she hadn't seen in years, I knew we had been right to resurrect *The Satirist*.

Shanti, handing out plates in one side of the room, would have said this was Ma looking out for us. She was there in the magazine, in the letters she had left for us to find, in the work clothes she had always treasured, and in the tea stain that refused to shift from the room that had played host to all her hopes. Shanti would have said this was our true inheritance, the magazine that was bringing meaning into all our lives. She would have been wrong, of course, and sentimental and superstitious, but for a moment, the thought brought tears to my eyes.

Ajay soon returned. 'What were you thinking?' he asked.

'What?'

'Pimping me off to that silly woman.'

I leaned back against the wall. The trickle of guests had

slowed down, and I could see things were beginning to wind down. The food would soon run out, all but the most determined drinkers would decline their next offer of a refill. One by one, people would return to their lives. I smiled. 'I thought the two of you would get along.'

'Really?' he asked, enraged. He pushed up the sleeves of his suit, and ruffled his neatly coiffed hair. 'You really thought I'd get along with that airhead?'

I patted down his sleeves. 'Careful now,' I said slowly. 'There's nothing wrong with Puneeta. She's attractive, and she's capable.'

'She's all gloss and no substance,' he sniffed. 'Typical marketing professional.'

'Careful,' I said. 'I'm a marketing professional.'

'Yes,' he said, looking at me through squinted eyes. 'Well, exactly.'

Mr Seth was next in. He hugged me, and I said, 'It's so good to see you, Mr Seth. I only run into Vivek now.'

'I wasn't going to miss this for the world. My two favourite girls launching a magazine; of course I was going to come to the party. Did you know,' he said, leaning in conspiratorially, 'Vivek wanted to come to this thing tonight.' He reached for a passing waiter and took a samosa straight off the plate. 'You stay and sweat in the shop,' I told him. 'What business do you have at this party thrown by my girls?'

'Very right,' I replied. 'I'm so glad you're here.' I meant my words. Mr Seth had been a background motif all my childhood, always ready with a sweet, always soothing with a kind word on days when Ma was angry with one of us.

'Ah yes,' he said, turning to business, 'I heard my son has been asking for money to display your magazine?'

'Well,' I said. I had been presumptuous too, palming him off with free advertising, but the old man was shaking his head.

'I've told him,' he said. 'He's not too old to be scolded by his father.' I giggled. 'Now, listen. There will always be a prime spot available for your magazine for as long as you want it. I don't want to think about payment until you start to make money.'

'Thank you,' I said. I hugged him. 'And there will always be a free advertising space available for Seth Supplies as long as the magazine is in operation.'

'Yes,' he said gruffly. 'Well. Next time, don't worry about Vivek. If you run into any problems, come straight to the boss.' Mr Seth swiped a kebab off another tray, and thumped his chest. 'Come straight to me.'

XV

I woke up in the middle of the night with a realisation. The person Maya had been in such deep conversation with was the boyfriend of her college days. Older, a little stouter, and with markedly less hair, but it was definitely Kunal.

I closed my eyes and tried to return to sleep, but it was no use. The image of the man kept returning to me; a tall, well-dressed figure with a hand tucked into his trouser pocket. He had been the same at university, though I had been more in the habit of observing his night-time shadow than his person, and though I tried to focus, and though I tried to think of reasons why a man talking to Maya wasn't necessarily her old boyfriend, I had no success. My heart rang with certainty. It was Kunal. It was! I had barely been able to get a look at his face, but I knew it was him. He had stood upright, ramrod straight, and I thought of that shadow I had seen night after night when Maya had first gone to college.

I closed my eyes. There it had always been as Maya dashed the flower from behind her ear, vigilant and utterly still, like a pool at night, a shadow that was only disturbed once my sister was safely back indoors. A picture emerged of the evening that had just passed, the noise of the tent, and its heat, and Maya, her colour raised, paying rapt attention to the tall, still figure she spoke to. Her hands rose constantly to her hair, which she fanned out over her sari and then smoothed behind her back. She smiled, she tilted her head, she played with her hair, and in all her motion, I was convinced she wasn't registering a single word that was said to her. Her colour was higher than I had ever seen it before, a little like she was in the grip of a fever, and I smiled happily.

I looked at my phone. It was past three in the morning. In a few hours, Sonia and Ajay would arrive to conduct a debrief. The magazine would be officially launched at eight; our plan involved going to the various retail outlets stocking the magazine to highlight the publication. A press release would be issued during the day in the hope that it would be picked up by one or more of the conventional news agencies. A newspaper Sonia had worked for had promised to carry a small report on the launch. A reporter had been sent to the launch party, as had a photographer, and we hoped this morning's newspaper would carry a mention of *The Satirist*.

I knew it was going to be a long day, and I knew I needed to get back to sleep, but I rose from my bed. The winter chill slammed against me, and it took an effort to carry on. The house was dark. There was no light from within the house, and none from the street outside. The lamp posts that guided the neighbourhood's security were shielded by the thick curtains Shanti drew in the evening, and I tiptoed quietly in the silence. I progressed through memory, and at Maya's door, I paused before I entered.

This had been me all my childhood, running from night terrors into my sister's bed. She would turn sleepily towards me, pat me on the back and lull me back to sleep. Now, though, I watched her restful face with something approaching pride. This was a discovery I ached to share with her. I wanted more than anything to wrest an admission from her that it had been Kunal she had been speaking to, but I didn't disturb her, mainly because I was scared of being proved wrong. I got into bed next to her, and as she shifted to make room for me, I heard her sigh. I *might* have been mistaken; the person she spoke to might not have been Kunal. She *might* have coloured from the crowds and their heat, but for the moment, as she drew me in to the warmth of her embrace, I knew I could rest safe in the belief that it had been her old boyfriend she had been speaking to.

I woke late. Maya must have tip-toed around me as she readied herself; I grew aware of the day as Shanti yanked open the curtains. She went about her work more noisily than usual, and I knew I must have resisted earlier efforts to wake me.

'Quick, baby,' she admonished. 'Everyone else is waiting for you in the office.'

I quickly put clothes on from Maya's wardrobe and ran downstairs. Ajay smirked as I rushed in, my feet still in my slippers. 'Good morning, princess,' he called.

On the table where Maya had first gathered up the books spilled from Papa's collapsed bookcase were rows of newspapers. 'No mention here,' Sonia said, her mouth held in a grimace, 'but here, see,' and she pointed to a slim column on a page inside one of the newspapers. I saw a photo of Raja Singh holding forth with Maya, and a caption below that read: *Raja Singh in conversation with founder of new magazine*. The accompanying article dealt more with the party's attendees than with the magazine itself, and though the rest of the team was disheartened, I pointed out that at least the event was covered.

'It's publicity,' I told them. I pulled out my phone and told them about the social media campaign I planned to mount. 'Facebook, Twitter, Instagram,' I told them, 'all are going to be bombarded with photos of last night.'

'But it will be like speaking into an echo chamber,' said Sonia. After the rush of the previous evening, she seemed visibly deflated. More than once I had caught her looking at her watch. 'It's no use,' she added, 'we're playing at journalism with our 500 copy print run. No one knows we exist.'

'Have some faith,' I countered. Within the hour I had posted the photos, tagging key attendees, and several had shared the content. 'It's not the overnight sensation you wanted,' I told her, 'but it was never going to be.'

'Look,' added Tasha-di, and I winced. She had consistently been bearish on *The Satirist*, and I feared she was totting up the money spent on the magazine and the launch party. She took Sonia's hands in her own, and said, 'The party last night was a success, no?'

'Well...'

'It was,' nodded Tasha-di kindly. 'I've been the harshest on this enterprise, but even I have to admit that last night was a success.' She looked at Sonia, still unhappy, and at the rest of the room.

'Yes,' said Ajay, reaching out to Sonia. He clapped her on the back. 'It was a resounding success. I had my doubts, of course,' and as Tasha-di squinted at him, he carried on, 'but everyone was there last night. All the media bigwigs, all the sponsors, everyone was there. I won't be surprised if tomorrow's news carries some more photos of the occasion. And,' he added, watching me as he spoke, 'Siya's efforts will bear fruit too.'

It was a quieter day than anticipated. The phones didn't ring with advertisers and with papers looking to cover the reception. I kept refreshing *The Satirist*'s social media feeds, but after the sparse mentions that had followed the launch party, no other reports followed. None of Raja Singh's feeds—his portfolio companies' social media accounts, his own personal ones—mentioned the launch. It was as if he hadn't attended, and as India woke up to the day's news, it was as if the launch hadn't taken place. There was nothing for me to do.

I rose to go to Mr Seth's store to take a few pictures of the magazine to post onto our accounts, and the others offered to accompany me. The cover story for the next issue was already assigned and no one seemed in the mood to work. We were all jittery, waiting without purpose. It was too early, we knew, for plaudits, but we were too nervy for any productive work.

At the store, *The Satirist* was prominently displayed. I took heart from this, then immediately worried it wasn't flying off the shelves. A woman hovered over a copy, and I approached her.

'This is ours,' I said, grinning at her, and as she quickly handed the copy to me, I shook my head. 'No,' I said, realising my blunder. 'I meant to say that this is a local magazine.' I pointed towards my bemused team, 'We set it up together.'

'Ok,' said the woman uncertainly. She looked at the proffered magazine, and Mr Seth popped out from the back of the shop. 'The magazine is free,' he told the lady. 'The girls refused initially,' he added, 'But I asked them repeatedly to make it free for the local area for the first few issues, and eventually they relented.' The woman looked up at me, still uncertain, and Mr Seth added, 'I'm very grateful to you for your generosity.' He thrust a copy in her hand, repeating, as if it were a mantra, 'It's free for the first few issues only,' and waved her off.

'Seriously,' he complained after the woman had left. 'These people are such lemmings. She won't want to pick up the magazine unless she's heard about it from her friends, and then she will rave about it to everyone she meets regardless of quality.'

'Thank you,' I told him, as he stood there, angrily shaking his head. 'Your support means the world to me.'

'Of course,' he replied, 'but people are idiots.' Someone passed by, a driver looking for cigarettes, and Mr Seth grabbed a magazine and shoved it in his face. 'Here,' he told him, 'give this to your *sahib*.'

The driver looked surprised, and Mr Seth explained to me. 'This is Raja Singh's driver. If he likes the magazine, there's no knowing what heights you can reach.'

The driver had set the magazine down by the till, and Mr Seth pushed it towards him again. He reached behind the counter to hand him a pack of cigarettes. 'Here,' he said, 'your cigarettes are on the house today. Just make sure Mr Singh's eye falls on this magazine.'

'Sir,' said the driver, thrilled with his free cigarettes. He tripped off, and Mr Seth winked at me. 'People *are* idiots. We just need to make sure the right idiots are seen to read your work.'

Shanti and Pradeep left for the village the same day. We were busy running around with the issue, and with my social media efforts. Ajay had taken to sitting outside the house's gates with a copy of *The Satirist* in the hope that he would influence a passer-by to give the magazine a chance, and it was he who first noticed Shanti coming from the servants' quarters with a suitcase. He offered to help her carry it, and when she refused, asked her if she was leaving, 'No,' she said, blushing at the attention. 'My son is getting married next week. We are going to the village.'

Maya and I came out at the noise. Shanti put her hands on our heads in benediction. 'Be good while I'm gone,' she said to us, 'take care of each other.'

Pradeep had emerged by this point. He carried a suit bag and dragged an ancient, battered leather case that had once belonged to Papa.

'Getting married, eh?' Ajay joshed, but Pradeep refused to look him in the eye.

Sonia, who had come out too, nudged us, 'He's getting embarrassed at the thought of his marriage,' she giggled. 'Just imagine.'

'The approaching nuptials,' I began, then took a look at Pradeep. His face was turned towards the ground, his hands balled up into fists, and I knew the inspection was excruciating for him.

'Come,' said Ajay, clapping him on the back, and I saw Pradeep refuse to look up. I was sure there would be more jostling, more bawdy teasing, but Ajay took the suitcase from Shanti's hands, and as she complained, telling him she was capable of carrying her suitcase, he pointed towards his car. 'Come,' he said again, 'I'll give you a lift to the station.' He put her luggage in his boot, took Pradeep's suit cover and draped it over the passenger seat, and as Shanti and Pradeep stood behind the gates, uncertain and alone, he gestured them in. 'Come now,' he repeated. 'It's a busy day for the magazine, and I don't want to be back late.'

This finally got them in the car, and with many expressions

of gratitude, the trio was off to the station. We stood watching them off, and Tasha-di smiled. 'Ajay is the good guy,' she said. 'Who would have thought?'

It was only later, after I had uploaded our photos onto social media platforms and interacted with the two news organisations who showed an interest in covering our maiden issue, after Ajay had returned, after Tasha-di had brought out the champagne to celebrate our first issue, and after our colleagues had departed for the day, that I asked Maya who she had been speaking to at the party.

She professed ignorance. 'There were so many people there.'

'It was a man.'

She shrugged, though a dark flush stained her face. 'There were many men there.'

I smiled in response, and though she pretended not to notice, her lack of composure was clear. She fidgeted, rising from her chair before sitting down again, tying and retying her hair in a bun. 'It was Kunal,' I asked as she rose again, 'Wasn't it?'

'Kunal?'

'You know exactly who I'm talking about,' I said. She looked like she would evade the question, and I asked, 'Was he there are the party last night?'

'Yes,' she replied.

'I knew it!' I yelled, as if the victory were all mine, and then said, 'Why did he come?'

'I don't know,' she replied, and it seemed like she was genuinely puzzled. 'I'm guessing Sonia told him about the party. He was at college with her too, don't forget.'

'But he came,' I exulted.

'He did,' she assented. There was a pause for a minute as we both sat nursing our thoughts. It had grown steadily dark, and neither of us had thought to switch on the lights. I saw her move in the dim light, her torso rocking back and forth against her chair before she added, 'He's got two children.'

'Oh.'

'He's separated, he says,' and as I hugged this little nugget of hope to me, she moved to crush them, 'but he's not divorced.' We were both silent, and her torso didn't cease its motion. Forward it rocked, like a pendulum insisting on the passage of time, and then relentlessly backwards. 'He's not divorced,' she repeated in a voice stilled of emotion, 'and he's still got two school-age children.'

XVI

Word of the magazine slowly spread. Mr Seth, our personal PR machine, called to tell me he had run out of stock. 'If you want,' he suggested coyly, 'you can have some more dropped around.' The magazine's social media account slowly gained followers. I made sure to post daily; Puneeta disseminated all my posts to the followers of the hotel, and slowly, more people began to respond to our output. My tweets were shared, and my Instagram and Facebook posts liked. We weren't setting the journalistic world on fire, not just yet, but we had reason to be hopeful.

~

We ran into Raja Singh a few days after the launch. He was with another person, a business associate, we presumed, and we smiled politely at him as he walked past. He acknowledged our greeting and didn't slow his pace, but said to his companion as he passed: 'These girls have just launched a magazine, Manu. I'll give you my copy…'

The two men had wandered out of earshot, but I squeezed Maya's arm. Raja Singh hadn't forgotten about our existence. He hadn't told his companion he loved our magazine, but he hadn't forgotten about us. That was something.

~

A week after the launch, Pradeep and Shanti returned. They brought with them Pradeep's new bride, a tall, slim girl called Saloni. Just like in her photo, I spied a burst of intelligence in her eyes, but she remained subdued that first day, cowed either by her distance from her parent's home or by the noise and sounds of Delhi. Maya and I sat her down, and over a cup of tea with Shanti, tried to make small talk. She sat at the edge of the sofa, knees primly glued together, as if worried about seeming too presumptuous. She wore a bright salwar kameez, the fabric a brash, synthetic red shot through with strands of gold thread. It was clear she was conscious around us, avoiding eye contact, tidying down the skirt of her kameez every time she spoke and making sure her plait was tidied away behind her back. I wanted to reach out, to squeeze her hand, to assure her we meant well, but I worried about putting her more on edge.

She barely spoke. She was polite, painfully so, replying to our questions with great parsimony. Everything was pronounced to be good. How did she like Delhi? It was good. How had the wedding been? Good. How did she like the mother-in-law who had been our second mother? Good. It was impossible to get any real information out of her, and at length, we gave up.

'They'll make a pretty pair,' I whispered to Maya as the new bride was escorted out by her mother-in-law. 'Neither will open their mouth.'

'Poor thing,' she said in reply. 'Imagine being put under the spotlight like that. There we were, thinking ourselves so kind to invite her to tea and ask her questions about herself, when she knew she couldn't claim a similar interest in us.'

'What were we to do? Show no concern?'

'No, no,' Maya said. I was surprised, both by the interest she had taken in the new girl, and by the empathy she was displaying. When I had called from London, it had often felt that she had no interest in my life. Ma had begun the era of polite disinterest, of course, but Maya had shown no sign of wanting to diverge from the example our mother set. Now, there she sat, feeling the new bride's discomfort, telling me we had to be kinder. 'We have to let the poor girl alone. Here she is, married to a stranger who has brought her to a strange city to live with his mother and two other strangers. The least we can do is cut her some slack.'

Saloni receded into the background. Her main role appeared to be to relieve Shanti's burden; she cooked and cleaned in the servant's quarters, and once Shanti's work was done, she no longer had to return to her rooms to prepare dinner for herself and Pradeep. During office hours for the magazine too, Shanti sometimes enlisted her daughter-in-law's help. Tea was constantly being ordered, plates of biscuits and snacks forever ferried around, and Saloni took on the role of courier for us. Messages to Pradeep—to buy more supplies, to run to a newspaper with an issue of the magazine—were delivered through his new wife.

She sometimes lingered in the library, longer than expected, and though instructions were issued, and the girl nodded to show she comprehended, we all noticed she was slow to move. I took it to be lethargy on her part, a slowness of the mind that belied the sharpness I had sensed in her eyes. She was often slow to return from her trips to see Pradeep, and though I associated this with the same sluggishness, Ajay was quick to disabuse me.

'Love,' he told me, returning from one of his cigarette breaks by the back of the house, 'is blooming in the garage.'

I wrinkled my nose at the smell, but he edged closer. 'I didn't think the boy had it in him, but I walked in to see him with his arms around his young wife.' Ajay snapped his fingers. 'How they jumped apart when I entered!'

'You,' I scolded. 'Be kind to them. It can't be easy trying to get to know each other in a goldfish bowl.'

He howled with laughter. 'The boy didn't look too pleased to be disturbed, if I'm honest.'

'Poor guy,' I said.

'Yes,' assented Ajay. 'He's married to a beautiful woman who is ten times cleverer than him'. He looked thoughtful. 'Poor guy.'

Later on, as Maya and I sat in the living room upstairs, I observed Saloni. She had come in with our dinner; this she now placed in front of us. 'Your dinner please,' she said, speaking in fluent English. She worked neatly, nodding as we thanked her. She watched us for a moment quietly, and as I looked up at her, she shot me a shy smile. 'Good evening,' she said in the same eloquent voice before she left.

Some days later, I noticed Saloni in the office. She had set down a tray with cups of tea, and proceeded to hand the drink around to all of us. Her work finished, she remained in the room. She wiped the tray down with a dishcloth; she dusted the desks, and slowly, she inched towards where the layouts of the next issue were kept. She was tall, and though she had a soft tread, her shadow fell on me, and I observed her out of the corner of my eye. She knew she was trespassing, and she moved slowly, her eyes darting around the office every few seconds. When she reached the table with the layouts, she seemed to relax. She leant over the pages, and I saw she was reading. She had a graceful neck, her face slender and evenly proportioned, and I found myself echoing Ajay's earlier thought: here was a woman more attractive and more intelligent than her husband.

Saloni bent again. I guessed this was to read in greater detail, but I saw that Ajay had noted her presence too, as I saw him rise and walk swiftly to where the layouts were. 'Hello, hello,' he said in her ear, and as she jumped in fright, I saw him smile.

'I was just leaving,' she said, forgetting her dishcloth in her haste. This fell to the floor, and I swooped down to pick it up.

'I'll return it to Saloni,' I told Ajay, who shrugged.

In the kitchen, Saloni apologised to me. 'I didn't mean to pry,' she told me as I handed back her cloth.

'I've seen you around the office before.'

She scrunched her face up apologetically, then noticing that I remained silent, she began to speak. 'My degree was in English,' she said. 'I love to see the magazine coming together.'

Shanti came up to us. 'Is all well?'

'I'm sorry,' Saloni said miserably. 'I won't come into the office again.' She wrung the dishcloth and folded her hands in apology. Her head was bowed, as if expecting admonishment, and as Shanti asked me what her daughter-in-law had done wrong, Saloni slunk off to the basin, where she started to wash dishes.

'She's a good girl, really' Shanti was saying. 'A bit dreamy sometimes, but her heart is in the right place.'

'I didn't know she had a degree in English.'

'Yes,' said Shanti carelessly. 'She's always reading the papers you girls throw out. I tell her it's bad for her eyes, but she won't stop.' Shanti looked at me. 'I'll speak to her again.'

'Don't,' I said. I walked to Saloni, who was washing the dishes with a savage energy. 'Saloni,' I told her. She stopped her work, but didn't look in my direction. 'Did you enjoy the magazine?'

'Didi!' she exclaimed. She dashed the water off her hands, drying them on her clothes. 'The piece on the restaurant was too much!' She pronounced the word restaurant curiously, res-too-ront, but her enthusiasm was clear. 'The pictures were too much,' she continued, 'the piece on the non-resident Indians—too much,' and then, sneaking a glance at me, she added, 'But there is one mistake I noted.'

Shanti, who had been observing our interaction wordlessly, came forward to scold Saloni. 'Baby doesn't make mistakes,' she said, but I told her I wasn't offended.

I walked back to the office to bring up the page Saloni had looked at, and asked, 'You saw a mistake here?'

'Yes, Didi.' Saloni dried her hands on her clothes once again before she took the proffered page. 'Right here,' she said, pointing at a line. 'Right where it says "The locations is perfect for the office crowd."' She nodded in emphasis. 'Here,' she repeated, 'can you see?'

I bent to where her finger lay, reading the words she had read out, and nodded.

'Didi,' she was saying, 'It should read "The location is perfect for the office crowd."'

'Yes.'

Shanti glared at her daughter-in-law, and a miserable Saloni said, 'I'm sorry, Didi.'

'Don't be,' I told her. There was a desk in the kitchen where Shanti worked out her recipes and shopping lists, and I sat Saloni down on it. I went back to the office, returning with the remaining pages of the coming issue, and said to her, 'I want you to go through these pages line by line.' Shanti looked concerned but Saloni paid me close attention. 'Find all the errors you can, and circle them.' She was looking at me wide-eyed, as if I had asked her to sabotage my own production, and I explained, 'What you are doing is one of the most important tasks in any publication. You are playing the copy-editor's role.'

'Coffee-editor,' Shanti said wonderingly.

Saloni didn't move, and I thrust the papers into her hands. 'Sit,' I told her, 'and come show me what you've found once you're done.'

The girl looked miserable. 'Didi…'

'It doesn't matter if the work is too hard. But if you find that this is something you do want to do, we would welcome another pair of eyes.'

Saloni kept shaking her head, but later that day, after the others had left the office, I saw her hover outside. 'Saloni?'

'Didi,' she said, 'I hope you don't mind.' She winced as she placed the pages in front of me. There were red circles on every page, with corrections next to the offending sections. 'I'm sorry,' she said again, her head hung low, and I got up to hug her.

'Saloni, don't you understand?' I yelled. 'If you hadn't spotted these problems, we would have printed the errors.'

'Oh.'

I sat back down to read her edits. Each one was valid, and her corrections showed she had read and understood the tone and content of each piece. 'Readers wouldn't look at the magazine again if it had gone to print like that.'

Shanti appeared in the room. 'I told the girl not to trouble you.'

She made to take Saloni by the arm, but I was shaking my head. 'Trouble me, Shanti? Saloni has saved my life.'

'No, no…'

'Yes,' I insisted. 'She has. If she has time to spare,' and here I looked at Shanti, who continued being sombre. I was aware that Shanti and Pradeep had been looking for a homely girl who would cook and clean for them; a Shanti, as it were, for their own unit. They had returned, instead, with a revelation, a woman with brains and with ideas. Saloni looked from me to her mother-in-law, not interrupting, and I repeated, 'If she has time, I would really value her input.'

Shanti frowned. She turned to Saloni. 'Do you like this…' She waved her hand in the air, as if scratching at an invisible itch. 'This coffee-editing?'

Saloni nodded miserably but didn't speak.

'You are sure?'

Once more she nodded.

'Then,' said Shanti, 'of course you must help baby.'

Saloni was the first member of *The Satirist*'s staff to draw a salary. Maya worried the fact that she was independently earning money would cause tensions in the marriage, but nothing was mentioned, neither by Saloni nor by Shanti. One morning a week, after her chores were finished in the servant's quarter, she would rush into the office and run her red lines through the articles we had compiled. She was efficient and ruthless, and always apologetic with it, which caused much hilarity in the office.

One morning, as Saloni quietly slipped into the office, Sonia asked her, 'Is Shanti happy for you to work here?' The question was a nod to family politics. Shanti had been in charge of the household all our lives, but there was a clear hierarchy.

She had started off as a maid, and though she was a treasured member of the family, her work was menial. And here her new daughter-in-law was, sitting with the others in Papa's old study. I had wondered if that fact rankled Shanti, but she had appeared happy enough for Saloni to work with the magazine.

'Yes,' she said, looking at me.

'She is,' I assented. 'I asked her if it was ok for Saloni to work with us, and her main concern was with whether Saloni was keen on the work.'

Ajay came forward. We were huddled over the layouts, and he bent down between me and Saloni. 'What about Pradeep?' he asked.

'Pradeep?' laughed Sonia. 'He's such a quiet little thing; I'd be surprised if he's even noticed that Saloni's working here.'

'I'm sure he's noticed,' said Ajay. 'Is he ok with you working here?'

I turned towards the girl. Since she had starting working, Saloni had grown in vigour. It was clear her work consumed her, and it was clear she was a valued member of the team. She skipped into the office, eager to find flaws in our grammar and structure, and though she was distant and respectful with us, I had once noticed Pradeep call to her when she was working. 'Bring me a cup of tea,' he had said to her, and she had refused. She had told him she was working, and though Pradeep hadn't made a fuss, I had seen his face darken. Nothing further was said, not at the time, but I wondered if the matter had been raised privately. 'I can talk to him if you wish,' I said to Saloni. 'I can talk to Shanti too. Surely they must see that you working for the magazine doesn't represent a threat to them.'

Ajay was shaking his head. 'But it does, can't you see? They are stuck outside the family rooms.'

'Shanti is family,' replied Maya stoutly.

'Sure,' said Ajay. 'But do you invite them upstairs for dinner? Do they invite you for the wedding? There is a clear distance in your relationship, and here Saloni is, a new bride, being invited to enter and sit—as an equal—in the inner sanctum of the family. So I'm sorry if what I'm saying doesn't accord with your version of equality, but Saloni's mere presence in this room does threaten the order as those two have known it.'

'It's fine,' Saloni was saying. 'Pradeep is not like that,' and though we all smiled at her, I began to wonder if there was any truth in Ajay's words.

XVII

Maya had a superstition she inherited directly from Ma. Anytime things were going well; when they made it back home just before a rain shower, when they grabbed the last pineapple pastry in the bakery, or when their favourite movie was on television; their hands snaked out to touch the first piece of wood they saw. It could be a table, or a door, or an ashtray, or even the legs of a bed, they didn't care as long as they touched wood. It was a stroke of luck by any other name. *Coup de foudre*, the French called it, but for Ma and Maya, it was always a miracle worth thanking providence for.

I had forgotten about their little totemic ritual, but now, as things started to go well with *The Satirist*, I noticed Maya touch wood every so often. Saloni would find a typo in the magazine, and Maya's hand would sneak out to caress her tabletop. A new sponsor was acquired, and once more, Maya would perform her subtle manoeuvre. It could be anything big or little; Pradeep back early from his rounds, Tasha-di in a positive mood, or Shanti preparing her favourite meal for dinner, and Maya's hand would be straight out and knocking on wood.

'Maya!' I would exclaim anytime I caught her, and though she would smile, she didn't change in her habits, and neither, it would appear, did I, as I would tut every time her hand reached out for the nearest wooden table or armrest.

'What's the harm in it, anyway?' she would chide me. 'Am I hurting you in thanking the heavens for our luck? Am I disturbing you? Is it inconvenient to you when another sponsor signs up, or when your Twitter account swells with yet another happy reader?'

'No, Maya, no,' I would reply, but I would continue to chortle. 'No, no, you keep on touching wood to bring us luck.' I laughed then, but soon, when our luck changed, I found myself wishing I hadn't been so smug.

Things *were* going well. Mr Seth continued to run out of his copies, and we considered having our print run increased for our next issue. On one of our morning walks, Maya suggested we think about the next step in our business. 'We'll remain free for the moment,' she said. She spoke assertively, making decisions, setting the tone of each issue, and I had to make an effort to recall the sister who had restricted herself to the shadows. 'Of course we're too young to be attractive to an investor, but there's no harm in planning, is there?'

I nodded. We turned a corner and walked towards the market, beyond which stood Raja Singh's palatial home. I thought of the offer he had made, of friendship, of counsel, and though I suspected his words had merely been pleasantries, I wondered if he did represent an avenue of help. 'I've got all the numbers,' I told Maya. 'I'll put together a forecast spreadsheet for you to look at.'

She smiled. 'Go for it. What's the worst that could happen?' We wandered in the direction of Raja Singh's house, pausing outside it for a few minutes. 'This is what you want,' she said to me.

'This house?'

'No!' She shook her head vigorously, then said, 'That genius. That finger on the pulse, that talent for the next big thing, for what the country wants. That's what you want.' I looked at her, taken aback by the intensity of her words. She'd always been so quiet, so derivative, and for the first time I wondered if she felt liberated by Ma's passing. She was studying the house now, and as we stood by the gates, a security man came towards us to ask us our business. We looked at each other, surprised, and as Maya shouted at me, 'Run,' we rushed away, giggling in our juvenile thrill, and raced back towards home.

It was the height of winter, and we were all waking later in the mornings. It grew light later, and cold with it, and we all resisted getting out of bed until as late as possible. Maya had begun to set alarms in my room, often far out of reach, and as the noise built up, I found myself hopping through the room, blanket wrapped around me, my body prickling with the sudden slap of cold against my skin. Alarms defused, I would return to bed, snuggling under the covers. I sometimes wished myself back in London with its central heating, but the truth was, winter felt sharper in Delhi. It was a relief to get into bed at night, and a distinct act of will to rise in the mornings. It still thrilled me to go outside in the evenings and find my breath turn to frost.

It had performed the same feat in London too, and more. There had been snow; there had been sleet, there had been darkness at three in the afternoon, but somehow, the cold was so much more the norm there that it didn't feel like so much of an aberration. Here, our diets changed, and though I had eaten enough winter soups and stews and drunk enough mulled wine, there was a joy in lifting our shawls from their mothballed cocoons in early autumn, I now noticed. The morning's first cup of tea felt sweeter. We doused our mustard leaves in butter, accompanying them with bread Shanti made with milled corn. We ate peanut brittle, and caramelised sesame seed snacks. Winter felt like an event in India, its presence feted as much as it was feared.

We suffered too. There were heaters on in all the main rooms; in the office and living areas, and as we walked from the warmth there into the cooler passages, or outdoors, we exposed ourselves to cold. Tasha-di came down with the first fever, and didn't come into the office for a week. Maya was next, and then Sonia's kids, and when Saloni didn't come in one morning, I thought she had fallen prey to the flu too.

When Shanti came in with tea, I asked her if her daughter-in-law was unwell. 'Saloni?' answered Shanti. 'No. no, she isn't.' She looked around the room. 'It's Wednesday, isn't it?'

'Yes.'

'She should be here.' Shanti picked up her empty tray and nodded at me. 'I'll just go and check what the matter is.'

She didn't come back for an age.

The office was lightly staffed. Tasha-di still wasn't back from her flu, Sonia was at home nursing her children, and Ajay was away on a shoot with Puneeta. It was just Maya and me in the room that day, and though we both worked, trying not to think what could be taking Shanti so long, both of our minds were on the matter. I kept looking at the clock Pradeep had fixed and put up on the wall; Maya's hand reached out to her tabletop in talismanic appeal, and still no Shanti appeared. I stood up, walking to the clock and then back to my desk, where I checked the clock on my laptop. I walked to the door and peered out.

There was no sound, and I called out to Maya that I would go and see where Shanti was.

The two women were in the courtyard behind the house. They spoke animatedly, and as I neared them, I heard Saloni cry out, 'But he wants me to sit and roll out rotis all day.'

Shanti replied, her voice acquiring a reasoning tone I recognised from a dozen childhood disappointments. 'He'll see sense,' she told her daughter-in-law, 'but just for now, you could…'

Saloni noticed my presence. 'Didi,' she called out loudly, and Shanti immediately clammed up.

She turned to me with a smile. 'Baby,' she said. 'We were just coming to find you.'

'Didi,' Saloni said again. Her voice was thicker than normal, a sign I initially associated with a sore throat, and then, as I took in her swollen eyes, I knew she had been crying. I looked at Shanti, who busied herself with her bangles. 'Didi,' Saloni was repeating, 'I don't think I will be able to work with the magazine anymore.'

I had been expecting news of a domestic row. I had even been prepared to believe Shanti or Pradeep had been unkind, but this announcement took me by surprise. I stood looking at her without speaking, and Saloni lowered her gaze, 'I'm sorry, Didi.'

'But surely you're not unhappy, Saloni?'

'No, no,' came the reply, but no further detail was volunteered.

I thought quickly. It appeared Pradeep was averse to Saloni working, but she was not likely to complain about her new husband in front of his mother. I thought of what Ajay had said about Saloni working with the family while her husband and mother-in-law were restricted to menial roles. Perhaps she herself was uncomfortable working in the office. Saloni's input was always valued, and though Maya and Sonia often mimed exasperation at the typos she found, it was obvious to us all that their complaints were made in jest. 'You know we all value your work, don't you?'

'Yes, Didi,' came the miserable response.

'And that Maya and Sonia only joke when they say they wish you hadn't found so many errors.'

'It's not them, Didi.'

This was something. There was someone who had upset Saloni. 'Who, then?' I asked. It wasn't Tasha-di; it wasn't me, surely. 'It's not Ajay, is it?'

The two women exchanged a brief look, and I knew Ajay had somehow caused offence. 'No, no,' Saloni was insisting. 'There's no problem with anyone else at all!'

'What, then?' I asked, but Saloni kept shaking her head.

'Please, Didi,' she said, her face averted. 'I just can't come to work.'

~

Saloni continued to come into the house. She continued to help out her mother-in-law; fetching us tea, bringing us snacks, but she didn't reprise her old role at the magazine. I didn't ask her directly for her reason for leaving the job, but a few days later, as Shanti came in with my morning tea, I asked her if Saloni was happier away from the magazine.

'To tell you the truth, she is,' Shanti replied. She set the tea down on my bedside table, and came to stand next to me. 'I think the work was too much for the poor thing.'

She spotted some clothes that had fallen out of my bed, and tutted her admonishment. 'Really, baby,' she said, but my mind remained on Saloni. 'She was so quick with her work, Shanti,' I said to her. 'It can't possibly have been too much for her.'

Shanti shrugged and bent to retrieve the clothes.

'It can't,' I insisted.

'I don't know, baby.'

'It can't have been too much work,' and she continued with the chores. 'If it was too much, why didn't she come talk to me?'

Shanti nodded, her attitude sympathetic, but as I continued to frown, she leaned forward. She tidied my hair behind my ears, she smoothed my forehead, and as I looked up at her, she said softly, 'Pradeep doesn't like Saloni working at the office.'

I laughed out loud. For Pradeep, who had called me Didi as long as I had known him, and who had never uttered a negative in my presence, to refuse to allow his wife to work in my magazine beggared belief. 'Pradeep!' I laughed, but Shanti continued to look sombre.

'I've tried to talk to him,' she said. 'I've told him that times have changed, and that Saloni should be allowed to work. I've told him over and over again that it is your company, and that there is no danger to her or to their relationship while you are in charge. And I've told him repeatedly that we only have a roof above our heads on account of your generosity...'

'Shanti!'

'It's true, though,' she said. Her hands remained on my forehead, but she spoke in a low, dull tone. 'I told him again and again how much we owed your family, but he refused to listen...'

'There must be a misunderstanding,' I said. It was impossible, this fit of pique. 'Does he think we're taking advantage of her?'

A vigorous shake of the head followed. 'I'll go talk to Pradeep; assure him how much we all value Saloni.'

'No, no, baby.' Shanti's hand lifted from my forehead, and a new, terrible thought occurred to me.

'He's not jealous of her, is he?' I asked. I'd seen it time and time again, the bruised male ego, but Shanti was shaking her head.

'Don't be dramatic, baby,' she admonished. 'It's always a tricky time; a new marriage, getting to know each other. Things will settle down in time.' She came forward again to my side of the bed, but didn't touch me. Her hands were by her side, worrying the fringes of her dupatta as she spoke. 'No, baby, really,' she said, continuing agitated. 'He'll see reason.'

I frowned. Was Saloni to continue to waste away until Pradeep was restored to his senses? I couldn't see his objection to his wife continuing with us, and then, as Shanti continued to look distraught, I thought of how Ajay had spoken of Saloni. 'He doesn't,' I asked, 'think that Ajay is causing trouble?'

Shanti sighed. She worked her dupatta fringe devoutly, as if running through a string of rosary beads, but in the end, she nodded. 'Pradeep doesn't like Saloni to be around Ajay Sir.'

I thought hard. I couldn't remember any particular interaction between Saloni and Ajay. There was some flirtation between him and Puneeta, and he teased me more than he did the others, but I couldn't remember any such incident with Saloni. She was studious, keeping to herself, focussing on doing her work and returning to her chores such that it was sometimes an effort to draw her out. There was no small talk; no asking after our health or our weekends. There was nothing but the taking of orders and smiling with a quiet pride as Maya and Sonia complained about the thoroughness of her work.

'Really,' I told Shanti, 'Saloni hasn't even looked at Ajay.' I watched Shanti closely, though she didn't speak. 'They've barely even spoken.'

Shanti didn't reply, and then, as I stared, she offered, 'I don't know, baby. Pradeep won't listen.'

'I'll talk to him if you like.'

'No, baby. We'll just have to be patient.'

Our conversation ended inconclusively, but the next morning, Saloni was at her desk in the office. 'I'm sorry,' she was saying breezily. 'I was ill yesterday,' and we all nodded in understanding. She didn't look at me, didn't mention our exchange of the previous day, but set to her work.

Shanti checked in on us, ostensibly to bring us refreshments, but I was certain she was keeping an eye on her daughter-in-law. I wasn't sure if she shared Pradeep's suspicions, or sought to reassure her, but she squeezed Saloni's hand as she passed her by, and the girl looked up at her with gratitude.

XVIII

The winter seemed never-ending. All across Delhi, people organised blanket drives, recycling old rajais and shawls and handing them over to those who lived on the streets.

Our colds persisted. Tasha-di was the first to fall ill, and Sonia's children were next. Her eldest was preparing for his Board papers. Everyone at the office still remembered the dread of preparing for the school exams; the early morning wake-ups, the cessation of leisure activities, the embargo on walks or movies or TV or books, the poring bent-back over books until late in the evening, until it felt like half the senses—touch, sight, feel—were impaired, and the others—sound and smell—painfully heightened. The weeks we devoted to preparing for our annual exams were bad enough, but the board exams held at the end of our tenth and twelfth years of schooling filled us with particular dread, even at a remove of twenty years. And here Sonia's son was, expected to revise when he was ill, down first with the flu, and then with a bug he caught off his sister.

Sonia herself was off for a month or more. She was nursing her children back to health and watching over her son's revision, and we considered her out of action until exams ended at the close of March. She hadn't been assigned any articles, and though the December and January issues carried her features, Maya took over Sonia's column for the February issue.

It surprised us, then, when Sonia came into the office early in March. 'It's not Maya's article, is it?' I joked. 'I know it's not up to your standards, but I did quite enjoy it.'

Sonia laughed. She had tracksuit bottoms on; her mother uniform, I remembered her telling me. There was no hint of make-up on her, no perfume, no high heels. 'How have you been, Sonia?' Maya asked. 'Are you surviving the exam season?'

A sigh followed, and then a quick wave of the hands. 'But forget that all,' she said, turning bright eyes towards us. 'I wanted to talk to you about these labour chowk men.'

'Labour chowk?' I asked, but then I looked at Maya, and knew she hadn't heard the phrase before either.

'Labour chowk,' Sonia repeated, masticating the words around her mouth, as if relishing their sound. 'Labour chowk,' she said again. 'You know it's been ridiculously hectic at home, right? Well, to make matters worse, last week, one of the curtain rails broke.'

This was a tangent, but Maya was quick to offer support. 'Pradeep,' she was saying, 'is very handy around the house.'

'No need,' smiled Sonia. 'Our cleaning lady went and sourced a handyman. I got talking to him, and I learnt that she had found him at the labour chowk.'

'What,' asked I, still unable to understand the purpose of her story, 'is a labour chowk?'

'Yaar,' Sonia said. 'All these labourers congregate in designated places to hawk their services for the day. You can get all sorts there—builders, carpenters, plumbers, anything. It's basically a daily open-air market for manual labour, and my cleaning lady had gone to the one in Chandni Chowk to find me a carpenter.'

'That's fantastic, I said, still unable to understand the purpose of the anecdote. 'Entrepreneurship in action.'

'Yes, yes,' agreed Sonia, but Maya and I could both see she had the bit between her teeth. She smelt a story where we couldn't sense one, and she eyed us impatiently, anxious for us to feel her excitement. She waited for a moment, her eyes flitting from my face to my sister's, but when no realisation dawned on us, she began to speak again. 'But it's more than that, don't you see? It's our society in a microcosm. It has everything; an immigrant's dreams of success, the deadening wait for occupation, the harassment, the discrimination, the cruel anonymity of big city life, mind-numbing poverty and gaudy ostentation existing side-by-side as they do in Delhi, and in the end, after all the sacrifices, after all the deprivation, the labourer's exploitation at the hands of the moneyed elite.'

'Woah,' Maya said. I knew she was worried that the story wouldn't resonate with our readership. The idea was good—no, great—but I wasn't sure if our readership would enjoy reading about it. We had started off wanting to turn a mirror to Indian society, but featured so many lifestyle stories that our consumers were just the moneyed elite Sonia was criticising.

Sonia's eyes were fixed on my sister, who cleared her throat. 'Well,' she said, and Sonia turned disapprovingly away.

'Maya!' She had begun to pace the office, and Maya guided her through to the garden room. The ground was cold here, and freer of the carpets Ma had loved to lay on the floors throughout the house. Sonia sniffed loudly. 'Can you see what I'm talking about?' she asked. 'These labourers come here as boys from India's deepest villages; from Jharkand, from Bihar, from UP. They crowd in these…' She shuddered. 'I went there, you know. I got the carpenter to take me there, and they were all herded in there, on top of each other, fighting, shoving, cursing, and then at the sight of a potential client, all straightening themselves out neatly and patting themselves like so many pieces of meat for sale.'

Maya was shaking her head. It was clear she was moved by the workers' plight.

'It's horrendous,' Sonia cried. 'At the start of the day, these people will go to your home to work for four hundred rupees a day. But as time passes and they remain unclaimed, their desperation rises. Mouths at home still have to be fed, and by midday, you can hire them for half the price.'

'Oh God.'

'That's what my cleaning lady did,' Sonia told us. 'She thought she was doing a great thing finding me such a bargain. The poor thing expected to work the entire day for Rs 200. He fixed the curtain rail, sorted out one of my desks, put back a shelf in my cupboard, and replaced all our bust light bulbs for the price I pay for a cup of coffee.'

'And,' said Maya, 'you want to do a profile.'

'I thought you'd never ask.'

Maya was frowning, looking at me, and I shrugged. Our issue for May was already filling up. And Sonia's human-interest story was unlikely to strike a chord with the local crowd. People liked their hard luck stories at a remove; wars in a faraway land, refugees unlikely to flood one's own borders. I checked my calendar. State elections were coming up, which we were planning on covering. We had decided to limit political features to one per issue while the magazine remained free to maximise its appeal, and I half-heartedly suggested, 'We may be able to fit something into the July issue. We were thinking of asking you to focus on the elections in the May and June issues.'

'Sure,' she replied. 'This feature can appear in the April issue. If,' she said, looking unusually coy, 'there's space for it, that is.'

'Aren't you going to be busy with the Boards?'

'Yes.' She sighed. She had sat down on one of the old wicker armchairs, and now she rose and began to pace again. There was a nervous energy to her that I recognised from a day or two before the magazine had gone to print. She had the same air of distraction, the same frenzied movements, smelt strongly of coffee, and had the same familiar circles under her eyes. 'I've written a draft already,' she said, and as I cried out, she wagged a finger at me. 'I've taught the boy to count,' she said sternly. 'I've taught him to read and to spell. I've done all I can for him; he will pass or prosper on the basis of his hard work now.'

She fixed me with a glare, and I wilted.

'It's not too much to ask, is it?' Her voice was plaintive, as if she was convincing herself as much as us. She had her maternal guilt to cope with as well as the weight of societal expectations. I'd never seen her husband agonise about making himself available for their children's revision.

'I make sure he's up at the right time; I make sure he's properly fed and taken care of. I don't let him study in the dark, I don't let him eat rubbish, I don't let him forget about his hygiene. But beyond that, there's little I can do. I can't revise for him. I can sit there in his room, surveying his every move, but what's the point of that?' She held her hands out in appeal, and we both nodded rapidly. 'He knows I'm at my desk if he has any problems. And I've been waking up early, earlier than him even, to fit in my work so I'm not distracted while he's revising.'

'How long have you been working on this draft?'

'A week,' she said. She reached into her bag, pulling out a sheaf of papers.

She held the papers out between Maya and me, and I took hold of them.

Raju rises at my approach, but his movements are measured. There is grey in his stubble, his teeth are stained yellow—with age, with tobacco, with a paucity of time—and his head trembles slightly as he talks. Everything seems a bit slow about Raju, and considered, and in another life, he would have been the village sage, the repository of local experience, doling out stories on holy days and handing out judgements on the indiscretions of youngers. We are at the Chandni Chowk labour chowk, a mart for human toil, and Raju is one of dozens of labourers who are following my movements with interest. They are all quiet, all respectful, but behind me, a refuse bin is overflowing, and I smell the stench of urine from the public toilet. How much, I ask him, does he charge for work? Anything you please, he replies, and I know he is not being glib. Employment is the prize here, and as I have already been talking to him for five minutes, he knows his chances are good. He will work for whatever paltry or generous sum I suggest, but if he demonstrates truculence now, he knows I have dozens of more biddable others to choose from.

I looked up to see Maya reading over my shoulder. She met my eye and arched an eyebrow. Sonia was watching us. 'It's rough,' she told me, 'And my structure is awful. But I'll tidy it up once I finish it.'

'It's beautiful,' Maya was saying, and I nodded.

'This Raju,' I asked, 'is he a real person?'

'Yes,' she said. He's the person who came to work for us.'

'Raju,' I said. It was a generic name, a little like Jane Doe, and I said, 'I wonder if that's really his name.'

'No it's not,' she explained, 'his real name is Rajeevlochan. It was too long for people in the city, and at first it was truncated by one employer to Rajeev, and finally by another to Raju. He's grown to like the name now,' she added, 'and let's face it, it's not exactly a name anyone is going to forget.'

'Do you have the time to work on it?'

'Raju is coming back tomorrow. He'll introduce me to a few of his friends. Their stories are the final burst of colour I need for my piece. I'll write it all up when the kids sleep.'

'So…' I began, worried about an appropriate deadline to suggest to her, when she broke in. 'I have it in hand, Siya,' she told me in an overbearing voice. 'I'll have it completed by this time next week.'

XIX

Sonia's article was featured in *The Satirist*'s March issue. She delivered the article two days after she came to see us, well ahead of schedule, responding to edits before we woke in the morning. The piece itself was well-received, with several people stopping us in the street to ask about labour chowks. Some, of course, were scouting for cheap labour, though most had been shocked to learn that labourers' services were traded in markets around the city.

'It's human interest,' Maya said as she told me about another reader who had complimented the article. 'And Sonia writes with such empathy that you can't help but feel for the human condition of her subjects. I'll handle the articles on the State elections. We must get her to focus more on articles in this vein.'

And she was right. Despite our initial misgivings about the change of tone her article heralded, the move had been the right one. One after another, we heard people approach us to talk about Raju's struggles. Raju was as needy as any other worker we saw on the street, but Sonia's writing had made it real in people's minds. In most people's minds. Mrs Bhatnagar, my old walking companion, provided a ready counterpoint to the norm. 'Just imagine,' she said as she accosted me outside the house. 'Delhi's like a souk of old—all this trading in slaves and spices and golds and perfumes.'

'Hardly,' I replied, but as I stepped off, she followed me.

'You've got a good readership now.'

This was spoken as a pronouncement and not as a question, and I nodded briefly. 'My daughter,' she was saying, 'she was in a hotel the other day, and she saw your magazine in the lobby. Very glossy, she said.' This too was said with approval. 'Very stiff,' she was adding, 'very good, thick paper.'

'Have you read the magazine?'

'No,' she replied. 'Normally I don't read magazines,' and I nodded. There was a turn towards the market a moment away, and I wondered if I would be able to get away.

'I need to check in at Mr Seth's place,' I said, but Mrs Bhatnagar tugged me on the arm.

'I don't,' she said, 'normally read these sorts of magazines, but I picked up a copy after my daughter spoke of it.'

I was nodding, smiling at her words, moving towards the market, when she added, 'But you know, you need to consider that it's all these foreign tourists who come and pick up this sort of magazine.'

'Well…'

'The hotel, you know, then all the tourists coming to this market. Is it good if they read this sort of stuff about India?'

'Well,' I replied, 'it's an Indian magazine, just like *Outlook* or…'

Mrs Bhatnagar was ploughing on. 'But I saw foreigners reading your magazine. They should not form such a negative opinion about India.'

I didn't tell her that Raja Singh had come up to me to praise the magazine's reporting. I didn't bother to mention the positive pieces we always gave pride of place. The features on Delhi's cultural scene, the literature festivals and the history walks, the reviews of the latest bars and restaurants, the ingenious rain water recycling system set up by two local school girls. She was talking now about our demonetisation article. 'I didn't read it at the time, of course, but I went and looked up back copies.' My pace had picked up, and as she hurried to keep up with me, I heard her grunt. Her face had turned red with her effort, but she wagged her finger at me, 'It was painful, of course, the entire demonetisation episode. Especially,' she said, stopping and looking at me pointedly, 'for those of us who were there at the time.'

'But it was the casual workers, the labourers, those who work in the shadow economy...'

'Oof,' she was saying, 'we all suffered, but we all knew it was for a good cause.' She widened her eyes. 'We had to crowd out all the black money in the system. Stop the terrorism that comes in from across the border...'

'Yes,' I said. It was difficult to argue against nationalism unencumbered with nuance.

'Do you think it's nice for foreigners to come and read such stuff about India?'

'Well...'

'You're new here,' the woman said with no apparent irony. 'You'll have been subject to propaganda outside India. But what you have to understand is that this is a new, ambitious government. It is bent on making India better. It is bent on effecting change. You've heard about the *Swachh Bharat* initiative. Write about that. The Prime Minister himself goes around sweeping the streets to illustrate the point. It's an entire mindset that is being changed, and it will take time. But you have to trust the Prime Minister, and you have to reflect India at its best.'

We had reached Mr Seth's shop. Another reader was waiting outside, a comment on her lips, and I quickly turned to Mrs Bhatnagar. 'Thank you so much for the chat,' I told her, reaching forward to hug her. She was taken aback by my gesture, but didn't otherwise react. The other reader—another broad, loquacious lady in late middle-age—stepped forward to talk to me about Puneeta's review. 'Is it true?' she asked, 'that Delhi has an Armenian restaurant now?' I confirmed the news, and then she took me by the arm. 'But what I really wanted to talk to you was about these labour chowks.' Her eyes grew wide. 'Are they real? Do they really exist?' I nodded, and she added, 'Can you really buy a whole day's labour for Rs 200?'

Ben loved Sonia's article. 'This is ground-breaking writing,' he wrote to me in his email. 'These are the real issues. Not just what new resort is opening in Bali.' I couldn't be sure if this was discontent with his life, but I didn't probe. I corresponded with Ben more frequently than I had for months, and this level of interaction, professional and familiar at the same time, felt doable.

He was now contributing to every issue of *The Satirist*, and most weeks began with either a submission or with edits. We didn't talk much about each other's lives. I didn't ask if he had a new girlfriend, or if his work was going well. When the lease on my property ran out, he retrieved the two boxes I had left behind. These were now stored in his parents' garage, but he hadn't asked me when I would be back to collect them, and I didn't offer him any information either. It meant something to me, and perhaps to him too, my possessions in his childhood home, and in the meantime we carried on our professional relationship as if there had never been any claims of love between us. There was no reprising our relationship of old, but the echoes that remained brought with them the most pleasant aspects of our life together; all the joy, all the warmth and none of its bitterness.

Tasha-di's health didn't improve. The seasonal flu she had contracted lingered, lodging itself in her lungs, and the last time we visited, she had a fever and a cough that wouldn't budge. We drove her straight to the hospital. A battery of tests was performed, and at its end, she was diagnosed with bronchitis.

'With people of an advanced age,' the doctor, a young man with an earnest manner, was saying, and Tasha-di rolled her eyes. I patted her on the back and nodded at the doctor. 'Well,' he was saying, clearing his throat, 'they have to be monitored much more carefully.'

Maya and I returned with Tasha-di to her flat. The place smelt musty, as if it hadn't been aired in ages, and I saw piles of paper on top of the coffee table. This is how it starts, I thought. With a fall, with an illness, with an inability to function as before. The light in the living room had blown a fuse, and when I asked Tasha-di where she kept her spare bulbs, she had pointed to a cupboard by the kitchen.

It was bare, and as I looked around in other shelves for bulbs, Maya asked me, 'You've changed bulbs before?'

'I've lived alone,' I reminded her. 'I've managed.'

'Exactly,' crowed Tasha-di. 'We've both managed.' She rose now with instructions on where she kept her spare bulbs, and Maya had to entreat her to sit back down. I gave up on my quest, and the three of us sat down, side by side in the dark, on Tasha-di's small sofa.

'Tasha-di,' Maya was saying in a patient, soft voice, and Tasha-di must have known what was to follow, as she began again to talk about how independent she had always been.

'My marriage ended forty-forty five years ago,' she recounted. 'It ended almost as soon as it began. And here I was, this childless, friendless woman, all alone in Delhi.' We had heard this story countless times, and normally were on the lookout for new titbits to be gleaned from her. One day she would let slip details of the last argument she had had with her ex-husband, and on another occasion, about the paltry divorce settlement he made on her. This once, though, we willed her silent. Her days of complete self-reliance were at an end, for a while at the least, and we needed her to stop battling the change. 'I had no friends here, and no family, not really, apart from my father's dead brother's widow. She was kind, and I always had a warm reception at her home, but everything else, profession, money, company, I had to take care of all alone. There was no community looking out for me, I can tell you this.' She glared at Maya, who had asked Tasha-di how she was managing on her own.

'Tasha-di,' I said, 'just move in with us until you recover.' She turned to me with a pained frown, as if I had betrayed her, and I grimaced. 'It's not for long,' I promised, 'and really, I'm mainly thinking of our convenience. We have to drive in daily to check in on you.'

She bristled. 'No one told you to…'

'No, no,' I said swiftly, 'Of course, but you know we want to make sure you're ok. Even during our busy periods, neither of us feels easy until we've seen you. But you know the magazine's next issue is out in a week. Maya and Sonia are flat out with assignments.' Tasha-di hadn't interrupted, and I carried on talking. 'Puneeta's review needs changing. We have too much to do at the moment, and it would be kind if you were to come home.'

Tasha-di let out a low groan. Her voice was huskier than we were used to, but she remained reluctant to move. 'Really,' Maya insisted. 'All our deadlines have slipped since you've been gone. I was hoping you weren't too ill to come into the office for an hour or two every morning to help set us straight.'

Silence followed. No one moved, not Tasha-di, nor Maya nor I. Her breathing had felt ragged to me, but there was no hint of a noise now. We sat there in the dark, unable to make eye contact, and I was scared most that Tasha-di had fallen asleep without resolving the matter. My hand went to the fringe of the shawl draped over the sofa, and as I ran my fingers through it, some of my movement's noise must have carried through to Tasha-di, as she said to me in a drowsy voice, 'You always loved that shawl, Siya.'

'Come stay with us, Tasha-di. We'll take your things with us so you can feel at home.'

'Silly child,' she scolded. 'My furniture is not going anywhere. I'll move into Civil Lines for a week or two until I return to normal.' Her speech was measured, her delivery slow, her words lofty, as if she was conferring a great honour on us, and we were both quick to assent.

'Yes, Tasha-di,' I said, and the matter was settled. Tasha-di would move in with us while our next issue was being finalised, and would move back to her home straight afterwards. We expressed our gratitude with sufficient enthusiasm, and she finally consented to being driven back to our home with us.

XX

Our big break came some days later. Things had been going well for a while; we were a few issues in, and these had been well received by *The Satirist*'s readership. Often when Maya and I were on our morning walks, we would be stopped by a resident who would praise our magazine. There was criticism too, typically meted out by the retired men who made their morning excursions with a fervour bordering on the religious, but the conclusion was clear; we had become local celebrities, and *The Satirist* the collective property of the entire neighbourhood.

One morning we were stopped by someone, a harried-looking man in his early forties. He first speed-walked towards us, distracted, plugged into his earphones, only spotting our approach and swerving at the last moment, and then, pausing as we moved to let him pass. He stopped right where he was, in the middle of the pavement. He removed his earphones, and the assured tones of a motivational speech wafted our way.

'Hey,' he called out, and though I initially thought he was addressing a stray dog or an interloper, it was soon clear he was talking to us. He moved swiftly in our direction, waving his hands to ensure we didn't move away. 'You're the publishers of the new magazine, aren't you?'

'Yes,' Maya nodded. '*The Satirist*.'

The man fell in step with us, explaining that he worked for an educational company in Delhi. 'We own several schools,' he told us, huffing through his exertion. There was a generous band of sweat on his brow, and his discarded earphones kept blaring out a stream of reinforcements. 'Remember,' I heard the disembodied voice pronounce, 'that you're the best. You,' it repeated, slowing down in emphasis, 'are the best.'

'We,' our companion was saying, 'are the best.'

I coughed, and he continued. 'We are India's fastest growing educational establishment. We've even entered into the college space now. Our graduates are just beginning to enter the job market.'

He looked at me, inclined his head, and it appeared a response was expected. 'Well done,' I responded. 'That's fantastic.'

'And that's why I wanted to speak to you. You take advertisements for the publication, I see.'

Maya spoke up. We were a minute away from our house, and I saw her tearing away and preparing to cross the road. 'Siya here,' she said, 'is your *man*.' She waved her hand cheerily at us, and peeled off back homewards.

The man turned to grill me. He asked me about our rates, about the length of the contract we sought, and about our editorial policy. As he spoke, his motivational mantras kept being blared out of his earphones.

'Well,' the man was saying. He hadn't introduced himself by name, but he now clutched my arm and retrieved a folded business card from his tracksuit. 'Here,' he said as I read his name. 'I'm Neil Sethi,' he added, presaging my actions, 'MD at the "Local Group of Schools".'

'Yes,' I replied, and as his head tilted in anticipation, I

added, 'That's fantastic.' He was waiting for a reply to his questions. I thought hard, naming a price well in excess of what I had discussed with Puneeta. 'All our sponsors sign up for an entire year,' I told him. 'Our sales process is just coming to an end. We're fortunate,' I added, as Neil gulped, 'that we've been able to choose the best quality of partners with the best packages to offer to our readers.'

I began to walk, and Neil followed rapidly. 'That's not a problem,' he promised, talking about free school tours for the magazine's readers.

I turned back towards home as he turned with me. 'Several of our partners have promised product promotions. Free samples, deodorants, shampoos, children's clips, that sort of stuff.'

'Sure,' he offered, 'Sure. We can rustle up something. A goody bag, maybe.'

'Maybe,' I replied. I pointed to the house. 'That's my stop,' I said to him. I lifted his card and nodded. 'My office,' I said, thinking of a still recuperating Tasha-di, 'will send you a proposal in the next few days.' He nodded, and I reached out to shake his hand. 'Goodbye,' I said to him, as he continued to nod. 'Nice doing business with you.'

The house erupted the moment I opened the door. Maya faced me, with Shanti right behind, and I knew my sister had raced the old retainer to the door when she had seen me approach. Tasha-di and Sonia were quick behind, and Ajay, though he tried to look insouciant, leant back against the hallway wall. Even Saloni, relegated now to the kitchen, hovered anxiously in the living room.

I didn't speak.

Maya's brows ascended to her hairline, and still I didn't utter a word.

'Well?' Sonia asked at length. 'What happened? What did he say?'

'We spoke,' I replied. Maya stamped an impatient foot, and I knew those at home had conferred. 'He was keen,' I added, and as Sonia snorted, I held up my hands. Shanti was shaking her head, Ajay smirking in the background, and I added, 'He was very keen. I told him we would need to get a commitment for a year, and that other sponsors…'

There was a laugh from Ajay, and I repeated, 'Other sponsors are throwing in samples for our readership.'

'Wah wah,' clapped Shanti.

'And?'

'And,' I said, 'he lapped it all up. I told him my office…'

Another laugh proceeded from Ajay, and we all turned to look in his direction. He piped down. 'I told him,' I carried on, 'that my office would contact him with a marketing proposal.' I held up the business card Neil had handed me, and they were all over me, my family and co-workers, hugging me, examining the card, slapping me on the back, as if I hadn't won the interest of a potential sponsor but had conquered the steepest, most treacherous peak. It felt that day like I was the hero of fables, like I was the loin-cloth wearing Gandhi wresting India from colonial rule, like I was the child plugging my finger into a wall and saving Holland from the encroaching sea. Anything felt possible that day, and I the person who had made the glorious future a tangible prospect.

Work grew more animated. All at once, we were full of plans. We always met in the garden room for short interludes; for a coffee break, or for a chat about a feature or the right theme for an issue, but that day it seemed to become the working nucleus of the operation.

I had been working on a marketing proposal. Puneeta's hotel group had been paying for sponsorship for the past few issues, but this engagement had been largely informal in nature. As each issue was sent to the printer, I thanked Puneeta for her article, and she confirmed the hotel would stock the magazine and sponsor the following month. Tasha-di teased that we were bribing the girl to sponsor us, and perhaps we were, but the arrangement hadn't required any inking. The hotel group always renewed their sponsorship, but we were always at risk of the deal coming to an abrupt end.

To mitigate the chances of this happening, I had been preparing a formal proposal. Everything in the magazine was decided by committee, and accordingly, I had booked in some time to show my proposal to Maya, Sonia and Tasha-di the following week. All of this was now expedited, and I had spent the hours after my walk going through my files, looking for sponsorship deals I had agreed to in my previous role. I lifted out the best worded sections, and was beginning to patch together key terms for our offering when Sonia tapped me on the shoulder.

'Come,' she told me. 'Team meeting,' and I followed her to the garden room to see Maya and Tasha-di already seated, their hands around warm cups of tea. It was still cold enough for us to drink more tea than in the warmer months, and as I saw the steam rise out of their mugs, I sighed.

'It's not fair,' I complained, pointing to the two armchairs they had ensconced themselves in. They pointed to a teapot and empty mugs, but I continued shaking my head in mock outrage. 'You've had the warmest of the tea, and you've taken the best chairs.'

'Come on,' Tasha-di joshed. 'Stop being a baby,' and I sat promptly down. 'Now,' she added, 'We must be serious. Where are you with the proposal?'

'We have a week to turn it around,' I told them, adding that it wouldn't do to sound too keen, but their excitement was palpable. We were all swaddled in our winter shawls, but as we spoke, mapping out plans and deadlines, these came swiftly off. Maya fanned her face; Sonia flushed red. The sun was bright outside, and streaming in through the glass doors Shanti had painstakingly cleaned, with the result that even winter's insipid heat was magnified as it fell on us.

'Open the doors,' called out Tasha-di. She had recovered well in the time she had been staying with us, and though she still spoke of returning home, we found that she mentioned it less with every passing week. Pradeep was regularly sent to her flat to return with items; a throw, a shawl, her favourite spice blend, and inch by slow inch, the first floor of the house began to accommodate elements of her life. The photo of her and Ma now stood next to our family pictures; her throw was flung over our old, ragged sofa. She made the place home, and she grew in confidence around the office too, taking over increasing amounts of the organisation. 'We'll have to put a screen door here for the summer months. We'll let in the air but not the mosquitoes.' She was asking Maya if she remembered the wire screen she had been in the habit of using in her flat, when I put up my hand to stop her.

'Siya?'

There was noise from outside, an exclamation followed by a muffled response. I stepped out of the room in my slippers, and as questions came from my colleagues, I gestured to them to be silent. It was a male voice, two, in fact, and though their exchange was rapid, I couldn't hear any of it.

I stepped forward. 'Siya?' came the call from the room, and the noise outside was stilled. No one spoke, no one moved, not those outside the room, nor those inside. I heard no footsteps either, and I closed my eyes to try and remember the source of the noise. Had it come from the garage to the left? Had it been outdoors, and so perhaps from the neighbouring house? The wind rustled through the branches, still bare after a lingering winter, and I heard a throat being cleared.

'Bas,' a voice spoke. It was male, definitely male, but muzzled, and I walked on, waving at the occupants of the garden room for silence. No further noise followed, but just as I turned the corner, I saw Pradeep leaning over Ajay. Ajay was pinned to the wall, his mouth covered by Pradeep's hand, and as Ajay noticed my arrival, he raised his eyebrows, and Pradeep turned towards me.

His hand fell off Ajay's mouth and he smiled at me. 'Didi,' he said, 'I was just, I was just,' and then, as inspiration abandoned him, he asked, 'was there anything you wanted, Didi?'

'We,' interrupted Ajay. He straightened himself up, smiled confidently at Pradeep, and patted him on the back. Pradeep shook him off. 'We were just discussing a cricket match.'

'Cricket?'

Pradeep nodded. This was the age-old ritual of omertà playing out, and I knew what their response would be before I repeated my question, 'Cricket?'

'Yes,' Ajay insisted, and as I stared, he said again, 'Yes, yes,

yes. This man says Kohli is the best batsman to ever have played for India, can you believe it?'

'Ajay...'

'I mean it, Siya. I think I was quite restrained in my reply, all things...'

But he was destined not to finish his sentence. The others came hurrying in from the garden room, and stood surveying the scene before them. The men were still standing inches away from each other. Ajay had a smile plastered on his face, but Pradeep looked upset. For all his falling in with Ajay's speech a moment ago, he looked like he was on the verge of an outburst.

His face was flushed; his hands balled up into fists. He was looking straight at Maya, his features distraught, and said, 'That's it, Didi, I can't take this anymore.' His words were more spittle than any genuine articulation, each word hurled out with great force, and I turned back to see if anyone else had comprehended any better than I had.

Maya stepped forward. 'Now, Pradeep...'

Pradeep turned to Maya and looked at her earnestly. 'I told you, Didi, didn't I? I told you I wouldn't stay if Ajay Sir spoke again...'

It was obvious the pair had discussed Ajay. There would have been another mention of Saloni, another perceived insult, and Maya would have stepped in to soothe Pradeep's nerves. His eyes bored into her, but she was still nodding in her placating manner, like when she had been in the habit of telling me as a child that my fears were unfounded. I'd fallen face forward one day at school, slicing open my knee. She had been right behind me. It had been break, I think, when the entire school spilled out into the lawns behind school, and I had tripped on the tarmac leading up to the lawn.

Maya had been in front of me, and eager to go off with her friends, but she had heard me fall and had returned to my side. The cut was gaily bleeding, my hysteria setting in, and children were gathering all around us to point and offer counsel. Maya would nod at all she heard, nod at my tears, and as she worked with a handkerchief to stem the flow of my blood, she would nod again, telling me my injury wasn't so bad, that she had suffered worse herself, my sensible older sister, trying to make me disbelieve the evidence of my own eyes.

Now she nodded at Pradeep's complaints, and I knew Ajay had reprised his teasing. I watched him as he leaned back against the wall he had so recently been pinned again, one leg crossing the other, as if he had no care in the world. There Pradeep was, nearly crying in his despair, telling my sister that though he was grateful to Maya for all she had done, he couldn't continue to live under her roof, and Ajay tilted his head, as if he were a removed but well-meaning observer of the spectacle.

My blood boiled. 'Ajay!' I called, my voice sharp, and he immediately straightened himself out. 'What's all this about?'

'Nothing,' he replied, as Pradeep glared at him. 'We were just having a chat…' Pradeep laughed out loud, a brittle sound, and Ajay nodded his head vigorously, 'Yes,' he added, the shameless villain, 'we were just talking about cricket.'

There was a low growl from Pradeep, a warning battle cry, and Maya looked to me beseechingly. *Help*, she mouthed, and I nodded. 'Come with me,' I said to Ajay, 'I have an errand to run, and you can give me a lift.'

He whistled in the car. The tune escaped me for an age, which added to my irritation, as instead of discussing his altercation with Pradeep, I focussed on trying to identify the song. It was definitely a Hindi number, and old, from the black and white era, and I dimly remembered a pomaded hero swaying through the streets as he sang the song. I shut my eyes to concentrate, and still the song escaped me. Had there been a heroine in the song? I couldn't remember one, but I distinctly remembered crowding around our old black and white TV set for Saturday morning's music hour. *Antakshari*, the programme was called, and we had grown up in the days of terrestrial TV, when the sole national media broadcaster focussed on family friendly television at all times. There were no scantily clad models on TV, no risqué music videos, no clashing in-laws. I had definitely seen the song on TV in my childhood, the music repeated every weekend, but the lyrics continued to elude me.

It was endlessly tantalising, a memory out of reach, like a soap bubble trailing into the ether as I chased it. Ajay's whistling slowed as we reached a traffic light, and he turned smilingly to me. 'How I loved that song as a child. Dev Anand,' he said, as the song finally flashed in my head, 'so happy, so handsome. So carefree.'

I shrugged.

'How long you've been away,' he said. He was looking at me, his eyes serious, for once not bent on a joke, and I looked down. His hand was on the clutch, and he had rolled his sleeves up. I could see the hair on his arms, and I turned away.

'Well,' I said, as the light changed and he shifted gear, 'I really need to understand what happened with Pradeep.'

'Oof,' came the reply. 'The man is too sensitive.'

'You've been needling him,' I said. 'You know he's not happy about your interest in Saloni.'

'Come on, now,' he retorted. 'Here you women are, acting

like feminists, when all you care about is protecting poor Pradeep's feelings. A girl comes in, intelligent, ambitious, and eager to work, and I admit I teased Pradeep in the beginning.' The car came to a stop in front of a parade of shops. 'He did well marrying her, and you know it, but after Pradeep erupted, I dialled down the ribbing. I, for one, would be proud to have a beautiful, intelligent woman by my side.' Ajay looked out of the window, where a parking attendant offered him a chit. He took the chit, nodded, and rolled up the window, 'But this Pradeep. This big, strong man, well he prefers to keep his jewel hidden.'

I had a sudden thought. 'You like her.'

'No,' he said, his words harsh. 'I do not like her. I admire her, yes, and I do think she's wasted on that oaf, but I have no romantic designs on her. I, I…' and here he dashed his hands against the steering wheel. The horn blared, a school of crows flew off the bonnet, and Ajay grunted. 'And I'm surprised at you, Siya. Taking his side when he's being so unreasonable.'

'It's not so simple,' I said, struggling to defend myself. Nothing he had said had been wrong, and all the anger I had built up deflated. 'There's Shanti to think of too, and she is like family.'

'Shanti,' he mused, 'another woman shielding a man.'

'I know,' I began, then stopped. He was right, Pradeep's conduct was indefensible, but there it was. Another car pulled up next to us, and the parking attendant hurried to the driver. They conducted their business, and then the attendant peered through our window. He seemed unable to decide if we were having a quarrel or an assignation. He eyed us for a few minutes, and then, as another car pulled up, he moved smartly in its direction. I turned towards Ajay, who had his hands firmly around the steering wheel. His knuckles showed white. 'Anyway,'

I asked, attempting levity, 'since when did you become such a feminist?'

Ajay nodded, smiled, laughed, waving away a half-clad child who came round asking for money. He lifted his hands to run them through his hair, and I noticed his knuckles remained pale. 'My father,' he said. 'My handsome, suave, successful father has been cheating on my mother for as long as I remember.'

'Ajay…'

He nodded, but his face remained trained in front of him. 'He was discreet in the beginning. We sometimes ran into his conquests. At a restaurant, in the cinema, in a parking lot. He was never embarrassed when running into them, introducing them to us as "friends", and it didn't strike me for the longest time that he appeared to have more female friends than male ones.'

He clapped his hands. I smiled, and he took up his narrative again. 'But then, I suppose the pretence grew tiresome for him. It's gotten to the stage now where he openly boasts about his "girlfriends". My poor Mum sits at home, eating herself fat, and that man talks about the diamonds he is buying his latest little plaything.'

'That's horrible, Ajay.' He shrugged, but didn't reply, and as the silence stretched between us, I asked, 'Why doesn't she leave him?'

'Because, Siya,' he said, adopting the same slow, pained enunciation he had used when talking about Pradeep, 'she has no options. She has no money of her own, no job, no assets. I offered to have her move in with me, but she just laughed at the thought. I live in a one bedroom flat in a very nice part of Delhi, but that's just it, a bachelor's pad. I told her we could move, but she wouldn't hear of it.' His hands were clasped around one another, and I saw his skin lighten with the pressure. He laughed once more, a mirthless, cheerless sound. 'Her parents think it's just a phase Dad…' Ajay paused, returning his hands to the steering wheel. A sound emitted from his throat, low and guttural, as if he was trying to expunge something unsavoury. 'Sorry, my father. My father. Well, my mother's parents advise her to hold firm, and part of me can't even blame them. They're middle class, and ageing, and they worry perhaps about my mother losing all the comforts she is accustomed to. But then again, perhaps they just don't want to have to shoulder her burden.'

'I'm so sorry, Ajay.'

'Don't be,' he said, his response rapid, almost as if it were instinctive, but then he paused. He nodded, lifting his hands from the wheel, holding his palms out for inspection. 'I'm not sorry,' he added, 'I live on my own, I visit my parents like a good boy every weekend, and when my father tells me how well he's doing, and how much money he's spending, I slap him on the back and congratulate him. He wants me to join him in his business, you know.'

'Oh Ajay,' I said, feeling the uselessness of my words, but he shrugged. He pointed to the shops in front. 'Come,' he said, 'get your work done otherwise our attendant friend here will be calling the police to report lewd behaviour. Cavorting in a car, no less,' he guffawed, as I frowned. He pointed at the parking attendant, who was looking towards us, and clapped his hands. 'Oh well done, well done,' he called out as he left the car. He went up to the startled man and shook his hand. 'Thank you,' he told him, 'for making sure India minds its morals.'

XXI

Pradeep was gone by the time we returned. Saloni was too, and it was a wan-faced Shanti who gave us the details. 'I tried,' she said, wringing her hands. A dishcloth hung over her shoulder, her eyes were ringed with kohl, and it was clear she had been crying. She looked at Ajay for a minute, then addressed me, 'Baby, you know I never wanted any of this. I wanted him to be happy, for Saloni to be happy, for them both to help you and Maya baby out. But,' and here she fixed Ajay with a slow stare before shaking her head.

This was all alien to her, for all her histrionics at home, she was essentially a docile creature, used to following tradition and respecting the status quo. She was always deferential with visitors, holding herself back in the shadows, and though Ajay had tried to befriend her, cracking jokes, making fun of himself, she had preferred to maintain her distance. Her actions here, placing the blame of Pradeep's departure on Ajay's shoulders, was like the reversing of her natural order.

'I tried to talk to him, baby,' she was saying. She came up to me, putting her hands in mine. 'I really did. I told him to be reasonable, but he wouldn't listen. He said he couldn't bear it any longer.' She didn't elucidate further, and her eyes didn't return to scrutinising Ajay, but her inference was clear.

'He'll see sense,' I told Shanti. 'The two of them needed a honeymoon anyway.'

Ajay laughed, we both turned to him, and he hurried off to the library. 'It might be the best thing for him,' I told Shanti. Her hands were still in mine, and I gave them a squeeze. 'It will be,' I insisted. 'It'll give him some time to cool off. And,' I added, 'it'll give him some time to get to know Saloni. He's a good boy, Shanti,' and she finally nodded. She looked at me, cupped my face in her hands, and lifted herself on tiptoe to give me a kiss. '*You* are a good girl, baby.'

Sonia's next feature was on Chitra Kashyap. A high-achieving Delhi teenager, she always aced all her exams before failing to attend her board exams one morning. Her parents went to her bedroom and found she had hanged herself in her bedroom using her bed cover. The police was called in, the school informed just as the other students were filing in for their examinations, the distraught parents were dosed up with sedatives, and for days no one knew the cause of the suicide.

Chitra's mother mandated nothing be touched in the unfortunate girl's bedroom, but as Delhi's dust laid quick siege to the place, the maid was finally allowed in to dust the room. It was she who uncovered the suicide note tucked under Chitra's pillow, and not understanding its importance, put it into her dustpan to be discarded. Chitra had forever been writing on long sheets of paper in her close, spidery writing, scrunching up her notes and hurling them into her dustbin, and this missive laid neatly to rest under her pillow had been mistaken for another such, until Chitra's mother entered the room and noticed the sheets lying on the maid's dustpan.

There had been no sign of upset, no failed romance, no tempestuous friendships, and at the end, no reason they could discover that explained her actions. Until Mrs Kashyap recovered the discarded suicide note left by her daughter, with the words that would burn into a nation's conscience: 'I know I'm going to fail.'

It had been a task getting her to agree to the interview in the first place. All the national papers had hounded her for weeks, but Sonia had told her she had a child sitting board exams herself, and this had thawed some of Mrs Kashyap's reserve. 'I understand,' Sonia had repeatedly told her. 'The late nights, the never-ending revision, the unhealthy emphasis on that one set of exams. The Facebook posts on sleepless nights; the Instagram snaps of unmade beds and messy desks. My son's skin,' she had complained, feeling her lack of grace. Her son was still alive, and out playing with his friends, but she ploughed on. 'It turned almost grey, he'd seen so little sun,' but this mention of the pressure India's children were under brought an invitation. 'Come, then,' Mrs Kashyap said. 'They're going to write about her anyway, all these news-hungry sharks. I might as well talk to someone who understands what it's like.'

Sonia had come in with flowers, had hugged an unresisting Mrs Kashyap, and had made all the right noises as the bereaved mother removed Chitra's note from the plastic casing she stored it in. She watched Sonia as she read, mouthing each needless, memorised word. 'There was no question of failure,' she cried as Sonia looked up. 'There was never any question of failure with Chitra.'

'Had she been under much pressure?'

'No, no,' came the reply. 'She was always a happy child. No trouble, no boys, no late nights, nothing. She was always very cheerful. She would come in from school, eat her fruit, and sit down to study. I never had to tell her to revise.'

'She put pressure on herself, maybe.'

'No, no,' came the stout reply, the words repeated over and over again. 'There was never any pressure.'

'What were her hobbies?'

Mrs Kashyap narrowed her eyes. 'Hobbies?'

'Yes,' said Sonia. She could have changed the topic, but this story had consumed her. Her own son had needed waking up every morning, and constant prodding to return to his books. There was always a football match, or the messages that lit up his phone to distract him, but here was this girl, who rose on her own, who spent her days at her desk, but had felt certain she was doomed to fail. 'A sport, maybe; badminton or tennis. A local friend she could take evening walks with. A favourite show on television,' but Sonia was met with a stony stare.

'She was happy,' Mrs Kashyap maintained. 'There was no sign of unhappiness.'

Sonia winced. She knew her next words would be seen as an attack. 'Was there an overachiever in the family who Chitra might have been aspiring to emulate? A parent, a sibling, a cousin?'

'We're all academic,' replied the mother. 'I have a PhD in Sociology, my husband is a Professor, her brother studies at IIT. But,' she repeated, as she had done over the course of the interview, 'Chitra was bright. She was happy. She never complained about any pressure.'

'No, no,' agreed Sonia, but as she got to writing her piece, she couldn't help thinking of the toll India's exams took on its children.

'No pressure,' her mother had kept on saying, over and over again, as if it was a mantra, and Sonia knew she was sincere. Mrs Kashyap had expected her bright daughter to perform, and her daughter had performed. She had never shown any sign of struggle, but her parents hadn't appreciated either how stifling her environment had been.

This was what India's schooling was doing to its children. The population was vast, the number of minorities claiming seats enormous, and for the rest, for the simply bright or the middling, and for those without the funds to access universities abroad, the chances of gaining a good education were vanishingly small. Exam results in the nineties were often not sufficient. You had to score near perfect marks, and everything else—friendships, hobbies, social skills—slipped by the wayside in the pursuit of the best exam results. Tutors were engaged, career coaches consulted, and students spent the best part of two years studying; studying when they should have been sleeping, studying when they should have been playing, studying when they should have been held hostage by their hormones, and studying when they should have been learning about themselves.

She wrote, then, Sonia, as her son finished his board exams. She wrote as he received and celebrated his mediocre exam results. She wrote the most sombre piece she had ever written, missing her deadline twice, and when Maya first read it, she forwarded it to me.

She came over to my desk as I read the piece. 'She's not pulling any punches, is she?'

I read out the passage Maya pointed to:

Chitra Kashyap was the child we all want our child to be. She was bright, determined and driven. Cheerful and responsible, she woke early to study, and stayed on top of her homework and her other commitments, but as I looked into her final months, I saw that Chitra hadn't had any commitments outside her schoolwork. There had been no space in her schedule for distractions. There had been no boyfriend. There had been no evening walks with friends. There had been no trips to the cinema or the bowling alley. There had been no sports, no drama, no swimming, no tennis, no teenage tantrums. There had been nothing but work, nothing but the cliff-hanger of the board exams to work towards, and in the end, when Chitra's doubts—redundant as they had been—began to set in, there was no outlet for her to take comfort in.

Citra's story is a tragedy, and we will tell ourselves it will never happen to us. We can point fingers. We can blame the parents. We can blame Chitra's personality. Chitra's story is essentially one of a lack of resilience. But if we bother to introspect, we will see that it is also a shameful indictment of a country that measures achievement not in terms of skills or kindness or long-term dedication, but in terms of the marks earned in a solitary set of exams our children spend their childhoods working towards. Where is the space in such a system for late bloomers? Where is the space for imagination, for creativity, for the mavericks, for the artists, for the innovators? Where is the space for a wobble, and where is the space for recovery? We are training our children to be factory workers—scientists, sure, highly paid coders or doctors or lawyers or bankers, sure, but not individuals. Chitra's tragedy is our tragedy too, and more than that, it is the story of India's failure to imagine more than one path for our young.

Maya was looking at me, smiling her small, sad smile. I sighed. 'That poor, poor family.'

'That poor, poor girl,' insisted Maya. 'The pressure these children are under...'

I nodded. All the time I was away, the news on India had largely been positive; the growth, the rising tourism numbers, the infrastructure being developed, the rockets launched into space, and I had thought our development had been even. I thought life was improving for all, for the rich as much as for the poor, for the rural poor as much for their urban brethren, for the young as much as for the old, but I had been wrong. India's development had only brought its divisions into sharper focus. The immigrant labourers were as vulnerable for exploitation as before, and the futures of India's brightest still balanced as precariously on a single event as they had always been. It was heartbreakingly thin, the gap between success and failure, the chasm between want and plenty, only that the gulf grew larger as India grew richer.

'Do you remember,' Maya told me, 'that time when we had tried to bake a cake?'

'When?'

'Oof,' Maya replied impatiently. She waved her hands at me, as if to spur my recollection, and I nodded in hazy memory. We had gone into the kitchen one afternoon as the rest of the household took its post-lunch nap, opening cupboards we forgot to shut, spilling milk and sneezing through clouds of flour, and turning the heat in the oven too high. We had smelt the cake burning as we waited for it to rise.

Maya laughed. 'Do you remember how blazing hot it had been when we opened the oven? The cake had been burnt to a crisp in minutes.'

I cupped my face as I remembered our shock. The heat of the oven had hit us as we pulled open the oven door. We hadn't bothered with oven gloves, and every part of us felt like it was on fire—my silver pendant, Maya's teenage spectacles, our nails and hair and very faces.

She nodded. 'That's the environment these poor children are growing up in. They burn without knowing how they suffer, and their parents don't know either until a child loses his or her life, or until you come in from the outside and see it's not normal and it's not needed, this pressure, this unhappiness, this relentless emphasis on paper perfection.'

'Yes,' I agreed, 'but it won't make for easy reading.'

'So?' I had never seen Maya this combative. She rapped her knuckles on my desk. 'A child has died. Is it the worst thing if Delhi's readers pause to think for a moment before returning to their lives?'

The article came out, and as with Sonia's piece on the labour chowks, was the one we led with. Ajay's accompanying cartoon showed a girl playing at teaching a doll to read. Sonia had quickly become our lead writer, with Maya focussing increasingly on the editorial function, on theme and layout and timing.

She made me change the column I had already written to a tongue-and-cheek look at India's progress from a newcomer's perspective. I wrote about the strides the country had been taking on the economic and cultural stage, and alongside each of my points, Maya added a statistic that revealed the whole truth behind India's unequal progress. Next to my paragraph about increasing GDP, she printed statistics on the country's more modest GDP per head. Next to my paragraph about the number of billionaires India now boasted, she printed statistics about the number of people living below the breadline. Next to my paragraph about the appeal of Bollywood's modern movies, she printed statistics on the number of rapes committed by India's repressed and entitled men.

Her own political column focussed on the derisory response by Delhi's politicians to Chitra's suicide. Maya was our ringmaster, and powerful as Sonia's article was, it was given context by Maya's careful choreography of the entire issue. She had aspired to emulate Raja Singh's talent, and as I saw her take control of *The Satirist*, I sensed that his genius lay within her grasp.

Sonia worried Mrs Kashyap wouldn't like the article. 'It's not easy reading,' she fretted. 'And I worry she'll think my tone too judgemental,' but a week after a copy of the magazine had been sent to the Kashyap household, Sonia received a call. 'Good morning, Mrs Kashyap,' she said, raising a hand to silence the noisy newsroom. 'No, please, Mrs Kashyap,' we heard her say, and we worried that Chitra's mother had been offended by the reporting. 'No,' she was saying, 'no, no,' and as I got up, ready to comfort my colleague, she spoke again. 'No, please, Mrs Kashyap,' she said. 'It was my pleasure. I wanted Delhi to know how hard school is for our children.'

Sonia didn't speak for a good while after she rung off. She took herself off to the garden room, where she remained for an age. We debated joining her, but it was clear she wanted to be alone. Shanti hovered outside, part curious and part worried, and when Sonia eventually emerged, it was obvious she had been crying. We fell silent, waiting to gauge her mood before talking. She sat down on her chair. 'She didn't read it until yesterday,' she said.

'She read it yesterday.' She paused, wincing, smiling, then nodding once more. 'She threw it in the bin after reading it, but retrieved it this morning. She read it again, once, twice, sharing it with her husband, who sobbed as he read.' Tears fell unchecked down Sonia's cheeks. 'She told me he hadn't cried since the funeral, but that he wept on reading the article. He hadn't spoken much in the weeks following Chitra's death. He had busied himself with all the admin surrounding their daughter's last rites, and then had thrown himself into work. Anytime she asked him how he was he told her he was fine, and that he was busy with work. She told me she couldn't explain why my article had unlocked so much emotion in him, but he had cried, cried without shame, cried without knowledge almost, and all while reading what I had written.' Sonia looked up at us, her eyes moist, her face shining with her tears. 'She thanked me,' she said, 'over and over again she thanked me.'

Mrs Bhatnagar had an opinion to express on Sonia's article too. She corralled me early one morning outside the house, and I knew she had been waiting for me. Maya had been too busy for her morning walk, and I had been late setting off, and it gave me a small pleasure to know that Mrs Bhatnagar had had to wait out in the street in Delhi's rising heat.

'Siya,' she cried upon sighting me, waving a copy of my magazine in her hand. Pleasantries were dispensed with entirely. 'I wanted to talk to you about this soo-cide article.' She huffed as she ran up to me, her face the colour of a ripe tomato, and as I professed ignorance, she repeated vociferously, 'Soo-cide, soo-cide, Siya, you know, that horrid article about that poor dead girl.'

'Ah,' I said, walking at a smart pace, 'Chitra Kashyap.' I knew what she was going to say before she said it. She had greeted me with a pursed face, like so many childhood teachers when I had failed to complete an assignment to their satisfaction. *Siya doesn't follow instructions*, I read on endless terse report cards, and the look I spied on Mrs Bhatnagar's face, spent and frustrated, was materially the same.

'Yes, yes,' said the woman impatiently, 'her.'

'It was a sad story.'

'That's my point,' said she. 'What was the point of writing such a piece?'

'But...'

'I've told you before,' continued Mrs Bhatnagar, pulling up her sleeves. She didn't quite bare her teeth, but her annoyance was clear to see. 'This sort of reporting does India no favours.' We had reached the market, and stood in front of Mr Seth's shop, where a woman came out carrying a copy of *The Satirist*. Mrs Bhatnagar scowled. 'And who is it who wrote the soo-cide article, anyway? I've seen her name attached to several of these doom-and-gloom articles.'

'Well,' I began, but Mrs Bhatnagar was wagging a stubby finger at me. 'Wasn't she the one who wrote about those silly labour chowks too?'

'Yes,' I replied proudly. The next month was to be our last one offering the magazine for free. We were quickly running out of money. My reserves were all but depleted, and though we were all working without pay, we were unable to so much as afford new printer cartridges. The magazine would have to start bringing in money. I saw another customer come out carrying a copy of the magazine and exhaled.

This thing did have potential after all. We'd lose some freeloaders, we'd lose some critics like my irate companion, but the true readers would persist, and hopefully, they would grow. And we would finally be generating revenue.

'This is not done,' Mrs Bhatnagar was saying. 'The rest of the magazine is negative too.' She lay a sweaty hand on my sleeve, and as I started at the contact, she carried on, 'Listen to me now. The magazine is displayed in hotels and in shops visited by tourists. It really is not helpful for outsiders to be seeing India in this light.'

'The readership of the magazine,' I explained patiently, 'is a Delhi one. We write articles suited to the needs of our market.'

Someone else exited Mr Seth's shop, another potential advertiser. This person now approached me, asking me when was a good time to talk. 'Now,' I said to her as Mrs Bhatnagar huffed. 'Now is a perfect time to talk.'

'You refuse to listen to me?' Mrs Bhatnagar called. I smiled as I walked off, giving her a cheery wave, but her final words came in a quick barrage, 'Don't say I didn't warn you.'

XXII

It was some weeks, a month or more perhaps, since Pradeep and Saloni had left, and we had gotten accustomed to functioning without them. Ajay picked up supplies on his way in to work, Tasha-di and I helped out with the copy-editing, and though some things slipped, we told ourselves we managed pretty well.

I hadn't asked Shanti how the couple was doing for fear of prying. Shanti didn't mention them either, and I suspected both sides felt a little bit of embarrassment about how matters had ended.

I did frequently wonder about Saloni, though. In some ways, she had the smaller adjustment to make. She had grown up in the village, and unlike Pradeep, would still have local friends, but all I had seen of her, from her quiet observations to her unfailing ability to pinpoint any weakness in our articles, convinced me that she was not meant for domestic life. She had always been respectful when in the office, always mindful of her position as Shanti's daughter-in-law, but this didn't stop her from running her red pen through huge swathes of Sonia or Puneeta or Maya's work. She was serious and honest, and conscientious with it, and utterly, intractably determined. Her marked-up pieces were handed back in with deference but no apology, and I wondered how she now occupied herself. Was she working or was she tending to her father-in-law's debauched house? Did she ever think of *The Satirist*, and of the mock outrage we greeted her redlined pieces with?

Sonia's May issue focussed on local elections, and the entire house buzzed with poll analyses and predictions. The latest battle to break out in the newsroom was over Maya's desire to go interview a renowned astrologer. He had predicted six of the last seven election results, apparently, and though Sonia and I thought her frivolous, she refused to budge.

'India remains a deeply devout country,' she told us, 'There is a reason why so many still consult astrologers. They are asked to weigh in on everything; auspicious times for a wedding, advice on whether to move cities or take a job.' I laughed, and Ajay, who had looked up from his work at the noise, nodded.

'Perhaps,' he said to Maya, 'I should go with you and ask when we will get better printing equipment for the magazine.'

'Patience,' advised Maya, though his point was well made. The magazine continued to be printed in the garage which also functioned as Ajay's photo studio. The situation wasn't ideal, and one we intended to change. 'Please,' Maya was saying, 'we will fix your space as soon as we start generating an income.'

'I'll take that on faith,' he rebutted, but he rose, driving her to the astrologer.

It was while they were gone that Pradeep and Saloni returned. We had no prior knowledge of their arrival, and neither, it appeared, did Shanti, as the first we heard of anything was a loud shout from the old retainer. 'Deepu,' she called out repeatedly, Pradeep's old childhood nickname, which was soon followed by a torrent of tears. Other indistinct noises joined hers; a sniff, a shuffle, a laugh, and Tasha-di and I ran out to investigate.

Shanti was squatting in the hallway, her head in her hands, her mouth distended with emotion. Pradeep sat next to her, trying to maintain his composure, but failing miserably. He gave into his mother, meeting her embrace, and as she stroked his head, tears streamed down his face. Saloni stood, slightly removed from the tableau, watching as mother and son talked. It was she who first spotted me.

'Namaste,' she mouthed, bowing her head, and I responded in kind.

Pradeep sensed our movement and looked up. 'Didi,' he said, rising to his feet. He appeared to search for the right words to say, and after a few aborted attempts at speech, he followed his wife's lead and folded his hands together.

Shanti rose too. 'Baby,' she said with gleaming eyes, 'Pradeep has come back.'

We didn't pry; it was clear that both Pradeep and Saloni were embarrassed by their dramatic departure and abrupt reappearance. We fell into our routine of old; Pradeep working as our chauffeur, and Saloni helping out with the copy-editing. Ajay behaved too, patting Pradeep on the back and telling him he was happy to see him.

We did, of course, wonder what the couple's weeks in the village had been like, and whether their stay with Shanti's husband had brought them closer or exposed the differences between them. Shanti was uncharacteristically tight-lipped, and though I was on the lookout for glimpses into the family's interaction, nothing was apparent. Saloni remained deferential to her mother-in-law, and restrained in her husband's presence. She was quiet and professional in the office, limiting herself to responding to interaction initiated by the rest of us.

It was Pradeep who, one morning, caught up with Maya and me on our walk, and said, 'Didi, I'm ashamed of how badly I behaved.'

'Come on, now,' Maya replied, 'we're happy to have you back.'

'No, no,' he insisted, refusing to be comforted. 'I wouldn't listen to your advice.' He folded his hands miserably. 'Forgive me.'

'Pradeep…'

Maya spoke again, 'What made you change your mind?'

He smiled. 'It wasn't until we were in the village that I saw how happy she had been here. She would race down to the office in the mornings, and there I had been, thinking it was Ajay Sir, when it was her work. Even in the village, she would mope around, spending her money on all the newspapers she could buy, running to any TV set that showed the news. She was happiest when she was learning, and it was then that I saw that she had been happy here.'

'Pradeep…'

His hands were folded again. 'I was horrible,' he said contritely. 'Please forgive me.'

In the garage too, amity prevailed. Ajay no longer complained about Pradeep's presence, and the driver, for his part, was mindful of when Ajay was in the space and working on his pictures. I suggested to Maya that perhaps the couple's break had been good for them, but she advised restraint. 'Everyone is on their best behaviour,' she counselled. 'Let's see how long it lasts.'

The flare up in the garage came, not from a breakdown in relations, but from a short circuit. A fire started late one evening in early June in the garage, and by the time we became aware of it, much of our magazine equipment had been destroyed.

I slept soundly, as I always did, but was roused by Maya shaking me awake. 'Quick,' she said, barely pausing to speak before she ran. 'Call the fire department.'

I raced after her in my stupor, not registering her instructions. We smelled the smoke before we left the floor, though my brain remained sluggish. Maya ran into the kitchen for dishcloths, handing one to me to hold over my mouth. 'Call the fire department,' she cried, shaking me into action, and I ran to the library's phone while she rushed outside.

By the time I had made it outside, the entire garage was enveloped in flames. I paused briefly to survey the scene, and an irreverent thought struck me, the terrible, cleansing beauty of the fire. Then I heard a shout, and steps rushing out of the servants' quarter, and I surged ahead towards the fire.

The fire department was determined, battling the blaze until it was out, but the damage was done. Equipment left on overnight—the printer perhaps, or the camera Ajay had left on charge—had sparked a circuit, and the house's ancient, exposed wiring had instantly caught fire, like summer forest kindling.

The fire itself had been contained by the firefighters, but we lost Ajay's camera and the equipment we used to print our proofs. As the firemen surveyed the damage after putting out the fire, one of them sniffed. 'This is all minor,' he said, 'but the structure of this building isn't secure. It's too old and too unloved.' I looked at Maya; the fireman's words would apply to most of the main house too. 'I would seriously recommend tearing it down and rebuilding it.'

Maya gulped. 'That was our plan. To rebuild in the next five years or so.'

The man laughed. 'It won't last that long. There's been too much damage.' He tapped at the wall and winced as bits of plaster fell off. 'I would have this seen to as soon as possible.'

In the morning, as the others filed in, surveying the damage, trying to find a positive in the developments, Sonia offered, 'At least you'll get your dark room sooner, Ajay.'

Ajay stood cradling his ruined camera. All the work he had done for the past month was lost. He stood there, smiling bravely, telling us everything was retrievable, when Tasha-di asked the question we had all been wondering. 'How did the damn thing start, anyway?'

The obvious culprit was Ajay. He was forever smoking outside the building, and forgetting to turn the lights off in the garage, or to lock up. But then, as Maya later pointed out to me, the fire had only taken place after Pradeep's reappearance. We had restored him to his former position gratefully, but what if he had been nursing a grudge against Ajay and had started the fire to frame the other man? I laughed as Maya expounded her theory. It was ridiculous, but then I thought of Mrs Bhatnagar's threat a couple of months ago.

'Don't say I didn't warn you,' she had told me. She had been on the scene early in the morning too, condoling with us, but not displaying any surprise, and later, as she had left our home, I had heard her hum. She would make the most unlikely culprit, old, slight and grey, but she had taken a real dislike to us and to our work, and the political environment of the day didn't leave much room for disagreement. What if she had bribed a worker to set fire to our garage?

Then again, it could very well have been one of the house's occupants; Maya, Tasha-di, me, who had been to the garage and forgotten to switch off a device. I had checked on the latest print run the previous evening, and both Maya and Tasha-di had visited the garage too. The possibilities for blame were endless, but we all knew the obvious culprit was Ajay.

I hadn't answered Benjamin's last text, but I now typed out a message: 'Fire destroyed all our equipment.'

The reply was instantaneous. 'Are you ok?'

'Yes, but we've lost our printing equipment and our camera. We can't afford to carry on.'

'It's not like you to give up.'

I stared at the screen. The entire house smelt of the garage's fire. 'We've lost everything.'

There was no answer for several minutes, then: 'My girl never gives up.'

Matters grew swiftly worse. The house had comprehensive insurance, but when Maya called to claim on it, she was told that the insurance didn't cover commercial premises. It would take a mountain of money to rebuild the garage, and it would all have to be done under our own steam. Nothing could be claimed for, not the printer, not the computer, not the camera, not even the paper we had lost to the fire.

We were officially out of money. The magazine, the family, the house, everything seemed to have hit a brick wall. We couldn't afford to rebuild the garage, nor could we afford to tackle our crumbling house. There were smaller purchases we could make—a new printer, a new camera—and I had enough money for them, but neither Maya nor I could see the point. We'd been working without pay for nearly a year, and as we sat looking out onto our decrepit garage, the magazine seemed a luxury.

'Let's face it,' Maya said to me. She had aged visibly over the week since the fire. There was more grey to her hair, and the lines around her mouth seemed more firmly etched. I don't know if it was because we were spending more time outside in the sun's glare, but the wear on her face was marked. Several tines I caught myself staring at her, and then, as I saw Shanti looking at me, I wondered if the fire's ravages told on my features too. 'The house is a death trap,' Maya was saying. She walked about our living room on the first floor, switching off lights. 'At any time, any of these fuses can trip and the entire place can go down in flames.'

'Come on…'

'I mean it,' she maintained. 'I'm half toying with the idea of sending Tasha-di back to hers. She'll be safer there.'

I told her she was wrong, and that she worried unnecessarily, but Maya was resolute. We weren't to spend any more of my money on new equipment to be installed in the house.

XXIII

It was while we were at our impasse that Saloni asked me about Ma. This was the first unbidden thought she had voiced, and she had spoken it so timorously that I had not heard her at first. We were in the library, meeting out of habit more than out of any necessity. We had stopped work on the magazine's July issue, telling ourselves we had paused for the summer holidays, but *The Satirist*'s dwindling viability didn't escape anyone. Saloni had busied herself in dusting a bookshelf, then had asked me a question before repeating it.

'What?'

'Was ma'am,' and here she paused, trying to work out how to frame her address. 'Your mother,' she said eventually, 'was she a journalist too?'

'Yes,' I answered. 'Or no. Not for years. She used to be one.'

'But,' suggested the girl. 'This was her magazine, no?'

'Yes,' I conceded. 'Yes,' and as she stared, bravely raising her lovely neck in her clear-eyed scrutiny, I offered to show her Ma's old proof copies.

We went up to the first floor and into my room. I saw her look around in her quiet manner, as if to absorb every detail, and realised she had never been here before. 'It's a little childish,'

I said, as she told me the room was beautiful. 'I've had it for as long as I can remember.'

I sat her down at my desk and went to get the proof copies from Maya's room. When I returned, I saw Saloni with a card in her hands. She jumped up as she saw me, dropping the card. Her colour was raised, and she was stammering out her apologies, 'It was here, right here, Didi,' she was saying, 'I didn't mean to look at it,' and I turned the card over to see that it was a business card printed on thick, expensive card, its lettering in an italicised gilt cursive. It consisted solely of a name: Raja Singh, and no title or affiliation. Below the name was an email address.

I studied the card. I had forgotten about him with all the chaos of the fire. I bent the card, feeling the thick luxury of the material. He'd offered his help, had been supportive. I took a deep breath and turned to Saloni.

'I'm sorry, Didi.'

'No, no,' I replied. I thought quickly. I hadn't imagined Raja's enthusiasm for *The Satirist*. 'It's a wonderful project,' he had told me when I'd last run into him in the market. 'And much needed in the current political climate.' Another smile, an encouraging arm on my shoulder, and that offer for help made again. I had dismissed it as an important man's empty words, but now I wondered.

'But Didi,' Saloni was smiling, 'it's the same Raja Singh, isn't it?' and as I looked up, surprised that she knew of him, she nodded, 'He's the one who gave TV India the money they needed to begin, and he's the one who put money in the GoTo service…' she struggled for the right words, 'He's the one who's everywhere, isn't he, like God?'

I changed the subject. I showed her Ma's old proofs, letting her read Ma's editorial and marvel over the subjects she had chosen for her inaugural issue. She asked me questions about the magazine: had Tasha-di really worked with Ma, why it had shut down, and as I parried her queries, my mind remained on Raja Singh's card.

I slept with the card next to my bed, and by the morning, I knew my next steps. I didn't consult Maya, worried that she would try to dissuade me. It sounded fantastic to me too, the idea of asking such a great man to finance our little magazine. But, I figured, there was no harm in reaching out to him. The magazine had shut down while we scrambled around for funding, but it had built up a good local reputation in the months it had been in print.

Raja Singh himself had praised a few of the articles when he had seen me in the market, singling out Maya's work on the elections and Sonia's article on demonetisation. And we had had wider recognition too. A couple of the bigger newspapers had carried reports on our articles, and Sonia's piece on Chitra Kashyap had been widely referenced. There were even rumours that she would be nominated for a journalism prize, and, as I told myself, our little team represented a promising investment for Raja. It was worth a try.

I emailed Raja Singh that very day and half forgot about the matter. I was sure that a reply, if it did materialise, would be days in coming.

There was the matter of the fire to resolve, in any case. Estimates for the rebuilding of the garage had come in for a ruinous amount, and for the moment, construction didn't seem like an option. Papa's antique cars, on the other hand, seemed to offer us a way ahead. Much of the fire had been focussed at the entrance of the garage, and the cars, tucked in as they were towards the back under their hoods, hadn't been affected.

Maya and I began to discuss getting rid of them to raise money for the magazine. Maya was resistant to the idea, restored as she was to her native aversion to change, but as I pointed out to her, Papa was gone, and neither of us were car enthusiasts. It seemed like a no-brainer.

I charged Pradeep with contacting garages to find potential purchasers. Ajay was asked to find out how much it would cost to purchase the equipment we had lost, and on one free morning, he asked me to accompany him to look for a new camera. We drove down in his car, stopping via a local shop to pick up his favourite gram flour snack.

'You are always hungry.'

'Always,' he replied, handing me a handful of the food. I munched on it, savouring the earthy nuttiness of the food, when he asked, 'How are things with that boyfriend of yours?'

'Who?' I stuttered, sitting up straight. He arched an eyebrow, and I knew he was talking about Benjamin. I shrugged. Benjamin had remained in touch after the fire. He had been kind, renewing his offer of free articles, telling me he could lend me money, but I had told him we would manage. 'Benjamin?' I asked as he stared, and I shrugged again. 'He's a good friend.'

'Right,' Ajay replied, and I grew conscious that my reply had not answered his question. He turned to the rear window, beckoning the guard to pay his parking ticket, and set off.

'I mean,' I tried to explain. 'We broke up ages ago.'

'Of course,' he replied, frowning, focussing on the road ahead. He squinted as he rounded a corner, his brows furrowing, and I wondered if he wore glasses. He never had any with him at work; and I thought that perhaps he was avoiding wearing them out of vanity. Ma had been the same all those years back, shunning glasses as her eyesight grew worse, clipping her grey hairs out at the root instead of acknowledging time's march, and I smiled as I watched him. Just imagine, Ajay and vain. 'How old are you?' I asked, and he swerved.

'What?'

'I never asked.'

He pursed his lips, as if put out, and indicated towards the road ahead, where a traffic jam had built up. He nodded in its direction, as if he couldn't be distracted, and drove. We were silent for a while, and I asked, 'What is it, then? Forty?'

He didn't respond. The traffic had come to a standstill, and we weren't moving. He checked his watch, a broad, metallic number, and stared ahead.

'Fifty?'

He shot me a look.

'Fifty?' I asked, incredulous. I had him pinned down as being a few years older than Sonia and Maya, in his early forties perhaps, but his priggishness about his age amused me. 'Really?' I laughed, 'You're fifty?'

'Really,' he answered, twisting his mouth with distaste. 'Really, really,' and as I continued to laugh, he added, 'just like you and that Benjamin of yours are just friends.'

I laughed once more but he continued to look forward. Delhi's traffic debris wove past us; emaciated cows, street urchins, hawkers peddling books and magazines, and motorcycles making a path through the stationary traffic. The lights changed, the traffic slowly started up again, and Ajay drove unblinkingly on.

We selected a new camera at the store. 'Money from the sale of the cars should hopefully come through soon,' I told him, thinking he brought me with him to pressurise me into prioritising his purchase. 'And when it does, your camera and a new printer will be the first items on our list.'

Ajay was looking at me, shaking his head and smiling. He picked up the camera we had selected, telling the salesman the choice had been made. The salesman, who had been listening morosely to my talk about not affording purchases, broke into a delighted smile. 'Yes, Sir,' he said, acting with greater vigour than he had displayed throughout the sales process. The camera was placed into its packaging, the case was taken out and examined, and as I worried about how to tell Ajay we didn't have money for the purchase, he held his credit card out to the beaming salesman.

'No,' I told him. 'We'll get it. Just not now.'

'Don't worry about it,' he told me. 'The last camera was mine too. I am simply replacing it.'

'But…'

'No buts,' he maintained, 'if you fire me, I will take my camera with me. I may be soft, but I'm not that soft.'

I returned home to find an email from Raja Singh. Ajay was still with me, perched at the edge of my desk in the library, and as I exclaimed, he leant over to see if all was well. It was just the two of us in the room, and I nodded towards the computer screen.

He read the email and whistled. 'I've never received an email from the great man in all the years I've been in the business.'

'I contacted him first,' I told Ajay. 'He told me that I could get in touch with him if I was ever in need, and I thought this was as good a time as any.'

Ajay whistled again, emitting a smooth, low sound through his lips, and I added defensively, 'The magazine has been getting good coverage. I figured he might be interested in investing in us.'

He smiled then, leaning back to look at me. 'Does Maya know about this?'

'No,' I said, reading the email again. Raja had invited me to a meeting at his offices. 'I don't want to get her hopes up.'

'I'll come with you.'

'There's no need,' I replied. The email had only mentioned me, and I knew my best chance lay in appealing to the editor's nostalgia about Ma. Ajay's presence would alter the dynamic.

Ajay was studying me carefully, as if mulling his next words. 'He's got a reputation, you know.'

'Come on,' I said, surprised by his chauvinistic attitude. I wasn't a cossetted little doll to be placed under lock and key. 'I'm quite able to take care of myself.'

'Let me drive you, at least.'

'Pradeep can take me.'

Ajay looked over the email again, tutting with disappointment. 'The garage owner is coming tomorrow, isn't he?'

I nodded, frowning.

'Pradeep had better stay put here,' Ajay said in a matter-of-fact voice. He checked the calendar on his phone. 'Your meeting is just after two in the afternoon. I'll drive you there on my way to the gym.'

'Ajay…'

'Yes,' he said, nodding rapidly. 'That's the best plan. Means no one is wasting any time.'

XXIV

Ajay was on time. He arrived before midday, and didn't complain about being hungry, and as Maya laughed, telling him she wished he had shown such dedication while the magazine was operational, he smiled. 'I'm starting my New Year's resolution to go to the gym.'

'New Year's resolution,' burst out one, while another laughed at the idea of Ajay, so habitually supine, working out.

'I know, I know,' he maintained, holding his hands up, 'I'm a bit late in my execution. But like they say, better late than never.' He parried Sonia's laughter, and Maya's too, and when the time came for me to set off for my meeting, he was waiting.

We drove in silence. Ajay had tried to talk early on in our drive, asking me if I was sure I wanted to go in alone, and as I insisted on seeing Raja Singh by myself, he turned silent. He switched the radio on and then off, he waved off beggars with an unaccustomed briskness, and he drove so slowly I was certain I would be late.

Once we reached, he asked again if he could come in with me.

'Come on,' I complained, 'we've discussed this before.'

He shrugged then, as if it didn't much matter to him. 'I have to be getting off anyway,' he said, turning to his watch, and I found myself hurrying out of the car.

'Thanks for the lift,' I said, a bit put off by his manner, but he had already reversed out of his spot and was moving towards the road. I straightened my clothes out and patted my bag, feeling its outlines for the present I carried. It was a Mont Blanc pen, a gift Ma had once received and so treasured that she had never lifted it out of its case. I had thought twice about presenting it to Raja Singh, but was mindful of Ma's constant reminder; 'Don't go anywhere empty handed.'

I had thought of taking a bouquet of flowers, but had thought it inappropriate for a business meeting. Thoughts of an alcoholic present—scotch or a bottle of wine—were similarly squashed, but then I thought of the pen Ma could never bear to use. Here was a man of letters, and one who I looked to lift us out of our trouble. I got up from my desk and went to the almirah in Ma's room, where the pen remained, behind Ma's collection of dupattas. I squatted, feeling behind the gauzy material until I came across a harder surface, the smooth, firm black box that sheathed Ma's Mont Blanc.

I would rather have consulted Maya, but my mind was set on bringing a solution to her. She had reacted to the fire with a phlegmatic indifference I had forgotten. Maya had changed in the months since the launch of the magazine. Gone was Ma's satellite, so afraid of change or of uncertainty, and I wanted desperately to present her with Raja Singh's offer of investment, or with news of whatever door he was prepared to open for us, as a fait accompli.

The Mont Blanc pen, then, had been selected. I patted it through my bag, looking around. Ajay was long gone, and the compound was starting to fill up. It was a tall building, and I assumed it housed several offices, and one by one, I saw people on cars, motorcycles, scooters, and even the occasional pedestrian file past me and through the glass doors set atop a shallow set of stairs. No one stopped to ask me if I needed any directions, and I followed the stream of people as they went up the stairs.

~

I waited at the reception for an age. The first person I spoke to, a bored looking, over-manicured woman in her early twenties, nodded listlessly as I told her I had an appointment with Raja Singh, and asked me to take a seat. It appeared she had recently painted her nails, as she kept blowing on them and waving her hands in the air to help the paint dry. If she placed a call or sent a message announcing my arrival, I didn't see it.

After a while, she sighed theatrically and rose. She surveyed the waiting area with disdain before turning her back and walking off into the interior of the building. A man replaced her, and I quickly rose to ask him about my appointment.

'Yes,' he responded when I asked if I had to wait much longer. 'Let me see.' He twirled his moustache officiously and asked who I had come to see.

'Raja Singh.'

The man's demeanour changed instantly. 'Mr Singh!' he cried, bobbing his head furiously. 'Why didn't you tell me before? You should never have been kept waiting.' He stabbed at some keys on the computer in front of him and rose. 'This way please,' he said, leading me to a set of lifts. 'Singh Sir is expecting you.'

~

I rode up to a reception area, where I expected another long wait. I patted my bag, feeling for the pen, wishing I had some anecdote to recount. Raja Singh and Ma had been good friends, apparently, but I had had no knowledge of their interaction, and I had had no knowledge of Ma having launched *The Satirist*. I smiled at the receptionist, who rose at my arrival. 'Miss Sharma?' she asked, and as I nodded, she reached out towards me. 'Follow me, please,' she instructed in cool tones. 'Mr Singh is expecting you.'

Raja Singh was on the phone. The receptionist let me in and left the room, shutting the door behind her. I surveyed the office, which was large and bright. There was a floor to ceiling window at one end of the room, a big wooden desk situated against a perpendicular wall to take advantage of the views over the Delhi skyline, and two seats on the opposite side of the desk. I considered seating myself opposite Raja, but worried about appearing forward. There was a large, low leather sofa nearer where I stood, but I decided against seating myself there for fear of appearing unprofessional.

I looked again at Raja, who gave no indication of having noticed me. He laughed out loud, throwing his head back, and I wondered if it made sense to clear my throat or cough to attract his attention. 'Send her over, by all means,' he was saying in his booming voice, his tone generous and expansive and full of promise, and I inched forward in the hope that my motion would attract his attention.

It didn't. He laughed again at something the person at the other end said, and repeated, 'No, no, it's no problem really. I'll be glad to help,' and as he shook his head in time with his speech, he looked to the left and saw me.

The call was over in a moment, and Raja Singh was up on his feet. 'The girl of the moment!' he exclaimed loudly, coming round to where I stood, and I knew he'd forgotten my name.

'Siya Sharma,' I said, and he nodded. 'It's so good to meet you, Sir.'

'Likewise,' he said, 'Siya Sharma,' and as I put my hand out to shake his, he put an arm around me, 'Siya Sharma,' he said again, and directed me to the leather sofa at the other end of the office. 'Sit,' he sat, patting my shoulder. 'Sit down, Siya Sharma,' and as I sat down, landing too hard and too low on the soft leather, he asked me if I wanted a drink.

I looked around. There was no cafetière in sight. 'Some water, please.'

He looked at me with a smile I couldn't decipher and walked to a table in the corner, where he poured water into a heavy-bottomed crystal glass. He handed this to me and said, 'I'm going to fix myself my afternoon scotch. Will you join me?'

I checked my watch as he observed me. It was a little after two, just past lunch. I shook my head, and his smile widened. 'Suit yourself,' he said, wandering back to the table, preparing his drink. His back was turned towards me, and I observed him as he worked. He was of middling height, and slight of build, but power radiated off him. It was hard to pinpoint, but it went beyond his well-cut suit and exquisite leather shoes. He smelt expensive too; of cologne liberally applied and of a daily massage in the morning. He turned back towards me with a smile, and I knew he had his teeth whitened and that he applied lip salve. His hands were perfectly manicured, his nails short, his cuticles gleaming, and I thought to myself that this was a vain man.

'Well, Siya Sharma,' he said as he sat down. For all his being a near neighbour, this was our first real interaction. Everything before had been noise and tumult, a brief word spoken of a morning, and this was my first real opportunity to get a measure of the man. He took a sip of his drink before resting it on a glass coaster and moved closer to me. I could smell his breath, the whisky on his tongue, and the cologne on his face, and I leant back a bit. He took another sip, setting his drink down carefully, and moved an inch closer. I started. 'Now tell me, Siya Sharma,' he said, 'what brings you here on this balmy afternoon?'

'Sir,' I said. He smiled, putting his arm across the sofa's back such that his hand fell around my shoulder. I twisted around, resting my back against the sofa's armrest, but returned his smile. This felt unnatural. I tried to think of the email I had sent to him. I had thought myself professional in my message to him. Friendly, of course, but there had been nothing in my language that could have misled him. And he had heard of the fire, surely. But then, I considered, as he looked expectantly at me, perhaps I was being prudish. He had embraced his old friend's daughter, had fixed himself a drink and had sat down next to me. I was making too much of this. I blinked, thinking of how I could bring the conversation around to the topic of the magazine, when he patted my knee.

'I forgot,' he said, patting my knee once, then again, then giving it a meaty squeeze. I told myself once more that I was reading too much into his actions, and he continued, 'How talented a journalist your mother was.'

'Sir,' I said. I squirmed, despite myself, moving my legs away from his hold, leaning forward to take a sip of water.

'Rupa,' he was saying in that deep voice of his, speaking the name out softly, sensuously almost, and though I smiled, I willed him to stop. Was there a hint of knowledge in his eyes?

A hint of male appreciation? I shook my head. I was imagining things. Raja Singh was clearly inappropriate, handsy in a way older men sometimes were, but that was it. I just had to deal with him and make my case for *The Satirist*. He was harmless, surely, and I wasn't to read too much into his overtures.

'She was a beautiful woman, your mother,' he said, and I nodded. 'Beautiful, and talented too.' He looked at me appraisingly. 'Tell me,' he asked, 'do you write as well as she did?'

'No, sir,' I replied. 'I don't really write. It's my sister Maya who has inherited Ma's talent.'

'Yes,' he nodded thoughtfully. He took a deep draught of his drink and opened his mouth. The smell of the whisky reached me. 'I've read some of her work,' and then, returning to his earlier topic, he said, 'your mother really was something.'

There it was again, the hint of something lascivious, and I screwed my eyes shut. It was all in my mind, this needling suspicion, and I had to focus. 'If I remember correctly,' he was saying. I smelt the whisky on his breath and moved a touch away. 'If I remember correctly,' he repeated, his words blending slightly into one another, 'she was working on launching a magazine too.'

'Yes,' I replied.

'It had such promise, that magazine,' he said. 'Its name is on my tongue.' He clapped himself on his thigh, and I wondered if it was a compulsive habit, the constant contact with flesh. His voice sparked with gravel. 'What *was* its name?'

'*The Satirist*,' I said, preparing to tell him that we had adopted the name for our own publication, when he spoke again.

'Of course,' he said in his deep, lofty voice, '*The Satirist*.'

There it was again, the familiar, knowing lilt to his voice, followed by the words that rooted me to the spot. 'That it never raised funding fills me with endless regret.'

He took another sip of his drink, and then another, draining his glass, setting it down with delicacy and precision in its place. He looked at me with a disarming grin, and though I nodded, I felt the blood rushing to my head. He spoke again, evidently asking me a question, as he paused and looked at me, but I could hear nothing. It was suffusing my senses, pounding in my head, the blood, the rush, until I felt certain I was about to faint. 'Siya,' Raja Singh was saying, 'Siya Sharma?' He lifted my glass of water to my mouth, and I took a deep sip. I coughed, I spluttered as he slapped me on my back, and I rose quickly. 'Siya,' he was saying, perplexed, and I turned around and ran out of the room.

I stumbled out of the building, past Raja's cool faced secretary, past the man who had conducted me to the lift and past the woman who continued to blow on her nails. Once outdoors, I stood blinking in the sunlight. I heard some noise in the reception. I worried that Raja had followed me and hurried down the stairs.

The sun was suddenly blinding, the heat oppressive, and I felt my vision blur. The world grew dark, and I walked blindly forward, breathing heavily, taking in huge gulps of air as if to rid myself of all traces of my encounter. I felt myself sway, nearly walking into a standing motorbike before righting myself. It was impossible what Raja Singh said, and yet there had been a knowing look in his eyes, and I was sure I hadn't misheard. The heat rose and I lurched.

'Siya?'

I walked on.

'Siya?' came the call, and as I continued ahead, I felt a heavy hand on my arm.

'No,' I said, shaking the hand off, but it remained in place.

'Siya,' came the voice again, and all at once I heard Ajay's worried voice, and turned to see him looking at me with concern. 'Siya,' he said gently, taking me by the arm and leading me to the car.

I laughed. 'What are you doing here?'

'Are you alright?' He asked, and as I smiled, he said, 'Really, you look awful.'

'I'm fine,' I said, as he squatted by me. I saw the dust on the ground, was sure his khaki trousers were getting filthy, but I didn't say a thing. I looked at him, so worried, his forehead creased, and registered that I appeared shaken. I didn't say anything, not then, not as he asked me what had happened, not as he asked me if Raja Singh had harmed me in any way.

XXV

We sat in the car park outside Raja Singh's office for an age. Ajay had switched the car on, preparing to drive, and as the air-conditioning had flared into life, the car's music system started up too. A loud Hindi number was playing on the radio, a catchy piece that had been played at all the wedding celebrations the previous year, and as the singer began to croon about her milky wrists, Ajay hurried to turn the volume off.

'Siya,' he said, his voice low.

'Let's go.' I didn't look in his direction, staring instead in front of me as office workers filed past us. My hands were on my lap, I was conscious of Ajay's eyes on me, and I began to snap my fingers to the rhythm of the song that had just been playing.

'Siya, did he…'

I switched the radio back on, and the final refrain of the song burst into the car. Ajay switched it off and I laughed. 'It's a silly song, anyway,' he complained. 'Imagine singing an ode to your wrists.'

'You have to feel for the songwriter,' I replied. 'Everything else has already been written about.'

'Siya.'

'There's nothing to say.'

'Siya.'

I could laugh again. He was as predictable as the song, his

response as unvarying. He leant towards me, reaching out to touch my hand, and I said, 'Let's drive.' He stared at me for a moment or more. I suppose he was trying to gauge my mood. 'That Raja Singh,' he began, and then, as I didn't respond, 'I never should have let you…'

The office complex's door opened, and we saw Raja Singh stride out. He didn't look around, and was quickly ushered into a waiting car. Off he drove, and I said to Ajay, 'Please, Ajay, please let's just go.'

He looked like he wanted to argue, but one look at my face convinced him otherwise. He started up the car, and we joined Delhi's gridlocked streets. Raja's car was right in front of us, his pomaded hair brilliant in the sun, and I slunk low in my seat. Ajay looked my way again, and before he could speak, I said, 'Just drive.'

He pointed towards the jam in front. 'What happened, Siya?'

I turned the radio on, feeling my petulance. There was a caller on the radio, speaking about wanting to break up with her boyfriend, and I turned the sound off.

'What happened?'

'Nothing.'

Ajay's grip on the steering wheel tightened. 'Did he do anything?'

'No,' I said. I thought back to our time together, the early drink, the insistence on sitting together on the low sofa. 'No,' I said again, more resolutely this time. I could tell him we had spoken about Ma, and that he had repeated a phrase I had read, but I didn't know if I would implicate Ma by doing so. He was looking at me, Ajay, and I said, 'We largely spoke about Ma.'

'But…'

The traffic light changed, Raja's car surged ahead, and we

joined the traffic flowing north. I turned the radio's volume up again to avoid conversation, and though Ajay tried to talk a couple of times, I didn't respond. I sang along to the music, and though I knew my lack of communication frustrated him, he didn't try to force the issue.

My phone buzzed as we left the car. It was an email from Raja Singh: *You left abruptly, and I hope you weren't taken ill. We didn't finish our discussion, and as I have already told you, I am happy to support Rupa's children in any way I can. Let me know if you want to reschedule our meeting. R.*

I had wanted to discuss my afternoon with Tasha-di, but now I vacillated. What if I had imagined Raja Singh's aggression? What if his actions had been as his email implied; benign and interested? I avoided Ajay, avoided my sister, disappearing instead inside my room, where I paced the floor. I studied Raja Singh's email: *I am happy to support Rupa's children in any way I can.*

And he had been supportive. He had been kind and welcoming and solicitous, but then, as I told myself that my discomfort was imagined, I paused. I looked out of my window, where I had so often spied a Raja Singh on his morning walk. He had sat by me, close, too close, had placed his hands on my knee when there had been no call to do so. He had leaned in, he had presumed on an intimacy that didn't exist. I studied the email again: *Let me know if you want to reschedule*, and recoiled. I thought of the words he had spoken: *That it never raised funding fills me with endless regret.* How sincere he had seemed, how distraught at the idea of Ma's failure. And all while he rested his hand on my knee. I shook my head and threw my phone into my bag.

No, Raja Singh, no. His words sounded heartfelt, they sounded plaintive, but there was no denying their artifice. There was no truth in them, no real substance, and there was no end to them barring his own selfish interest.

Back downstairs, I took Tasha-di aside and told her about my meeting with Raja Singh, asking her if he had been Ma's benefactor.

We were in the garden room, the scene of so many of the two ladies' evening sessions. Tasha-di fingered the fringe of her dupatta as I spoke, her face impassive, her eyes fixed on me. She didn't interrupt me, didn't react to my story, but then said, 'Darling, I wish you hadn't gone to see that man.'

'Was he Ma's benefactor?'

Another oblique response followed. 'Was he civil with you?' She knitted her brows, and I saw she was trying to worry out the right words. 'Was he respectful?'

This I took to be much the same question as Ajay's, and my discomfort rose. The rushed words of the letter I had found swam before me: *That you considered my conduct overfamiliar fills me with endless regret*. Had this been what Tasha-di alluded to by asking about a breakdown in civility? A hysterical note entered my voice, 'Tasha-di,' I called out. 'Please tell me.'

'Beta…'

'Was Raja Singh the man who wrote Ma those letters?'

'Beta,' she repeated, neither a confirmation nor a denial.

I rose from the bamboo armchair, pacing the worn floor of the room. 'Beta,' called Tasha-di in a plaintive voice.

'Enough,' I said, my voice rising. 'I've had it with all this hand-wringing, Tasha-di, and with all this beta, beta, beta.' She looked like she'd been stabbed, and I rounded back to where she sat, 'I want to know what passed between Ma and this man.'

Evening had crept in around us, and the room was beginning to grow dark. I could have switched on a light in a second, but I didn't want to move, and Tasha-di was finally beginning to talk. I sat by her feet as she cleared her throat. The other two were upstairs, and I worried an interruption might break Tasha-di's flow, but she spoke in a low, still voice, 'I didn't really know Raja Singh. He was an acquaintance of your Ma's from her college days. Your Ma was an impressive journalist and Raja...' She grimaced. 'Raja, of course, was starting to emerge as a business superstar.' She paused. 'He had magic in his fingers; anything he touched turned to gold.' Mrs Bhatnagar had said the same thing, and now Tasha-di added, 'He was fearless, that man. He saw India changing as the economy was liberalised. He sensed that consumption would rise, and the new precious commodity would be access. He poured money into India TV when only the national broadcaster existed. He put money into online magazines before the internet really took off.' She paused. 'He had true vision, that man. He became synonymous with the Indian growth story.'

She was talking about Raja Singh as if he was the one who had died. 'They say excellence breeds excellence,' Tasha-di was saying. 'The people he invested in rose to prominence over the next few decades, and when your Ma thought to launch *The Satirist*, he was the obvious person for her to approach.'

She fell silent. Her fingers were working the fringe of her dupatta, running from one end of the cloth to the other. I worried that the edge would fray, but she seemed consumed by the task, and as the dark grew around us, I heard her above me, her hands busy with her cloth.

I heard footsteps approach and turned to see Maya switch on the lights. 'What are you two doing in this gloom?' she scolded. She laughed to see us so strangely positioned, then as we both continued solemn, asked if all was well.

'Siya went to see Raja Singh at his office today,' Tasha-di said, and Maya came to sit by her side. She sat with her hands neatly arranged on her lap, her head cocked a little, just as she had as a child in readiness for a story. 'Siya,' continued Tasha-di, 'asked me if it had been Raja's letters you girls had found among your mother's things.'

Maya's lips parted in anticipation.

'And?' I asked.

Tasha-di didn't answer me. 'I was telling Siya,' she said, 'about how brilliant Raja Singh is.'

'I know that,' said Maya quietly.

'I was telling her,' Tasha-di ploughed on, 'about how he has always been two steps ahead of the Indian consumer.'

'Tasha-di…'

She looked at me, bit her lips and nodded. 'Ok,' she said. 'Ok. Those *were* Raja Singh's letters you found. It *was* he who agreed to fund the magazine.' She looked at the both of us again. 'It was he who set us up, finding us our office, introducing us to suppliers and printers and sponsors. He was like a Godfather to us…' Tasha-di trailed off, though her head continued to bob gently, like a baby in a rocker, or like one of the dancing hula toys in Maya's car.

'Tasha-di,' I said. 'I want to know what happened between them.'

Maya was silent, her eyes on our aunt's face. Her hands were still neatly placed on top of each other on her lap, her position unchanged from when she had first sat down, and it seemed to me that she hadn't moved, hadn't played with her hair, hadn't scratched herself, hadn't rearranged herself, hadn't so much as breathed for fear of disturbing Tasha-di's flow. She didn't speak now, but her lips parted, and I turned to look at our aunt.

'I'm coming to that,' she said unwillingly. 'It all looked so good at the start. Raja Singh loved the concept of *The Satirist* and the idea of a woman-led team. He said it was just the thing India needed.' Once more she fell silent. There was a rustle at the door, a footstep or a shadow of one, and we all looked in its direction. I moved towards the door, but there was no further noise, and I paused for a while. Tasha-di had cleared her throat, and I was fearful of missing her testimony. There was no further noise, no door opened, and at length I returned to the armchairs and perched myself on my sister's armrest.

'It all,' Tasha-di was saying, 'looked absolutely perfect. We had funding from Raja Singh, we had our team of journalists, and we had our cover. Our layout—,' she pointed up, and to Maya's room where Ma's layouts rested—'was finalised, and it seemed our dreams were finally coming true. A few days before the launch...' Here again Tasha-di paused, wrestling with her memory. Maya didn't speak, and as I leant forward in my impatience, I noticed my mouth was parted. 'About a week before our launch,' Tasha-di continued, 'Raja called your mother into his office for a meeting.'

Another pause, another refusal to look up or around. 'She was gone a couple of hours. Yes,' she said, 'a couple of hours at the most.' I expected her to furnish details of what had transpired at the meeting, but she began to speak about the time Ma had been away. 'I'd initially thought she would call me once she was back, but I was so excited about the launch that I returned here in the evening. Your Ma had been gone an hour by this point, and I expected her back at any moment. Your father was away on business, and you girls…' Tasha-di smiled. 'Do you remember that time, girls? I'd come in, and it was just the three of us until you had to go off to bed?'

Maya shook her head noncommittally. It was such a regular occurrence, Tasha-di's presence in our home that it would have been hard for us to pinpoint any one occasion. She was as constant as daybreak, and to our ungrateful memories, as unremarkable.

'Well,' Tasha-di said, 'Anyway. After you girls were taken away, I sat here.' She pointed to the seat Maya and I occupied, 'And I waited.'

There was a knock on the door and Shanti popped her head around the door. 'I wanted to see if you wanted anything.'

We shook our heads, and Tasha-di burst out laughing at Shanti's retreat. 'It was just like this on that evening too. Shanti checking up on me every so often, and your mother…' Here she smiled at me, and I rose. Tasha-di's recounting had been unbearable. Her digressions had been endless, but worse still were the details she was now beginning to provide. The thought of Ma, of my mother alone with Raja Singh in his office was revolting. I had been there, right next to his whisky smelling breath a few hours ago, and the thought that my defeated, inward looking mother had suffered a similar fate was unthinkable.

Maya spoke now. 'What happened, Tasha-di?'

The older woman nodded. 'She returned after a couple of hours. She was surprised, I think, to find me here, as she initially sat in the hallway on one of your leather armchairs and only came in here to turn out the lights.' She nodded, as if buying time, as if weighing her words, as if she knew her account would change the way we viewed our mother forever. There was another long pause as Tasha-di consulted her memory. 'I forget too, but there was no hiding her distress. Her hair was dishevelled, her breathing ragged, and all I could get out of her for the longest time was that Raja had made a move on her.'

This was all alien to me. The idea of Ma in disarray, the vocabulary Tasha-di was using; this was all from a set, from the imagination, and not from any life Ma or her dearest friend could ever have known. And yet, there Raja Singh had been earlier in the day, reminiscing about Ma and about their relationship, shuffling closer to me until I had nowhere to move. Ma, so protected, so cherished, would never have been able to deal with an onslaught like that. 'He,' I asked, 'tried it on with her?'

Tasha-di swallowed. 'I don't know the details. But he didn't behave properly with her.'

This could have been a lunge or an attempted kiss or an arm around Ma. This could have been anything or nothing, but Maya was up, pacing the floor, her hands cupping her face. 'I never knew,' she said, 'I never knew.'

Tasha-di was nodding. 'She always tried to protect you girls,' and all at once the pieces fell into place. Ma's aversion to boyfriends, her resistance to our travelling outside India for our studies. Her furies, her irrationality, her eventual shrivelling into herself.

'I never knew,' Maya was saying, and I could see it playing out in her mind. Maya, who had never taken a risk, who had given up a boyfriend to avoid offending her mother, who had never stepped out of line, now thought of her mother alone in a predator's office. 'But,' she said as a new thought struck her, 'Raja Singh is such an icon.'

'Yes,' agreed Tasha-di, 'he's such an icon.'

Maya came to sit on the armchair, but continued to cup her face. She didn't speak, nor did I, but Tasha-di seemed to have unlocked some great reservoir that she had held within her for years. 'That was the problem, if I think about it. He was such an icon, and he had to remain an icon. The incident would have blown over if your mother had let it…'

Maya gasped. 'She should have let him…'

'No!' exclaimed Tasha-di. 'Not that. Never that. But he was her funder, he was her mentor, and her reaction—to threaten exposure…' She stopped talking, and for the first time that evening I sensed her agitation. Her words played through my mind—*her mentor, her funder*—and I thought of the Raja Singh I had encountered earlier in the day, so suave, so warm, so generous, and so, so close.

It occurred to me that she didn't know the details of what had taken place. She had never stepped inside his office, had possibly never even interacted with him for any real length of time. She was not to know the power of the man, or the constant oppressive nearness of him. Perhaps she thought it was merely an ill-conceived compliment, a presumption of interest, a misunderstanding that Ma had overreacted to. She had lost out too as Ma's dreams ebbed away.

'I'm not explaining myself very well,' she resumed cautiously. 'Of course what happened that night was abhorrent.' She winced, and I sensed her next words, 'But still.'

I got up and looked at Maya. She was still up, still pacing the floor, and now she paused at Tasha-di's words. 'But still?'

'The man made a mistake. He apologised for it.' I watched as Maya stared at Tasha-di. Tasha-di blinked. 'He wrote to apologise for it, Maya.' Maya guffawed, and Tasha-di shook her head sadly. 'It was a bad, bad business, but what did your Ma get out of her heroics?'

'Ma's heroics?' Maya spluttered. She opened her mouth to speak further, then clamped it firmly shut, and turning on her heels, hurried from the room.

'She's just like her mother,' said Tasha-di sadly. 'So emotional, so ready with the grand gestures, but really, where does it leave them?'

I thought of Ma and Maya and the regime of silence they had instituted. We hadn't spoken for years, and I had been left in no doubt that my departure had disappointed them. But what had it gotten them, that decade or more of glorious isolation? That puritanical rigidity of thought. They remained ideologically pure, sure, but alone too, cocooning themselves in their crumbling house.

'She never paused to consider,' Tasha-di was carrying on, 'what all was at stake. She never bothered to think that there was another way. That she could refuse Raja's advances without rupturing ties, that she could launch the magazine, and then, when she was established, when she was a credible force, then she could effect change. No, no, she didn't bother to think before she acted, she had to have her one principled stand, and so, in the end, she simply faded into the furnishings.'

My head hurt. All the events of the day were still fresh; Raja Singh's oily presence, Ajay's kindness, Tasha-di's revelation, and I wasn't nearly ready to begin to make sense of them. And then to hear Tasha-di speak as she just had, so critically of poor Ma's actions hit me with all the force of a body blow. What else was Ma to have done? I still wasn't sure what exactly had taken place that evening between her and Raja Singh, but I had no doubt about Raja Singh having been capable of aggression, and yes, as

I paused to think of it, of more. He would have tried seduction, that and coercion, he would have stooped to blackmail: all of these were within the realms of possibility. All of these things could have happened to my mother, but for Tasha-di to turn a stony face to her best and truest friend seemed inconceivable. And yet, there she sat, her fingers firm on the fringes of her dupatta, neither looking at me nor looking to soften her stance.

'Siya…'

The door opened, and I turned gratefully in its direction. It was Ajay, who was leaving. 'I just wanted to check,' he began, and noting Tasha-di's eyes on him, he said, 'if you needed anything.'

I rose and walked to him. 'Nothing,' I replied, 'but I'll walk you out.'

XXVI

Conversation was stilted. We all ate in our rooms that evening, and if Shanti had overheard our conversation, she didn't mention it. The next morning, Maya rose and went for her walk without checking in on me. I didn't remain in the upstairs lounge, but went straight down to the office, where I found a contrite looking Tasha-di who rose upon my approach. I saw she was slower in her movements. Her arthritic knee was giving her trouble with the change in the weather, and she appeared to have slept badly. Her face was pouchy, her hair uncombed, and still I turned away as I saw her.

'Please,' she said plaintively. 'Please, Siya, I expressed myself badly.'

Maya had returned from her walk, and perhaps wishing to be alone, had come into the office. She saw Tasha-di and me together, and turned to leave. 'Please,' Tasha-di repeated, 'it breaks my heart that I hurt the two of you last evening. I who should have been there for you. I who lived through everything, and who held your mother's hand through all her pain.'

Maya let out a peal at this.

'No, no, I mean it,' insisted Tasha-di. 'We went along with all your Ma wanted. We shut the magazine down, we cut off all links with Raja Singh.'

'Ma never worked again,' Maya returned.

'No,' agreed Tasha-di. 'No she didn't. But it's not all black and…' She saw the hostility on my sister's face and stopped. She returned to her seat and arranged her clothes, carefully smoothing her tunic over her lap. 'Your mother never worked again,' she said in a soft, composed voice, 'but the rest of our team lost their dream too. I lost out too.'

Maya was on the point of walking out. She turned to stalk out of the door, returned with an unarticulated barb then turned to leave again, before she finally came back in and shut the door behind her. She walked to Tasha-di, who was watching her with a curious passiveness, without judgement and without expectation. Maya hugged her, bending awkwardly over the older woman. 'Sit,' Tasha-di said thickly. 'That silly man has upended everything once again.'

Maya sat, not next to Tasha-di, but on an armchair facing her. I remained where I was standing, uncertain how long our thaw was going to last when my sister began to speak. 'I'm not a heroic woman,' she said in a limpid voice. There was a denial on my lips, but she held her hand up, and I sat down next to Tasha-di. 'No, really,' she was repeating, to give herself courage as much as to underscore her point, 'I don't have my mother's drive or her imagination. I don't have my sister's courage,' and here she looked at me with a gaze that was half affection and half exasperation, 'or her sheer bloody-mindedness. No,' she said, smiling to herself, nodding a little, 'I've always occupied a smaller space. I was the quiet child, in awe of the brilliant people around me,' and I was ready with a dozen rebuttals, examples of when I had looked up to my older sister, but she was shaking her head. Anything I said now, any tenderness I offered would be no more than the kindness offered to a child who had lost a favourite toy.

'Always in awe,' she was saying, 'but happy with my own more compact footprint.'

'No...'

She smiled, and her voice rang out over ours. 'And that's the key. I was content to be unexceptional. I wanted to be able to study, and then to work to the best of my abilities. But when it came to my studies, my brilliant, battle-scarred mother held me back and I didn't fight back. Somewhere in me, I remembered a vigorous Ma, and I was so protective of the shell she had become that I didn't dare oppose any stupid, paranoid thing she said.'

Tasha-di nodded sadly at this. 'It broke my heart...'

Maya was speaking over her. There was a briskness to her, an impatience, as if she had to finish her monologue and interruptions were not to be tolerated. 'Her fears became mine, and slowly, I turned inwards as she had done.' She looked at me, and the smile returned, at once loving and frustrated. 'Siya wasn't the same, though. She refused to accept the boundaries Ma tried to bind us by. She was rude and unpleasant and stubborn and impossible, which Ma wouldn't tolerate, but my little sister charted her own path. We are told so often to stay within our bounds, to not question authority, to follow tradition, to not disobey our elders...'

Maya paused, and I held my breath. This was the first hint I had heard of Maya's dissatisfaction with Ma. Tasha-di was up on her feet, but my sister shrugged.

'It's alright,' she said, smiling her small, sad smile. 'It really is,' and then, after a look around the room, she shook her head. The revelations of the previous evening were fresh in her head,

I could tell. She felt guilt too, for the anger she had felt at Ma's authoritarianism, the mutinies she'd contemplated, the teenage tantrums she had thrown. I saw her smile splinter, wavering and faltering before us, and I was by her side, hugging her, trying hard to make my quiet, unobtrusive big sister forget her hurt.

She was shaking now, shuddering against me, pushing me away. 'I've always,' she was saying, 'tried to do the right thing. I stayed at home, I took care of Ma as she aged.'

Maya was nodding. 'I'm fine now,' she said to me in her quiet voice, and I returned to my seat. 'I *am* fine. I have remained safe. I haven't been assaulted. I haven't been raped. I haven't been discriminated against.' Tasha-di was shaking her head sadly, and Maya laughed a joyless laugh. 'But I find I've had to pay the price for all of Ma's disappointments. I'm sorry Tasha-di that your business didn't work out.' Tasha-di was shaking her head, shrinking back into her seat, and Maya said, 'No, I really am. Who would understand a loss imposed by Ma if not me?'

Tasha-di was sobbing, she was up and by Maya's side and holding her, and my sister was smiling bravely. I thought of the spurned scholarship, and of a rejected Kunal. I thought of the children Kunal had had and that my sister never would. I thought of all the articles that had been turned down because Ma had fallen ill or had been in need. I could have been there. I should have been there to share the burden, but I would never have been able to be in Ma's house and breathe.

I looked at my sister, who was exhaling softly. I had thought her the favoured child, always loved, always close and precious, always consulted and petted and cherished, but I saw now how suffocating Ma's love was, and how it had limited Maya.

My sister had never been in search of a big life. She had

never courted the sun, but she had deserved some light of her own.

Raja Singh didn't disappear from our thoughts, but other problems came to dominate the day. The print store called with their usual monthly reminder; we would need to send in the next issue's proofs by the end of the week.

'End of the week!' Sonia laughed when she arrived at the office. 'Next issue!' She, in some ways, had been hit hardest by the fire. She had scaled back her commitment to *The Satirist* while her son sat his board exams, but had returned to work brimming with ideas. She had dreams of spin-off publications; magazines aimed at millennials, and others for students and for the global traveller. The fire represented for her the final, inalienable shattering of her deferred dreams. 'That's it,' she groaned loudly, her head hitting her desk, and Maya rushed to her side.

'Siya tried,' she began, 'she approached Raja Singh yesterday to try to interest him in investing in us.'

Sonia looked up at this. Ajay, who had been playing with his new camera, set it down and cast me a fleet look. He rose, as if to walk towards me before changing his mind. He remained by his desk, shuffling behind his chair, his hands dangling impotently by his side.

'And?' asked Sonia.

'And nothing,' replied my sister. 'That man…'

Ajay was moving in an instant, rounding the corner to where Maya was. 'I knew it,' he growled, 'that man's reputation. Why?' he added, turning to point at me. 'Your sister was shaking all the way back home.'

This was news to Maya, who came towards me. 'Did he try something with you too?'

'Too?' asked Sonia. 'Who all has he touched?'

I looked at Maya. Ma's life following her run-in with Raja Singh had been shrouded in secrecy, and neither of us knew how to broach the topic. This had been Ma's story, a topic so painful to her that she had retreated from the world and had tried to cloister her offspring, and we both shied away from the thought of uttering the words—rape, assault, harassment—even though we hardly knew which precise label applied.

'No, no,' I was saying, just as Maya said, 'Ma,' and we both fell silent. No one else spoke.

No questions were asked, partly because the others hadn't known Ma, and partly because her daughters' presence precluded them from forensic analysis. We didn't look at anyone, the daughters of the victim, feeling an unreasonable discomfort at her ordeal.

'Maya,' Sonia said at length, 'I'm so sorry. That man has a terrible reputation,' and as my sister didn't reply, she repeated limply, 'I'm so sorry.'

Maya looked straight at me. 'Did he try anything with you?'

'No,' I said, feeling pathetic. He had been too close, he had been inappropriate, but mercifully nothing else. Nothing worse. 'No,' I repeated as she stared. Ajay was looking our way, and I said again, 'He was a bit creepy, but he didn't so much as lay a finger on me.'

'Your poor mother,' Sonia was saying, 'your poor, poor mother.'

We sat in silence watching the room grow dark before Sonia thought to ask about the outcome of my meeting. 'What did Raja Singh say to you? Will he invest?'

I thought of my quick exit from the office. 'No,' I replied, and Sonia smiled bravely.

'It was always a long shot, I suppose. But,' she added, looking around at her desk. It was normally cluttered, full of post-it notes she stuck on every surface to remind herself of the trajectory of her articles, 'There's no point in fooling ourselves anymore.' There it was again, her brave nod, her maternal look conveying stoicism to a tremulous child. 'It was a worthy initiative, *The Satirist*, but there's no way we will be able to keep it going.'

'No,' I agreed. I'd run out of money. 'I,' I began, when Saloni interrupted.

'I'm sorry, Didi,' she said in her diffident manner, 'how much would it cost to print next month's magazine?'

Sonia emitted a brassy sound. 'Next issue, girl,' she hooted, 'we have no articles!'

'Still,' Saloni persisted. 'How much does it cost?'

I thought hard. 'Maybe we can use cheaper paper for one issue.' I tutted and hit my forehead with my palm. 'Of course we can't. This is to be the first proper paid issue.' I looked around the office; took in every worried face. 'We can't,' I said, shaking my head at Saloni. 'We can't afford to print. It's foolish to pretend we can bring another issue out.'

It was Saloni who came to our rescue. The very next morning, in she trudged, holding a pink satin envelope. It was luridly bright, luminescent with a blueish pearl-like tinge, like the envelopes of cash guests thrust into the bride's hands at weddings. This she proudly tucked into my hand, asking me to open it. Only Maya and I were downstairs, going to the office more out of routine than from any real purpose, and I looked at my sister as Saloni proudly nodded. I rose to see Pradeep in the doorway, his hands folded in greeting.

'What is this?' I asked, pretending to complain, but Saloni's excitement was infectious. The envelope bulged, but it was impossible. 'What is it, Saloni?'

'Just open it, Didi,' Saloni instructed, and I lifted the envelope's flap to find myself staring at a bundle of cash. I looked up at Maya, who had come to stand next to me. 'But,' I started, frowning, and then, 'how,' and 'why,' and as Saloni laughed to see my stupefied face, I finished with, 'but what even is this, Saloni?'

Saloni was engulfed in laughter and didn't reply. I looked to Pradeep, who blushed voicelessly at my scrutiny.

'I thought,' said Saloni, who was slowly regaining control over her features, 'that we had to get the new issue out. And we weren't going to let the magazine die for the sake of a few rupees. '

Maya had taken the envelope from my hand, and was totting up the notes. 'It's well over a hundred thousand,' she told me.

I was blubbering now, 'How did you even get this?'

'It's ours,' said the girl simply.

'Ours?' I asked, and Pradeep came into the room.

'I'm sorry, Didi,' he said, his hands clasped together. 'We wanted to help.'

'But…'

'Please, Didi,' pleaded Saloni, 'don't be angry,' and as I tried to worry out how the pair could think either of us angry about the gesture, she continued, 'we had some money saved up.'

The money they had saved up emerged to be the gifts they had received at their wedding and the money they had saved from their wages. It represented all the hopes the couple had intended to one day crystallise. 'Saloni!' I cried, registering my protest, and I sighed to see her wince.

'I'm sorry, Didi,' she said again, 'but I couldn't bear the thought of *The Satirist* shutting down for the sake of one issue. And this is the issue where we'll finally start to make money.' She blushed at the collective word. Saloni didn't look at me, continuing to speak as if to ward off a reprimand. 'You have done so much for all of us. And the magazine means so much to the both of you and, well,' here she looked up at her husband, and finally at me, 'it means a lot to Pradeep and me too.'

'Oh, Saloni.'

'Didi, there's nothing stopping us from publishing our next issue.'

I was taken by her enthusiasm, but Maya rang the dull note. 'Nothing, no,' she agreed, 'nothing but the copy.'

~

I returned the envelope to Saloni. We would use the last of my savings instead, and bolster the sum through our household budget. The house remained a problem, as did the garage, but Saloni's belief infected me. The magazine felt to be on the cusp of independence; it deserved a final push. 'The next time,' I said, 'you have a flash of genius, please discuss it with me. Imagine draining your savings for this.'

A call was placed to Sonia, who had emptied out her desk. 'We're in business,' Maya called, her voice ringing with delight. 'That funny, quiet, brilliant Saloni has saved the day!'

~

Our next stumbling block was the content of the magazine itself. All the sponsors had months left on their contracts, but we had no actual articles to populate the magazine with. I had an old article of Benjamin's that I hadn't used, and Puneeta could be relied on to turn something around quickly, but beyond that, there was nothing.

We were sitting in the garden room. Tea was drunk, the parlous state of the nation's politics was discussed, when Sonia suddenly said, 'I know what we can write,' and looking at Maya, she said. 'We can make your mother our lead story.'

'My mother?' Maya asked, and then, as if in need of clarification, she added, 'Ma?'

'Yes,' nodded Sonia. 'Your mother. She was a trailblazer. A woman journalist in a world where men have always wielded the pen. The person who first breathed life into *The Satirist*. We're going to tell her story, warts and all. We're going to sing her praises, talk of her failings, and we are not...' She looked around the room sternly, as if daring us to disagree, 'We are not going to shy away from the topic of her abuse.'

'I don't know,' hedged Maya.

'I have a daughter too,' said Sonia calmly. 'She's clever and passionate and idealistic and so keen to make the world a better place.' She paused. 'She has drive, that girl, and dreams, and I want to make sure there aren't any limits placed on her ability to achieve them.'

We nodded, all of us, my pragmatic aunt, my fatalistic sister, the banner-waving Ajay, and the die was cast. The next issue was to focus on Ma's story.

XXVII

Civil Lines hummed that rushed, frenzied week. We were always behind schedule. Ajay had to go out for shoots with a camera he was still getting to know. Sonia and Maya were busy with their lead story—Sonia focussing on Ma's career and Maya's feature dealing with the founding of *The Satirist* and Raja Singh's assault.

I had never seen Maya as involved in an article before. Her process was always an immersive one, and I had always thought her akin to a character actor when she wrote a profile or a social commentary. She seemed to inhabit the skin of her subject, appeared to feel their triumphs as equally their pains. In the case of the mother she had been both treasured and hemmed in by, her focus bordered on the obsessive. Always quick to empathise, in writing the story of Ma's life, she saw Raja Singh's attack as an assault on her freedoms too.

She woke early, she skipped meals, she seemed to forget how to make small talk. One day, I found her looming over my desk in the office. 'I've been thinking,' she said to me, 'we need to report the assault to the police.'

And it was I who now urged restraint, I who took her to the living room upstairs and poured her a glass of water. It was I who told her that the assault had taken place nearly two decades back, and that the police, never the most proactive in the first place, would be loathe to mount an action against a well-connected figure on behalf of a deceased woman. Maya shook her head. 'The letters, Siya,' she told me with a wild look in her eyes. 'The hope in the beginning, the plans, the articles planned. It was just like when we were setting up *The Satirist*. And then,' she gulped, gathering her breath and her thoughts. I lifted the glass of water to her lips, and she took in a deep draught. 'And then…' She trembled, shivering even though the room was hot. 'And then…' She shut her eyes, took in a deep breath. 'That letter, Siya, it ended everything.'

I sat down by her, putting my hand in hers. The loss had been hers too; the wounds hers as much as they had been Ma's. 'I know,' I told her, feeling useless. 'I know.'

I began to worry about the legal ramifications of Maya's article. We were potentially laying ourselves open to charges of libel, hearsay and defamation, and when I voiced my concerns, Sonia was quick to agree. 'Perhaps we should seek legal advice.'

Maya blushed. 'My aunt,' she said, her voice uncharacteristically indistinct, 'Kitty Bua is a lawyer.'

'That's great,' nodded Sonia. 'Is she a local?'

'No,' replied Maya, 'Well…'

I saw where this was headed. 'Kitty Bua,' I broke in, 'lives in Mumbai.'

'Oh,' said Sonia. 'Ok. Of course,' she said, casually, so matter-of-factly that I could almost believe the thought had just struck her, 'But you know that Kunal lives in Delhi, right?'

Maya didn't say a word. She didn't look up from her bare desk, and so it was left to me to respond. 'Kunal who?'

'You know,' she replied, nodding avidly, as if the act would spur my comprehension. 'He was at college with us…' She looked at Maya, but getting no encouragement, said, 'He was with Maya and me, and we all…' once again a look was cast at an unresponsive Maya, 'we all sort of hung out together.'

Maya spoke in a tremulous voice. 'You're in touch?'

'Yes,' Sonia said. 'He came along for the magazine's launch. I don't know if you saw him there.'

Maya shrugged, a something or a nothing, but her face burned up and I knew she was consumed with the thought of him. 'That's a great idea,' I told Sonia. 'We need honest advice, and it seems like your friend will be best able to provide it to us.'

'But Kitty Bua…'

'Kitty Bua,' I said firmly, 'is in Mumbai. There's no harm in contacting this Kunal guy.'

The die was cast, Kunal was called, and a meeting was arranged for the following morning. In the meantime, we proceeded as if the article were to pass muster. Drafts were written, Saloni's red pen ran ragged through them, edits were submitted, and still the magazine wasn't finalised. There was more clear space than I would have liked. I thought to contact Benjamin for another article when Ajay piped up. 'I can,' he suggested, 'put in a photo essay I've worked on. Homelessness in Delhi.'

This was such a surprise to all of us that the room burst out laughing. 'A photo-essay on homelessness?' I called, 'You?' and he shrugged.

'I had some free time,' he told me, but as I shuffled through the photos, a different story emerged. Ajay had been observing a young family living on the streets and had captured them through the seasons; surviving Delhi's harsh winter, huddling under plastic sheets during the monsoon deluge. The children grew in his photos, their hair bleaching with the sun and poor nutrition, the girl growing taller and more obsessed with grooming as the weather turned warmer.

'Do they know you're doing this?'

'Yes,' he said, offended. 'Of course. I'm not a stalker, you know. In fact,' he said, proudly, 'they were quite happy with the attention. They took me in, showed me their bags and all their contents. They gave me gram flour sweets on their birthday. They've become minor celebrities in their community with their own paparazzo.'

He spoke with a quiet pride I hadn't seen in his work before. 'This is good,' I said, and as he shook his head, I said, 'no really, it is. It belongs in the *National Geographic* or something like that. You sure you want to print it in a rag magazine like ours?'

'If you want it,' he said, as if it didn't much matter to him. Then he added under his breath, 'At least it means you won't have to run to that Benjamin fellow.'

The following morning, Maya woke earlier than me. This was par for the course; she had always been an early riser, and Ma's article had only made her more restless, but her energy felt frenzied this time. Her movements felt more staccato. There was a rushing around, the pulling open of wardrobe doors, the smell of perfume sprayed on wrists, and the sound of skittish footsteps taken on high heels.

By the time I ventured out into the first floor sitting room, Maya was ready. 'You didn't wake me up for my walk,' I complained blearily before I took a proper look at her. She was washed and clothed, even though it was before nine in the morning, and had worn a *salwar kameez*. Our usual attire for the mornings was tracksuits, though we usually changed into jeans for the office, and it was a revelation to see Maya in a freshly ironed salwar kameez, her dupatta trailing beneath her as she sat.

Neither of us wore salwar kameezes much when we were growing up; Ma's increasing insularity had meant we didn't socialise much. I hadn't seen Maya's outfit before, and wondered if it was one she had saved for special occasions. 'You didn't wake up, sleepy head,' she laughed, and I realised she was talking about our walk.

'But I didn't hear…' I pointed out, but she just carried on laughing, and I knew she was bent upon joy. There was a lightness to her voice, and a dewiness to her skin. Her hair felt at once fuller and more lustrous. The whites were still visible, but somehow, they didn't detract from her attractiveness. She looked girlish and skittish and radiant, so different from the haunted Maya I had seen over the past week, and I hoped, hoped beyond hope that Kunal was as anxious about our meeting that day.

Downstairs, Ajay whistled at Maya's apparel, but all else continued as normal. The final edits were made to the month's articles, and the layout was finalised. The fate of Maya's profile rested in Kunal's hands, though, and as I turned to my sister, I wasn't sure if she was more impatient for or anxious about his arrival.

When he did arrive, there was pandemonium. Maya shook his hand without looking at him, and Kunal burnt as if scalded by her touch. They didn't speak to each other, and Sonia and

I, their willing cupids, could do no more than stand like two gooseberries by their side, smiling encouragingly until we felt our cheeks would burst.

It was Tasha-di, in the end, who took matters forward. I wasn't sure if she was innocent of the history between the pair, or if she was simply focussed on the magazine's fate, but her briskness at least got us all off the hallway. 'We take our meetings in here,' she told Kunal, ushering him into the garden room. 'It's a strange little space,' she added, 'too hot in the summer and too cold in the winter, but it suits us.'

'It's lovely,' he replied. He spoke efficiently but politely, and was attentive to all that was said, but there was a sparseness to his speech that I liked.

We sat, then, and Maya's article was placed before Kunal. He winced as he saw the headline: *Raja Singh: The Emperor has no clothes*, but made no comment and carried on reading. He looked up once, studying the grills on the window facing the courtyard. His face whipped to where Maya stood. 'Was that what we could see…' he began, but catching our eyes on him, he trailed off. 'Right,' he said, putting his glasses back on. 'Well,' and he took up the magazine to peruse once more.

I felt a little for him. Here he was, surrounded by four others—Maya, Tasha-di, Sonia and me—and even if his intentions were innocent, and his purpose purely a courtesy, our hanging over him like he were so much carrion felt a little distasteful. I rose, telling the others I would organise tea and snacks, but as I moved towards the kitchen, I ran into Shanti straining against the garden room door.

'What are you doing?' I called, but she waved her dishcloth impatiently at me.

'Shh,' she commanded. There was a lull in the conversation,

and she pulled me to the kitchen. 'I recognised the boy,' Shanti told me accusingly. 'It's the same one who Maya baby used to meet in college, isn't it?'

'Shanti,' I said, but my smile must have betrayed the truth to her words. 'Please prepare some refreshments,' I said lamely, but she had already turned her back to me.

'Go back, Baby,' she said to me. 'I have work to do.'

Kunal ran his pen through vast swathes of the article, instructing us on what we would be able to print. For all his bashfulness around Maya, he was certain about his advice. Raja Singh wasn't to be mentioned by name, nor was any explicit reference to be made to his various enterprises.

He rose at the conclusion of the meeting, and as Maya stepped forward to thank him for his help, he said, 'You were always a wonderful writer, Maya.' He paused as he spoke her name. 'But I want to make sure *The Satirist* comprehends the changes that need to be made to rule out the risk of legal action.'

'Of course…'

'I mean,' he said, colouring. His eyes were intent on my sister. 'If you want, I can drop in at the end of the day…'

Maya was smiling, nodding, shaking her head. 'I don't want to inconvenience you.'

'No, no,' he said, as if the matter was settled. He picked up his case, muttering 'It's no trouble at all,' to all our expressions of thanks, and made his way out of the house.

XXVIII

Contrary to our expectations, the issue came out on time. Maya's profile was pared down, and another few articles dealing with the issue of workplace harassment were added. One of Sonia's former colleagues added her own account of being passed over for work after spurning an advance, and Sonia too wrote movingly about how opportunities had dried up for her once she had given birth. 'I hadn't meant to stop working,' she wrote, 'But all at once I wasn't being assigned out-of-town pieces. All at once my editors decided I wouldn't be able to commit to covering a year-long election campaign.'

Benjamin came through too. He managed to procure a friend's article on sexual advances made to her in the newspaper she had worked for in London. I accepted the gift of the article with gratitude, though I refrained from asking him who this friend was and how he had met her. I handed her article to Maya to edit, and when Maya told me the work was of an excellent standard, I smiled with pleasure.

The article on Raja Singh was pared down more than Maya would have liked. The title 'The Emperor has no clothes', was changed to 'Her story', which she complained sounded anaemic. All mentions of Raja Singh's name were removed. I was a little disappointed too. The smell of the man; his liberally applied aftershave, the whisky on his mouth, his breezy email afterwards all still lingered, and the thought that he was not going to be exposed rankled with me.

But then, as I read the article, not the proofs I had seen in their various iterations, but the actual physical piece as it appeared in the magazine, I had to acknowledge that the effect of Kunal's efforts was to make Ma's story more raw. The focus had lifted from Raja Singh's villainy; it now rested on Tasha-di and Ma's hopes as they had drawn up plans for *The Satirist*, and on the chaos that had followed her backer's spurned advances. Maya and I had never discussed the folding of Ma's magazine in any but the most abstract terms. We had looked at the proofs as the ruins of a failed business, but had never actually addressed the reasons for that failure. And in the aftermath of my last meeting with Raja Singh, after new details trickled out from Tasha-di about Raja's rancour, about the calls he placed to friends warning them about Ma's unprofessional attitude, we had focussed more on bringing the next issue out than on tackling how Raja Singh effected the complete destruction of Ma's life. The Ma I remembered; the introvert, the homebody, the woman who taught us to shy away from life was Raja Singh's creation, and this fact didn't entirely strike me until I held Maya's piece in my hands.

The fact that Raja Singh was not mentioned by name made the writing stronger. It made the threat more immediate. The story was no longer just Ma's story; it applied to anyone who worked or hoped to work in an office environment. The culprit was not any one single person; it was a careless superior, it was the man you shared a lift with, it was your boss or your boss' boss.

HER STORY

She has been planning for this moment her whole life. She is the exceptional girl at school, sharp and focussed and driven. She is good with words, quick with her emotions, and in a hurry to change the world. Sometimes her words trip out of her mouth, struggling to keep pace with the keenness of her thoughts. She has edited the school paper, has volunteered for endless charities, has set up rainwater harvesting schemes for her local area. She has made sure her maid's daughter is sent to school and that she stays in school.

As she has grown, she has dreamt of impacting more people. She has worked as a campaigner and as a journalist, and step by step, she has planned to set up her own publication. She has written pieces that have focussed on the burning issues of the day. She has not been daunted by opposition, and has volunteered for the most hostile interviews, travelling to the most inhospitable corners of the land to build her resumé.

Slowly, as her profile has built and her dreams taken form, she has partnered with a friend to breathe life into a new magazine. They work ceaselessly on their concept, meeting after they finish their day-jobs, negotiating the demands of work and family. They build a team and plan their first issue. Once this is ready, she approaches an investor, and he agrees to fund her new publication.

A magazine with a woman editor, he tells her, is an ideal worth striving for. The investor has a knack for picking winners, and now he tells the girl he believes in her. All is set, and the girl's fondest dream is on the point of being realised.

The week before the publication is due to be launched, the girl's mentor calls her into his office. He pours her a drink, he sits next to her, and he tells her how much he has always admired her. The girl thanks him, and as he moves closer, she inches away. He puts a hand on hers and she shrugs it off. He moves closer once more and she inches away again. They continue this dance until there is nowhere left for the girl to move to.

We all know how this story ends. There is no happily ever after for the girl. Her name is Rupa Sharma, and she had been on the point of launching this magazine's precursor a generation ago before she was called into her mentor's office and assaulted. When she resisted her assailant's advances, the offer of funding was revoked. She tried to return to employment, but her erstwhile mentor placed calls to his friends and colleagues, and she found she was never able to work in journalism again. Rupa Sharma was a broken girl with a shattered dream. She was the girl who retreated into her home as her world grew darker and never left it again. She was the mother who shielded her children because that was the only way she knew to keep them safe.

You can choose to think of Rupa Sharma as a failure who accepted defeat. She gave up the minute she encountered an obstacle. But then, she dared to look at the sun when so many others chose to follow a pre-set path.

Rupa Sharma was a dreamer and a trailblazer. She was a journalist, a mother, and a friend, and this is her story. It is a story of fierce ambition coming up against a brute, repressive predator. But her story is not hers alone. It is also the story of every girl who goes to school despite being told she won't amount to anything. It is the story of every girl who resists being married off in her teenage years. It is the story of every girl who wants to continue working after marriage and after bearing children. It is the story of every girl who dreams not of being rescued by a prince but of rescuing others. It is Rupa Sharma's story, of course, but it is equally ours. It is yours and mine, and if we don't act to effect change, it will be our daughter's too.

The minute the magazine hit the stands, it was clear that the article was resonating with readers. Ma's story, *Her Story*, was being read by women as their story. The article that followed, Sonia's ex-colleague's account of a career curtailed by an unwanted advance, was in the same crushing, confirmatory vein.

We worried there would be fewer readers now that the magazine was no longer free, but Mr Seth called us to order more copies. 'It's nearly sold out,' he told me, his excitement palpable. 'And you won't guess who I just sold a copy to—Mrs Singh.' I took a deep breath. Singh was a common enough name; it didn't necessarily mean Raja Singh's wife was reading our magazine. But then he said, 'She's a pretty, flimsy little thing,' and I knew it was the same person. 'She just told me these sort of stories fascinate her. Women's issues, feminism, and so on.' Mr Seth chuckled. 'Who would have thought it?'

I saw instant signs of reader engagement. I had uploaded key quotes from all the main articles on our social media channels, and our Twitter account was the first to light up with mentions. The quotes I shared—'It is the story of every girl who dreams not of being rescued by a prince but of rescuing others.' and 'It is Rupa Sharma's story, but it is equally ours. It is yours and mine, and if we don't act to effect change, it will be our daughter's too.'—were retweeted thousands of times. Normally I would be lucky to have a quote retweeted a dozen times, but here Ma's story had created a hashtag of its own. The story was trending, and the tag #HerStory was ranking above all the other stories emanating from India that day.

Other voices amplified the hashtag.

One reply to one of my tweets read: 'I was assaulted at an interview, and not hired because I resisted. #HerStory'

Another read: 'I was turned down for a promotion because I was of marriageable age and sure to be planning a family. #HerStory'

They came in drips and then torrents, stories of workplace discrimination and gender bias, stories of harassment and neglect, stories of gaslighting and trivialisation until I couldn't keep up with the updates anymore.

I fielded calls all morning. Magazine editors called to express their commiserations, but also to gossip. Did I know the identity of Ma's assailant? I pleaded ignorance, but more often than not, Raja Singh's name entered the fray. He was India's venture capitalist before venture capital was thought of; the angel investor to hundreds of dreamers. His reputation was well known, too, and the older people I spoke to recollected Raja's involvement in *The Satirist*'s first incarnation. One by one, I parried the questions thrust at me, but the queries about her attacker's identity remained. Who was it? Was it someone still active in journalism? Was it someone still wielding power? Was it Raja Singh?

Maya's article was sought for syndication by publications all over the country. By the following morning, her words would be translated into Telegu and Tamil and Bengali and Marathi and Punjabi and Urdu and be read in homes in all the urban and rural corners of India's great and sprawling land.

She had repeated offers to appear on television, and though

she initially declined them, Sonia urged her to reconsider. 'It's good PR for your mother's story,' she said, and then, 'and it's good PR for the magazine too.'

'I worry about being put on the spot,' replied Maya. 'It's all very well Siya fielding the calls and refusing to answer when they ask if Ma's assailant is Raja Singh, but I would give the game away instantly.'

'No you wouldn't…'

'I would.'

I nodded. Her life had been so sheltered that she hadn't had the need to compromise or pretend. 'She would,' I said. 'I would come along with you if it helped, Maya,' and as my sister nodded plaintively, I said, 'but I'm already behind with my follow-ups. I've had more requests for comments and for quotes than I can deal with.'

'I'll come with you,' offered Sonia. 'It makes sense for the two editors of the magazine to appear on these shows. It will allow us to sell the magazine and not just the story.'

The first show they appeared on was a panel. Chaired by a boisterous, opinionated woman, the other panellists were veterans of the media industry. The article was read out by Maya, and after the initial hand-wringing, talk turned to the reaction the article had been attracting. 'The piece itself,' read out the anchor, 'has appeared in publications across India and as far away as the Maldives and Thailand. Don't forget,' she said, nodding as she looked across at her panel, 'that this is a small, local Delhi magazine. A rag, if you will, that had to be given away for free up until a month back. But this issue has touched the nation, I can tell you,' and here the screen began to display the comments that had flooded our social media accounts. 'This is from Indore, this,' said the woman, peering at her screen, 'rape, rape, harassment, dismissal, rape.' She paused, turning straight to the camera. 'It's everywhere.' She paused, and as I wondered if an account of her own was to be unveiled, she said, 'It's always been there, and it appears it still is.'

They spoke of the impact of the story, and Sonia leaned forward to give the magazine a plug. 'This, in some ways, is Maya's Ma's final victory. This is the magazine she conceived of, and it is finally gaining attention because of her ordeal.'

'Ah, yes,' said one, 'I remember Rupa. She was a most promising writer.'

There were other nods, other words or regret and commiseration offered, until the anchor turned to Maya, 'What do you know, Maya, about the nature of the attack?'

Maya flushed deep. She opened her mouth but didn't speak, and it was Sonia who surged in. 'The reason this story has struck such a chord…'

'There's the matter of accountability, though,' said the sole male panellist. 'A finger has been pointed, an inference drawn.'

'We've not mentioned any name.'

'Now, now…'

'That's just semantics,' the man insisted. 'It's pretty clear who you're thinking of. There is only one man of the right age and profile to have invested in Rupa's magazine.'

'That's not true,' said Sonia robustly, but the man was waving his hands in the air.

'Who are you trying to fool, child?' he said dismissively. 'It's clear as day that you are trying to pin this on Raja Singh.'

The newspapers the following morning were full of news of the panel, and though Maya refused to appear on TV again, it appeared the connection had been made. In publications up and down the land, 'sources' emerged to claim that Ma's attacker had indeed been Raja.

A letter from Raja Singh's lawyers arrived the same day to announce they were launching a lawsuit against us. And just like that, we went from reporting the news to being the news.

A frantic call was placed to Kunal, who rushed over to look at the letter, but he was as bemused as the rest of us were. Raja Singh cited the article as libellous and defamatory. 'But,' Kunal pointed out, 'he's never once mentioned by name. We've only ever referred to him,' and here he picked up the magazine and read slowly through it, 'as a leading investor. Don't tell me there's only one rich man in all of India.'

'No,' Maya agreed, 'but he is *the* obvious candidate.' She had been incandescent after the panel, certain that legal action was going to be launched. I'd tried to allay her fears, but had known she was right. The reporting afterwards, on the television, in the papers, on drive time radio too, centred on the identity of Ma's assailant. Her story had gripped the nation. Many identified with her ordeal, and one by one, the 'experts' being called on to talk on Ma's behalf pointed the finger of blame at Raja Singh.

Maya was shaking her head, still angry at herself. The magazine's last issue had been more of a departure for her than for any of the rest of us. She had been so used to resting in the shadows, and while the rest of us had been exposed to a greater or lesser degree to the outside world—I in a strange city abroad, Sonia in the job market after having her children, and Tasha-di too, who had chosen to walk alone—Maya had always been sheltered from pain. With the magazine too, she had let Sonia take the juiciest stories, and the fire she had displayed on Ma's behalf had been one I had never before sensed in her.

'We did the wrong thing writing like that about Ma,' she complained now, more recognisably the Maya I had grown up with, 'for this shame to be her lasting legacy to the world!'

I shook my head. The shame did not rest with Ma. Sonia was ready with a riposte, but I spoke up, 'None of this was Ma's fault, Maya,' I said. Tasha-di wrinkled her nose, and I was reminded of her judgement on Ma's impracticality. 'None of this was Ma's fault,' I repeated, 'and it is still going on. It's going on in every corner of the globe, as the reaction to your article is constant proof. It's going on everywhere there is a power imbalance. And,' I said, looking at my aunt, 'it is going on everywhere well-wishers advise the victims simply to accept the status quo.'

Maya spoke again. 'Ma's memory…'

'This is the ultimate tribute to your Ma,' said Sonia. Maya had uncovered facts we had never known. Ma had won every prize in college, had travelled widely to cover her pieces—accompanying delegations to America, to the Hague, to Berlin and Geneva, and had been the youngest journalist in India to launch her own publication. All these mountains Ma had climbed, and the world knew none of it. 'And it is you who shone a light on it.'

And still Maya looked worried. 'Raja Singh is a colossus. There is no one else to match him, nor his reputation for having a wandering eye. It's no wonder that everyone thinks it was him we were writing about.'

'But,' repeated Kunal, 'there is no direct mention of him!' His frustration was tangible, and he picked up the letter to read through it again. 'His lawsuit has no basis,' he insisted, but news of the action had already spread. Journalists were camped outside the house, the phone didn't stop ringing, and my own mobile was lit constantly up by social media updates. I checked my apps to see Ma's hashtag #HerStory trending again. Below it, a new hashtag had sprung up: #IBelieveHerStory.

Every few seconds, my phone pinged with the same message from strangers; 'How can I help? #IBelieveHerStory'

On Sonia's mobile screen, an interview with Raja Singh's wife appeared. For all our proximity, I'd never met her, and was surprised to see she was young, a good decade or two younger than her husband. The white she wore suited Delhi's heat, but also symbolised the Hindu colour of mourning, and I wondered if the effect was intended. 'All these allegations,' she was saying, 'are rubbish.' She blinked rapidly. 'I've never even heard of these women, never even read the magazine, but I can vouch for my husband's honour.'

Kunal left for work but was back within a minute. 'My plan was to walk back home before going to office, but it's impossible.' We looked at the front gates, where the throng had grown. My phone was buzzing constantly now with media requests, with messages of solidarity, with offers of help. 'Come,' I told him, 'I'll spirit you out through the servants' quarters.' We moved quickly through the ruins of the garage to Shanti's home, and as we entered, I asked him, 'What are our options?'

'We'll fight the lawsuit,' he said resolutely. 'This man is just using bullying tactics.'

'We don't have the money for a long battle, Kunal.'

I spoke without thinking, but Kunal was quick in response. 'My firm will work pro bono...'

'I didn't mean...'

'It's not right,' he said, and I saw at once what drew Maya to him. He had that same purity of ideals, that same precious, dogged intransigence. 'For a man of his means to try to intimidate you is not fair. And besides,' he added, 'I and your sister go way back...'

'I remember.'

He coloured. 'Yes,' he said, 'Well, you see then why I can't let her go through this alone.'

I was on the point of asking him about whether he was now divorced, but we had reached Shanti's back door, which stood ajar. Kunal nodded briskly at me and let himself out.

XXIX

There was no let-up in the media circus over the following days. Ma's hashtag continued to trend, and the journalists outside the house maintained their presence, until I finally learnt that Shanti had taken it upon herself to supply tea and refreshments to the hordes twice a day.

I complained that she was just encouraging the frenzy, but she tutted disapprovingly at me. 'These boys and girls are bringing attention to your mother's story,' she said. 'Can't I so much as give them a cup of tea?'

The threats from Raja Singh grew more serious. A second lawsuit was launched, this one against Maya personally. Kunal represented her against this action too, but as news of her ordeal spread, people began to share their own stories of harassment and intimidation. The magazine's social media feeds were never quiet, and elsewhere in the country, movements were being organised.

In UP, by the Gangetic plains, a politician who had been accused of rape was thronged in the street. Facing him was a hundred strong crowd of women waving banners that read #IBelieveHerStory.

In South India, a venerated actor was accused of demanding

sex from aspiring actresses. A crowd assembled in front of his house waving banners that read #IBelieveHerStory.

In front of Raja's office complex too, crowds of women congregated waving banners that read #IBeliveHerStory.

Others gathered in front of our house, fed and watered by Shanti, and waving banners that read #IBelieveHerStory.

Early one morning, before the media circus started, I walked to the front gate. I'd only been there a minute when I saw Mrs Bhatnagar moving towards me. I smiled quickly, and I was on the point of escaping back indoors when she called out to me. 'Siya,' she said, 'Siya, I have to congratulate you on that wonderful magazine of yours.'

'Mrs Bhatnagar?' I replied, stunned.

'It's a hard world, you know.' She wiped her brow, adjusted the bangle on her wrist. 'My daughter Rashmi,' she told me, 'is a feminist too. Everyone is, nowadays.'

Sonia began receiving messages of support from women in the media fraternity. Women began to contact her—acquaintances, strangers, former colleagues—with their own stories. Ma's report had resonated with hundreds, no, thousands of others, and very soon, other accounts of assault began to emerge. And Raja Singh's ploy of coming after us backfired; far from silencing us, it emboldened his other victims to name him as a sexual abuser.

There were over a dozen others who now contacted Sonia, several of whom were ex journalists. These women now offered to join us, telling us they would man the magazine for free, and that they would contribute to any legal fund required.

Maya told me we had to launch a website. 'We finally have traction,' she told me, 'and if we can't afford to print, we'll publish online.'

This was her thinking with her editor's hat, but I worried about the cost of hiring a website designer. 'This may not be the best time,' I pointed out. 'We have to marshal our energy and our resources to fight Raja Singh.'

Maya laughed. 'Who's the dour one now?' she asked. 'Building a proper website can wait, but I've purchased our domain name and created a WordPress site. It's not the most elegant looking, but it's a landing site for *The Satirist*, and it's a source of information for our supporters.'

I nodded slowly. Had she always been there, this prodigy, this positive, proactive superwoman?

Maya was carrying on. 'Puneeta will link our social media updates to the site too, so we'll be good to go by the afternoon.'

'As you say, madam,' I said as she smiled. 'What's the worst that could happen?'

A meeting with the other women who had claimed to be assaulted by Raja Singh was organised for the day after the lawsuit was launched. Twelve women streamed past the media scrum at our front gate, each of them sporting a top with the words #IBelieveHerStory emblazoned on them. 'He wants to silence *The Satirist*,' shouted Abha, one of the women who claimed to have been attacked by Raja Singh. 'Let's see him try and silence us all.'

'He raped me,' she told us when we were gathered indoors. We had just introduced ourselves, shaking hands, muttering first-time pleasantries, accepting or rejecting offers of a cup of tea, when she stood up, looked around the room, taking in the group—consisting of other educated, middle-class women, of Shanti too with her rituals and her superstitions, and of Ajay—and had spoken calmly and without emotion. 'He raped me, you know,' she said, and it was those around her who shook with the serenity of her words.

Abha's testimony was key in that it was a first person account, and its narrator attractive, articulate and unburdened by unseemly feelings of guilt. Just like with Ma, she had been invited to Raja Singh's office. In her case, the pretext was her career. Abha had been a recent graduate, and had been hired to work as a researcher along with five or six other graduates at India TV. Raja Singh wasn't at the offices regularly, but any appearance was treated as a state visit.

Abha, then, was an insignificant first year hire. Flattered to have attracted the notice of Raja Singh, she didn't query his motivation, but went happily to his office. He offered her alcohol, which she was too daunted to refuse. He complained of backache, and suggested they move to a sofa. 'It was low, the sofa, and worn leather,' and I knew instantly that Abha was speaking the truth.

She had seated herself at one end of the sofa, near a low table, and he came to sit right next to her. 'Our knees touched,' Abha told us, and I nodded. She had edged away, but he had stretched out, his arms snaking around her, his thigh rubbing against her, and had begun to tell her how impressed he was with her work and she hadn't dared to move away. He spoke of a lead she had followed, and she was so gratified that he had remembered her work that she ignored his hand massaging her shoulder.

'And then,' she said, 'he was on top of me.' Her forensic

level of detail stopped, as did her testimony. I looked away. She didn't speak for a long while, and then, as if to impart courage to herself, she nodded. 'It didn't last long, and afterwards, I tried to tell myself it hadn't happened. I didn't tell anyone, not my parents, not my boyfriend, and the next time Raja came in, he acted like nothing had happened. He didn't behave proprietorially; didn't behave as if he had any claim on me. He came in as he did in the middle of the day and ignored all the junior reporters. He barked orders at the various producers, took one cursory look around the newsroom and wandered back to the car.

'When we next spoke, at a company social, he was cordial but distant. The disparity in our positions was clear. It was as if the attack hadn't happened. Very soon I began to question my memory. I rose in *India TV*, being promoted above a more senior colleague, and I wondered if maybe I had invited Raja Singh's attention. I hadn't refused his invitation.' She took a deep breath, but continued to look firmly at the floor in front of her. 'I hadn't flinched when he put his arm around me, and hadn't stopped him when he began to massage me.' There she was, staring at an imaginary spot on the floor, nodding in her deliberate, unsentimental manner. 'I could have stopped it, and then I told myself I hadn't wanted to.'

'Oh, Abha,' Maya said, going round to where she sat, but the woman was so straight backed, so averse to making eye contact that Maya just hung back in the end.

Abha began to speak again. 'A few months after my promotion, I was covering an event in Mumbai, and I received a call from Raja. It turned out he was in Mumbai himself, and staying at the same hotel as I was.' There it was again, that slow, insistent nod, that tucking in of her lips. 'He suggested meeting for a drink, and I agreed.' She laughed here, a loud, manic sound. 'Because let's face it, how could I refuse? I went down to the bar, but the barman came to me with a message. Raja was running behind schedule; could I go up to his room?'

There was a knowing intake of breath at this, and Abha shrugged. 'So off I trudged up to his room. I told myself I was forewarned, and that there was no danger of Raja making the same mistake again. But as soon as I walked in, alarm bells began to ring. There the man was, dressed in a bathrobe, his hands around a tumbler of whisky. He took me to his window to show me his view of Mumbai's glittering skyline, and his hands were carelessly placed over my shoulder. I could see the scene playing out in slow motion, you know,' and as those around the room nodded in shared memory, she went on, 'almost as if it were happening to someone else. I knew his next move. He would offer me a drink. He would return to my side, moving closer, his hands on my back, on my waist, his robe falling open…' Abha's breathing grew ragged, but when she spoke again, she turned her glittering eyes on all of us. 'It all happened as I anticipated. I had just drunk my first sip when his overture started. I shook my head, though he didn't seem deterred. He kept whispering his words of predatory seduction into my ears, his eyes half-closed, his speech slurred, and in the end, I rammed my tumbler against his bare chest. The contact jolted him, the cold glass against his skin, and I bolted. I took off, the tumbler still in my hand, and ran all the way back to my room. I finished my assignment, refusing to accept any calls from Raja, refusing his invitation to have breakfast together the next morning, and returned to Delhi as soon as my work was finished.'

Sonia whistled at the speech. 'Well done, Abha.'

'Well done,' Abha said with a rueful smile. 'I was sidelined soon after. All the plum assignments went to others, and, I couldn't help noticing that the others were often young, inexperienced women. Others were promoted over me, and though I was never officially told I was not being put forward for the best assignments, I knew that I would never rise in the company. Raja never looked at me again. I was moved to a small satellite office in Bhopal where I dealt mainly with corruption scandals that never made the cut for the shows, and when I was offered a job back in Delhi by a second-tier channel, I ran to take it.'

Abha's story was recounted over and over again that afternoon. Fresh pots of tea were produced, and women wearing their #IBelieveHerStory t-shirts spoke unbidden. The stories varied. Some were touched by Raja Singh; others burnt by innuendo and stonewalling. But details were beginning to emerge that tied the various accounts with each other; a power imbalance, a drink offered, a retreat to a weary leather sofa.

I looked at Tasha-di as she heard the testimonies. She didn't speak, didn't interrupt, didn't offer advice or criticism, but her attention was fixed on each woman as she spoke. Her mouth grew slacker as the day progressed, her shoulders hunched, and I could conceive of her imagining her criticism of Ma misplaced.

One by one, the women in the room nodded as they heard new accounts. I closed my eyes. The smell rose in me of Raja's pomade, of his ludicrously glossy mouth and of the stench of his scotch. More tea was poured, more voices were added to the din, and as Tasha-di finally nodded, her mouth slackening, I knew she saw the cost of all that Ma had endured.

XXX

Raja Singh was mobbed outside his office the next day. The crowds had been growing every day, but they maintained a distance, and restricted themselves to waving their banners and chanting their support of Ma. This time they clustered around him, denying him a clear path to his car. Mikes were thrust under his chin, demanding a comment on the article and the lawsuit, and though Raja initially thrust them away, eventually he began to speak. 'This is all a waste of my time,' he said angrily. We had been in the garden room, and were called to the upstairs lounge by Tasha-di, who had been watching the news all day. All the channels were full of the allegations and the lawsuit. The photos from the previous night, of the women arriving in their #IBelieveHerStory shirts had been running constantly, and the minute Tasha-di spotted Raja Singh on her screen, she called out to us.

We ran up to hear him say, 'I'm on my way to the airport. All this noise,' and looking disdainfully at the assembled rabble, he said, 'is just a way for a failing magazine to try and get some attention.' He laughed hoarsely. 'That's all it is; a way for a bunch of failures to have their fifteen minutes of fame.'

I clucked at his words, but he turned to stare right at the camera. His eyes bored into me, and he said, 'The founder of that rag came to see me a few days ago. Begged me for funding, and this, I suppose, is her revenge for my turning her down. Complete fabrication, the lot of it!'

Ajay arrived in Civil Lines within moments of the Raja Singh ambush. 'That's it,' he said, clapping his hands, 'we're off to the airport.' He was full of nervous energy that day, fidgeting, snapping his fingers, urging us to move. He took some items of clothing out of his bag, shoving one at each of us, and we saw they were the same #IBelieveHerStory t-shirts that the women had sported the day before. 'I might have mobilised a hashtag,' he said sheepishly as I stared. 'And it took a few simple clicks to organise a print on demand facility.'

There were cloth tote bags to go with the t-shirts, and it was the work of a moment to put them on. I got on the phone to Abha and the other women, asking them to come down to Civil Lines.

'But how are we to get to the airport?' asked Maya. 'Our cars can only carry a few.'

'We can organise a bus, surely,' I said, turning to Saloni, who rose.

'Leave it with me,' she said, 'I'll get Pradeep to organise transport.'

Our social media platforms were abuzz with the day's developments, and with the soundbites that had been created.

I drafted a short note.

We have not sought to identify or shame any one individual, but to report on Rupa Sharma's plight. Justice was denied to her during her lifetime, but we will not remain silent on her behalf.

We believe her story, and we are not going to be cowed down by big money or by armies of lawyers. We demand justice, and we demand the truth. We will meet at Delhi airport at 2pm today to face Rupa's aggressor. We believe Rupa's story. #IBelieveHerStory

I posted the message on all the platforms I could find and forwarded it to several journalists.

'Hurry, Siya,' I heard Tasha-di call. 'The bus is ready.'

'Just a second!'

Women assaulted by Raja Singh had been coming forward from other parts of India too, from Mumbai and Bangalore and Jaipur and Kolkata. A prominent Mumbai-based journalist reached out to me as I was on the point of shutting my laptop; 'What can I do to help?'

'Rally the troops,' I replied. I copied in all the others who had contacted me offering to mobilise. 'It's not just my mother who suffered. And it's not just Raja Singh who raped women. Let us all speak our rage.'

We took the first convoy; Tasha-di, Maya, Sonia, Saloni and I, squashed into Papa's old jeep. Ajay and the other women followed in a bus driven by Pradeep. Shanti was part of the rear-guard, proudly sporting her t-shirt, waving her tote bag as if it were a banner.

We arrived just in time to see Raja Singh being ushered into the VIP section of the airport. He turned around to observe us for a moment, and for a moment our eyes met. He surveyed the sea of people by me; dozens in their #IBeliveHerStory t-shirts, countless reporters and camera-people, and took a deep breath.

He exhaled, his eyes fixed on me, and then his lips curled. His teeth flashed white, like a feral animal, and he threw his head back in laughter. Then a hand appeared on his back, pulling him forward, and he disappeared into the airport.

I looked around at the faces around me. Family, friends, strangers and allies, all roused in protesting a historic injustice. 'Look,' Ajay said, yanking at my sleeve. He pointed towards a bank of screens by the far side of the waiting area. They were set to the news, and the news was full of our movement. Our movement, I thought as I looked at him. 'Our movement,' I said, and he shook his head. 'Your movement,' he said to me, 'you've created something.'

The cameras panned away from the scenes at the airport, and to a crowded scene in a different city. 'Is that,' I asked, 'is that…' and he nodded.

'That's the Gateway of India,' he smiled. 'That's a protest being held in Mumbai in solidarity with your Ma. And,' he added, as the scenes on the cameras changed again, 'that's Chandigarh, and that…' he took a moment to identify a new scene, 'that's Chennai.' The news station flitted through images in quick succession, and though Ajay tried to keep up with the new protests, 'That's Patna, that's Ranchi,' he soon lost count. The filled grounds represented giant metropolises and tiny provincial towns, but in one scene after another, the essentials remained unvarying. Women out in their thousands in the t-shirts that had been created in validation of Ma's story.

We were at the airport for an age, waving our banners, making way for disembarking passengers. The journalists stayed with us throughout, and local vendors began ferrying free cups of tea to us. 'Why are you doing this?' I asked one, and he folded his hands together.

'I have a daughter too,' he said, his eyes bright.

The TV channels continued to report our story as the evening rolled in. Two young girls arrived at the airport in Ajay's #IBelieveHerStory t-shirts, waving as they walked past us, and I asked Ajay, 'Who is selling all the t-shirts?'

'You are,' he replied. I shot him a bemused look, and he nodded. 'I opened an account in *The Satirist*'s name. Hundreds of thousands of the t-shirts have been sold, Siya. Those who're buying them know they're investing their money in a good cause.' He put his hands on my arms, and I was aware of Tasha-di's eyes on us. 'You can fight Raja Singh's action now. You can rebuild the garage. You can carry on with the magazine. And,' he said, as he saw me well up, 'You can finally start paying me a decent wage.'

All newspapers the next morning were full of reports about the protest. By some estimates, up to ten million women had taken to the streets of India. Maya came into my room to wake me up for our morning walk. 'Get up, lazybones,' she called, and I smiled. I patted the bed, and she came to sit down next to me.

She shook her head at my sloth, but then she nestled under the covers next to me. 'Read the papers,' she told me. 'We're on every front page,' and I smiled.

The day could wait. Kunal would be coming in soon for our daily meeting. Raja Singh's lawsuit would be defended, and robustly. He had greater resources than we did, and chances were he would either drown us under litigation or outspend us. He could and would try all the tricks in his book, but we had won the war of perception. Without mentioning Raja Singh's name, we had put him on the defensive, and all of India now knew him to be a sexual predator. India had awoken, and India's women were roused. They were not going to settle for silence any longer.

The Satirist would run, and if the emails promising support and sponsorship were to be believed, would flourish. Our journalists would be paid. Tasha-di had spoken last night about launching a charity for victims of sexual assault, and Shanti had offered the spare rooms in her quarters as office space for the venture. Kunal would ask Maya out, years after their last parting, and though both were measured and vulnerable, they would try their best to make a go of things.

Benjamin would send back my belongings. He wanted to write a profile on the #IBelieveHer movement we had launched, and wanted to come to Delhi. He had emailed the previous evening with the offer, but I hadn't yet replied. I could just see Ajay's reaction to Benjamin's email. 'Sure,' he would say, 'the man just wants to visit his ex-girlfriend's town to write an article.'

I smiled. All that could wait. There was work to be done. Lawsuits to be fought and the next issue to be brought out. The garage to be rebuilt. The caved-in walls and the closed rooms to be dealt with, but they could all wait.

I had my sister next to me, and for the first time in years, I know what my purpose was. The rest could all wait.

ACKNOWLEDGEMENTS

I had been thinking of writing a novel set in a decaying house, but it took a chance conversation in the shadow of the house that provided the inspiration for Nathaniel Hawthorne's *The House of The Seven Gables* to convince me that houses carry the imprints of their owners' trauma. My thanks to the lady for her conversation and her insight, and to the memory of the 2019 New England summer that has helped sustain me through an interminable 2020.

My thanks, as ever, to Claire Roberts, agent, friend and oracle, and to Rosanna Forte, who championed an early version of this book. And to Sayantan Ghosh at Simon and Schuster India, who felt such an instant connection with *Civil Lines* and the lives and fortunes of its inhabitants. I owe a debt of gratitude also to the S&S India family for their belief in this book, and to Himanjali Sankar for her painstaking proofing of the manuscript.

I owe thanks too to the indomitable women I have known, particularly at my alma mater Newnham. They are too numerous to name here, but have shown through constant example that excellence isn't incompatible with generosity of spirit.

Finally, I thank my family for their forbearance, and the virtual schooling provision at my children's schools for allowing me to reclaim my working hours through this pandemic.